精闢文法分析還不夠，本書同時收錄

豐富例句及精準的表格化釋義，

讓你除了深度學習，

還能搭配實戰演練收服所有考試！

Preface 作者序

近年來，英文學習多提倡英文口說表達能力，以培養能用英文進行口語溝通表達作為重要教學目標，白話一點來說，就是要改變啞巴英語的尷尬狀況；然而有些人誤以為可以不再學習文法，少數教師在英語教學中也因為過分追求教學過程的口語能力，強調功能、表達，忽視文法教學，因而造成不良後果：由於輕視基礎文法知識，在口語表達、寫作時就容易出錯。

其實，經過多年的探索、研究，英語教學界已形成共識：由於多數的台灣人缺乏英語接觸的習得環境與時間，學習英語必須借助文法這個重要工具。因為文法作為一門科學，是語言的組織規律，它賦予語言一套結構系統，指導語言正確、貼切地表達思想和傳遞資訊，是在口語表達中發揮創造性能力的依據與根本。

簡單來說，學好文法便可以大大幫助英語學習者掌握語言規律，更流暢地進行聽、說、讀、寫等實踐，意即，好的口說能力也需要相當的文法基礎，不然就只是單字胡亂被拼湊在一起而已。因此，培養正確運用語言知識的能力，可以說是在打地基，地基穩了，房子才能蓋得漂亮。

這本《萬用英文文法30天完全攻略：逆轉你學了10年都還搞不懂的文法概念》就是在這樣的心境之下誕生的。全書以 30 天為依準，注重語法知識結構的連貫性和系統性；淡化對語法概念、定義的講解和記憶，強調實例、比較、實踐和應用。本書克服了一般市面教材中語法教學內容分散、不利於系統化學習，造成前學後忘、效率低下的弱點，並注意對講解的語法知識進行適時總結、歸納，著重在條列和表格式的說明，以圖像作為輔助，最後再透過實戰的演練和解析，使讀者得以建立起新、舊知識的聯繫，將「短暫記憶」轉化為「長時記憶」，提高學習成效。

　　文法學得不好，當然不代表口說能力就會很差，但是溝通仍有達不達意、漂不漂亮之分，希望學習英文的人，都能注意到文法對於聽、說、讀、寫四大面向的全面性幫助，並不斷挑戰自己，

User's Guide 使用說明

1 精準的**分門別類**，讓你一眼就懂

本書從概述開始，讓讀者可以先快速理解該單元的背景資訊，再逐一按照學習邏輯，以大量例句作為輔助，不僅可以學得精準，還能用得到位！

Day 01　名詞 Noun

第一節：概述

名詞是用來表示「人」、「事物」或「抽象概念」的名稱。例如：Olympics（奧運會）、mascot（吉祥物）、France（法國）、Internet（網際網路）、cybersource（網路資源）、athlete（運動員）、scientist（科學家）、panda（熊貓），以及dream（夢想）等等。

第二節：名詞的種類

名詞可以根據其意義分為專有名詞和普通名詞兩大類。

1. 專有名詞：

表示特定的某個（些）人、某物、某地點或機構的名稱。例如：Taiwan（台灣）、AIT（美國在臺協會）、Coca Cola（可口可樂）、Olympic Games（奧林匹克運動會）等等。

2. 普通名詞：

表示某人或某類事物名稱的是普通名詞，如house（房子）、doctor（醫生）、photo（照片）等等。

(1) 普通名詞又可分為以下三種：

集合名詞	表示一群人或一些事物的總稱。class（班級）、group（小組）、army（軍隊）、family（家庭）。
物質名詞	表示無法分為個體的物質。例如：milk（牛奶）、cotton（棉花）、water（水）、snow（雪）。

010

抽象名詞	表示抽象概念（動作如：victory（勝利作）、happiness（

重點深度學

1. 有些名詞在特定場合可又可定義為另一種名詞也會有所不同。例如：
   • ice（冰）→ an ice
   • paper（紙張）→ a

2. 有些抽象名詞可以加上
   • beauty（美）→ a
   • youth（青春）→ a

第三節：可數與不可

一般說來，普通名詞和集a family（一個家庭）、an an物質、動作、抽象概念的名詞writing（寫作）、health（健和集合名詞）有單複數形式。

1. 可數名詞：

可數名詞大多數有單數常是在單數形式後字尾 s 式如下表：

3 擷取**重點深度學**，讓你精益求精

本書除了重點提示之外，還貼心附上讓讀者可以進行自我挑戰的文法學習，舉凡特殊用法，或是該文法概念的例外使用方式，都能幫助讀者深化研讀技巧！

2 貼心**重點提示**，給你必學文法要點

在特別需要注意的地方，本書皆以重點提示的方式呈現，除了可以提醒讀者該
文法解釋的關鍵之處，還能加深印象，強化文法使用的力道！

重點提示：必學文法小要點

提示1.

　　許多名詞通常是不可數的，在一定情況下又可變為可數名詞；
有些可數或不可數名詞的單複數形式表示不同的意義。例如：

- **tea**（茶）→ **teas**（各種茶）
- **steel**（鋼）→ **steels**（各種鋼）
- **coffee**（咖啡）→ **a coffee**（一杯咖啡）
- **snow**（雪）→ **snows**（積雪）
- **water**（水）→ **waters**（海水，大片的水）
- **green**（綠顏色）→ **greens**（青菜）

4 隨地**實戰測驗**，文法解析即刻救援

在每個單元後，本書皆收錄十題精心設計的試題，讓讀者可以隨
時檢測自己的學習狀態，隨後的文法解析也能讓讀者即刻調整讀
書方針！

Content 目錄

Day

01

名詞
Noun

Day 01 名詞 Noun

🚩 第一節：概述

名詞是用來表示「人」、「事物」或「抽象概念」的名稱。例如：Olympics（奧運會）、mascot（吉祥物）、France（法國）、Internet（網際網路）、cybersource（網路資源）、athlete（運動員）、scientist（科學家）、panda（熊貓），以及dream（夢想）等等。

🚩 第二節：名詞的種類

名詞可以根據其意義分為專有名詞和普通名詞兩大類。

1. 專有名詞：

表示特定的某個（些）人、某物、某地點或機構的名稱。例如：Taiwan（台灣）、AIT（美國在臺協會）、Coca Cola（可口可樂）、Olympic Games（奧林匹克運動會）等等。

2. 普通名詞：

表示某人或某類事物名稱的是普通名詞，如house（房子）、doctor（醫生）、photo（照片）等等。

(1) 普通名詞又可分為以下三種：

集合名詞	表示一群人或一些事物的總稱。class（班級）、group（小組）、army（軍隊）、family（家庭）。
物質名詞	表示無法分為個體的物質。例如：milk（牛奶）、cotton（棉花）、water（水）、snow（雪）。

抽象名詞	表示抽象概念（動作、狀態、品質、感情等）的詞。例如：victory（勝利）、friendship（友誼）、work（工作）、happiness（幸福）。

重點深度學： Day 01 進階挑戰

1. 有些名詞在特定場合可定義為個體名詞，在另一種場合下又可定義為另一種名詞，例如「物質名詞」，且在釋義上也會有所不同。例如：
   - **ice**（冰）→ **an ice**（冰淇淋）
   - **paper**（紙張）→ **a paper**（報紙；論文；考卷）

2. 有些抽象名詞可以加上冠詞，使其變成可數名詞，例如：
   - **beauty**（美）→ **a beauty**（美人；美的東西）
   - **youth**（青春）→ **a youth**（青年人）

🚩 第三節：可數與不可數名詞

　　一般說來，普通名詞和集合名詞是可數的，稱為可數名詞。例如：a family（一個家庭）、an army（一支軍隊）、a tree（一棵樹）。表示物質、動作、抽象概念的名詞大多數不可數，稱為不可數名詞。例如：writing（寫作）、health（健康）、glass（玻璃）。可數名詞（個體名詞和集合名詞）有單複數形式。

1. 可數名詞：

　　可數名詞大多數有單數和複數兩種形式，複數形式通常是在單數形式後加字尾 s 或 es 構成。規則的複數構成形式如下表：

(1) 一般的可數名詞的複數

加法	情況	範例單字
直接加s	❶ 一般情況	cup(s)杯子、girl(s)女孩、hand(s)手、face(s)臉、day(s)日子
直接加s	❷ 以兩個母音字母結尾的詞	zoo(s)公園、radio(s)收音機、bamboo(s)竹子、studio(s)錄音室、kangaroo(s)袋鼠
	❸ 某些以o結尾的外來詞	photo(s)照片、piano(s)鋼琴、tobacco(s)菸草、Eskimo(s)愛斯基摩人
	❹ 某些以f或fe結尾的詞	roof(s)屋頂、chief(s)酋長、gulf(s)海灣、cliff(s)懸崖、proof(s)證據、belief(s)信仰、hoof(s)蹄、safe(s)保險箱
直接加es	❶ 以s, x, ch, sh結尾的詞	class(es)班級、bus(es)公共汽車、box(es)盒子、watch(es)手錶、brush(es)刷子
	❷ 某些以o結尾的詞	hero(es)英雄、tomato(es)番茄、potato(es)馬鈴薯
變y為i再加-es	以 y 結尾的詞	factory—factories工廠、baby—babies嬰兒、city—cities城市、country—countries國家（但keys鑰匙例外）
變f為v再加-es	某些以f或fe結尾的詞	leaf—leaves葉子、life—lives生命、shelf—shelves架子、wife—wives妻子、thief—thieves小偷、knife—knives小刀、loaf—loaves條、half—halves一半、wolf—wolves狼、self—selves自己

不過，有些名詞複數形式不是以加s或es構成，它們的不規則構成方法主要如下表：

構成方法	範例單字
改變內部母音	man→men男人、woman→ women女人、Frenchman→ Frenchmen法國人、tooth→ teeth牙齒、mouse→ mice老鼠、goose→ geese鵝、foot→ feet足部
字尾加en	child—children孩子、ox—oxen公牛
單複數同形	two deer兩頭鹿、two fish兩條魚（註：two fishes 表示「兩種魚」）、two aircraft兩架飛機、two sheep兩隻綿羊、two Japanese兩個日本人、two Chinese兩個中國人

重點深度學：Day 01 進階挑戰

要學習複數變化，我們還可以透過「發音」來掌握：

情況	讀音	範例
在〔p〕〔t〕〔k〕〔f〕等無聲子音後	〔s〕	maps、desks、cats、beliefs
在〔s〕〔z〕〔ʃ〕〔tʃ〕〔ʒ〕〔dʒ〕後	〔ɪz〕	faces、matches、bridges、roses
在其他情況下	〔z〕	days、boys、fields、knives

(2) 合成名詞的複數

(a)將合成名詞中的主體名詞變為複數。例如：passer(s)-by 路人（們）、looker(s) on（旁觀者）、son(s) in law（女婿）、runner(s) up（亞軍）、editor(s) in chief（總編輯）

(b)將最後一部分變成複數。例如：go between(s) 中間人、drawback(s) 缺陷

(3) 集合名詞的複數使用

　　單數形式的集合名詞被看作一個整體時，相當於一個普通的單數可數名詞，具有單數概念，作主語時動詞用單數；被看作若干個體（成員）時，具有複數概念，動詞用複數。例如：

- **Our group consists of ten members.** 我們組由十人組成。
- **Our group are having a meeting now.** 我們組（成員）正在開會。

　　類似的集合名詞還有：hair（頭髮）、fruit（水果）、class（班級）、audience（觀眾）、company（公司）、club（俱樂部）等等。

　　還有幾個單數形式的集合名詞具有複數意義，只能與複數動詞連用：police（警察）、cattle（牛）、poultry（家禽）、people（人民、人們）。例如：

- **The police are looking for him.** 警察在找他。

　　但 people 作「民族」解釋時，則相當於普通的個體名詞，具單複數形式，動詞需根據主語的單複數來做判斷。例如：

- **The Inidan people is a brave and hard-working one.**
  印度民族是一個勤勞勇敢的民族。

2. 不可數名詞：

　　一般說來，物質名詞和抽象名詞是不可數的，因此沒有複數形式，一般也不用 a, an。下列名詞常用作不可數名詞：advice（建議）（但 suggestion可數）、bread（麵包）、cash（現金）、clothing（衣物）、equipment（設備）、fun（玩笑）、furniture（傢俱）、harm（傷害）、information（資訊）、knowledge（知識）、luck（運氣）、living（生活）、machinery（機械）、money（錢）、news（消息）、paper（紙）、permission（准許）、progress（進步）、courage（勇氣）、traffic（交通）、travel（旅行）、trouble（麻煩）、weather（天氣）、work（工作）、milk（牛奶）、water（水）、sand（沙子）等等。

　　若不可數名詞出現複數，則表示某種特別的意義。例如：

(1) 用以表示不同的類別

- **There are many famous teas in China. Longjing is one of them.**
  中國有很多著名的茶的種類。龍井是其中的一種。
- **They sell mineral waters.** 他們出售各種礦泉水。

(2) 複數形式表示數量多

- **He stopped, watching the broad waters of the Yangtze River.**
  他停下來，看著長江浩瀚的江水。
- **Several children are playing on the sands.** 幾個小孩在沙灘上玩。
- **Light rains began in the heat of April.** 在炎熱的四月開始了綿綿不絕的小雨。

(3) 有些抽象名詞的複數形式表示概念的具體化

- **She told him about all her hopes and fears.**
  她和他談了種種希望和憂慮。

3. 常用複數形式的名詞：

(1) 表示由兩部分構成的東西的名詞：

這些名詞常常只用複數形式，表示數量時常用「數詞+pair(s) of」，如 scissors（剪刀）、trousers（褲子）、shorts（短褲）、scales（天平）、sleeves（袖子）等等。例如：

- **A pair of trousers costs me a lot of money these days.**
  如今買條褲子要花我一大筆錢。
- **I like this pair of scissors. How much is it?**
  我喜歡這把剪刀，多少錢？

需要注意到的是，這類名詞作修飾語時常用單數。例如：

- **There is a shoe factory nearby.** 附近有家鞋廠。

(2) 有些以ing結尾的詞使用時常用複數：

belongings（所有物）、earnings（收入）、savings（積蓄）、findings（調查結果）、doings（行為）、surroundings（環境）、feelings（感情）、greetings（招呼）

(3) 有些詞的複數形式可以表示特別的意思：

- air（空氣）→ airs（神氣）
- paper（紙）→ papers（論文、文件、報紙）
- custom（風俗）→ customs（海關）
- people（人們）→ peoples（民族）
- damage（損壞）→ damages（賠償費）
- look（看）→ looks（外貌）

(4) 某些特定的名詞常以複數形式出現，如：

arms（武器）、clothes（衣物）、twins（雙胞胎）、outskirts（郊區）、troops（部隊）、resources（資源）、tears（眼淚）、contents（內容）、thanks（感謝）、congratulations（祝賀）

(5) 有些名詞在一定的片語中常用複數形式，如：

- make / take notes（做筆記）
- make announcements（宣告、通告）
- in high spirits（情緒高昂）
- as follows（如下）
- make friends with（與……交朋友）
- shake hands with（與……握手）

重點提示：必學文法小要點

提示 1.

　　許多名詞通常是不可數的，在一定情況下又可變為可數名詞；有些可數或不可數名詞的單複數形式表示不同的意義。例如：

- tea（茶）→ teas（各種茶）
- steel（鋼）→ steels（各種鋼）
- coffee（咖啡）→ a coffee（一杯咖啡）
- snow（雪）→ snows（積雪）
- water（水）→ waters（海水，大片的水）
- green（綠顏色）→ greens（青菜）

- **time**（時間）→ **times**（時代）
- **work**（工作）→ **works**（著作）
- **spirit**（精神）→ **spirits**（情緒，酒精）
- **iron**（鐵）→ **irons**（鐐銬）
- **change**（變化）→ **changes**（具體的幾種變化）
- **arm**（手臂）→ **arms**（武器）
- **hope**（希望）→ **hopes**（具體的幾個希望）
- **hardship**（艱苦）→ **hardships**（具體艱苦方面）
- **difficulty**（困難）→ **difficulties**（具體幾個困難）
- **suggestion**（建議）→ **suggestions**（具體幾條建議）

提示 2.

下列的名詞在英語中則一定不可數，如果要表示一定的數量，要借助單位詞。例如：

a piece of chalk / news / work / bread / paper / advice / cloth / furniture / thread / coal / meat
一支粉筆／一則新聞／一件工作／一塊麵包／一張紙／一項忠告／一塊布／一件傢俱／一根線／一塊煤／一塊肉

a cake of soap 一塊肥皂
a bar of chocolate 一塊巧克力
a grain of sand / rice / truth 一粒沙子／一粒米／一點真理

還有一些意思相近的詞，一個可數，一個不可數。例如：

可數名詞（單個）	不可數名詞（總稱）
a coat 一件外衣	clothing 衣物
a job 一份工作	work 工作

有些名詞雖然形式上是"s"或"es"結尾，意義上卻是單數，作主語時的動詞變注意要用單數，例如：news（消息）、maths（數學）、physics（物理）、politics（政治）等等。

第四節：名詞在句中的作用

名詞在句子中可以當作主詞、主詞補語、受詞（或構成複合受詞）、形容詞、同位語、稱呼語和副詞。

(1) 主詞：

- **China opens a new chapter in space exploration.**
  中國在空間探索上開啟一頁新的篇章。
- **Big Ben in London will celebrate its 150th birthday in 2009.**
  倫敦大笨鐘將在2009年慶祝它150週年的生日。
- **Aspirin and vitamin C help fight colds and flu.**
  阿司匹林和維生素C有助於抵抗流感和傷風。
- **Curiosity is a scholar's first virtue.**
  好奇心是學者的第一美德。

(2) 主詞補語：

- **A laptop is my good friend.** 筆記型電腦是我的好夥伴。
- **Knowledge is power.** 知識就是力量。
- **Observation is the best teacher.** 觀察是最好的老師。

(3) 受詞：

- **They planted more than 1.2 million trees last year.**
  去年他們種了120多萬棵樹。
- **I mowed the lawn.** 我除了草。

(4) 形容詞（修飾語）：

- **He is my pen pal.** 他是我的筆友。
- **Dancing is an exciting art form.** 舞蹈是一種令人激動的藝術形式。

(5) 同位語：

- **Tom's father, a successful lawyer, went to Europe yesterday.**
  湯姆的父親，一位事業成功的律師，昨天到歐洲去了。

(6) 稱呼語：

- **Come in, Miss Smith.** 史密斯小姐，請進。

• **Amy, pass me the dictionary, please.** 艾咪，請把那本字典遞給我。

(7) 副詞：

• **The sports meeting lasted a week.** 運動會持續了一整個星期。

• **The telephone rang a second time.** 電話響第二次了。

第五節：名詞的所有格

　　英語的文法中，名詞通常有三個格：主格（作主詞）、受格（作受詞）和所有格。其中只有所有格有形式變化。名詞中表示所有關係的形式叫名詞所有格。名詞所有格的構成形式有以下三種：

1. 表示有生命之物的名詞所有格在詞尾加「's」

Mr. Wang's telephone number 王先生的電話號碼

his father's study 他父親的書房

(1) 以s結尾複數名詞的所有格只在名詞後加「'」，如：

Teachers' Day 教師節　　**the students' opinion** 學生的意見

(2) 不以s結尾複數名詞的所有格要加「's」，如：

Women's rights 婦女的權利　　**Children's Day** 兒童節

(3) 複合名詞的所有格，在最後一個名詞後加「's」，如：

her son-in-law's photo 她女婿的照片

（比較複數形式：sons-in-law 此處s加在核心名詞後面。）

his sister-in-law's friend 他嫂嫂的朋友

(4) 如果一件東西為兩人或三人共有，則在後一個名詞或最後一個名詞後面加「's」；如果不是共有的，則每個名詞的後面都要加「's」，如：

Jane and Betty's room 珍妮和貝蒂的房間（共有）

Bill's and Tom's books 比爾的書和湯姆的書（不共有）

(5) 在表示「店鋪」、「某人家」、「診所」等時，通常會加上「's」，以省略掉名詞所有格後面的名詞。

at the tailor's 在裁縫店

at the barber's 在理髮店

the Li's 李家

at my uncle's 在我叔叔家

at the doctor's 在診所

(6) 有些表示時間、距離、國家、城鎮、機構的名詞後面也可加「**'s**」，用來表示所有格。

today's newspaper 今天的報紙

half an hour's lecture 半小時的講課

Taiwan's democracy 台灣的民主

Beijing's parks 北京的公園

2. 表示無生命的東西的名詞通常會搭配 of 構成片語

the title of the song 歌名

the workshops of the plant 工廠的工作坊

the middle of the river 河中央

有生命的東西的名詞也可以用of片語來表示所有格，特別是當這個名詞較長或有較長的形容詞時。例如：

the works of Marx, Engels, Lenin and Stalin 馬恩列斯著作

the name of the girl over there 那邊那位女孩的名字

3. 名詞所有格有時可以和of構成片語

有時所有關係還可用「片語of + 's所有格」形式表達。但這種屬格用來表示人的所有關係，而不是物。例如：

a friend of Ming's (= one of Ming's friends) 明朋友當中的一個

some sons of Mr. Hamilton's (= some of Mr. Hamilton's sons)
漢密爾頓先生的幾個兒子

若要將「'」和「of」這兩個表示所有關係的用法放在一起，主要會是在下列兩種情況下使用：

(1) 它所修飾的詞前面有一個表示數量的詞（例如：**a, two, some, any, no, few**等），如：

two aunts of Bob's 鮑伯的兩個阿姨

a picture of my mother's 我母親（擁有的）一張照片

（她有好幾張照片，這一張照片上的人不一定是她本人。試比較：a picture of my mother 我母親〈她本人〉的一張照片）

some inventions of Edison's 愛迪生的一些發明

Several students of Lao Yang's acted in the play.
老楊的幾個學生參加了戲劇的演出。

(2) 它所修飾的詞前面有一個指示代名詞，使句子表示讚賞或厭惡等感情色彩。

- **That little daughter of your brother's is very clever.**
你弟弟的小女兒非常的聰明。
（比your brother's little daughter 更帶有讚美的意味）

- **That dog of Robert's is really clever.**
羅伯特的那隻狗真聰明。（比Robert's dog更有讚嘆意味）

- **Get away those dirty hands of yours!**
快把你的髒手拿開！（比your dirty hands 有更強的厭惡情緒）

- **I'm all for this idea of yours.**
我完全贊同你的想法。（比your idea 更具欣賞意味）

- **Tom hated that pride of Mary's.**
湯姆討厭瑪麗那種驕傲的態度。（比僅用Mary's pride表現出更大的厭惡情緒）

1. _____ will be the presenter in the seminar.
   A. A friend of Mary's   B. Mary's a friend
   C. Mary's one friend   D. A friend of Mary

2. _____ father is a movie script writer.
   A. Nina's and Mary   B. Mary's and Nina's
   C. Nina and Mary's   D. Mary and Nina

3. The handmade pair of jeans _____ sold for three thousand dollars.
   A. was   B. were   C. did   D. does

4. f luck _____ on my side, I shall be able to play a part in the movie after the audition.
   A. is   B. does   C. are   D. have

5. The furniture _____ twenty thousand dollars. I can't afford it.
   A. costs   B. costing   C. spends   D. spending

6. Three million dollars _____ a large sum of money. Be careful when you carry so much cash.
   A. is   B. are   C. was   D. were

7. There is _____ work left. We can finish it pretty soon.
   A. many   B. few   C. much   D. little

8. He offered _____ to us.
   A. piece of useful advice   B. a useful piece of advice
   C. useful advice   D. a useful advice

9. Though the hope of overthrowing the tyranny _____ frail, the activists stilled started a revolution.
   A. was   B. were   C. have been   D. had been

10. The literary works of the author _____ highly regarded. Some of them _____ into movies.
   A. are; were adopted   B. are; were adapted
   C. was; has been   D. are; have adapted

1. 正解為(A)。本題考的所有代名詞。這句話的意思是說「瑪麗的一個朋友會是這場研討會的發表者。」

2. 正解為(C)。本題意思是「妮娜和瑪莉的父親是一位電影劇本寫手。」名詞所有格的寫法，兩人的父親只有一人，表示是共同擁有，所有格的 's寫在第二個名詞的後面。

3. 正解為(A)。這句話的意思是「這件手工牛仔褲以三千元的價格售出。」這裡考的是一件牛仔褲雖然jeans加了s，但是以單數看待。

4. 正解為(A)。這句話的意思是「如果幸運的話，這次試鏡之後我就會能夠在電影中演出一個角色。」這邊考的是luck 是不可數名詞，後面接單數動詞。

5. 正解為(A)。本題的句子是「這件家具要價兩萬元。我負擔不起」。這邊考的是家具furniture是不可數名詞，後面接單數動詞。

6. 正解為(A)。句子的意思是「三百萬是一大筆錢。帶那麼多現金在身上要小心。」這裡考的是three million dollars 是一個整體，看作是單數。

7. 正解為(D)。這句話的意思是「只剩下很少的工作要做。我們可以很快就完成」。Work是不可數名詞，前面接much或little，但是根據上下文的提示，應該選的是little，很少的意思。

8. 正解為(B)。這題的意思是說「他提供一個很好的建議給我們。」這裡用「a piece of advice」 表示「一則建議」而形容詞useful 就加在中間，應寫作a useful piece of advice。

9. 正解為(A)。本句意思是「雖然推翻暴政的希望很微弱，行動份子還是發起了革命。」句子當中的主詞hope是不可數名詞，用單數動詞。

10. 正解為(B)。本題題目的意思是「這位作家的文學作品備受推崇。其中有些被改編為電影。」這裡考的是完成是動詞的單複數，因為works作品是複數的，第一個空格要填 are 或 were，第二個空格填複數形式的被動語態。

Day

02

冠詞
Article

Day 02 冠詞 Article

第一節：概述

冠詞是置於名詞之前，進而幫助說明名詞所表示的人或事物的一種虛詞。它本身不能單獨使用，而中文裡沒有冠詞，所以將中文句子翻譯成英文時，要注意冠詞的使用。

1. 冠詞的種類

冠詞有兩種，分別是不定冠詞(a/an)和定冠詞(the)。不定冠詞和定冠詞的區別可用下列例子說明：

泛指	特指
He bought a car. 他買了輛汽車。	He rode to work in the new car. 他開著那輛新車去上班。

泛指	特指
Good medicine tastes bitter. 良藥苦口。	Take the medicine. 把這藥吃掉。

(1) 不定冠詞

不定冠詞一般修飾單數可數名詞，有 a 和 an 兩種形式。不定冠詞後面所接的單字若以母音開頭時用an[æn]，以子音開頭時用a [ə]。例如：

子音開頭用a	母音開頭用an
a small island 一個小島	an island 一個島嶼
a country 一個國家	an American 一個美國人

(2) 定冠詞

定冠詞 the 用於特指，一般的可數不可數名詞都能用定冠詞修飾。它有兩種讀音：若定冠詞後所接的單字是以子音開頭時讀[ð]，以母音開頭時讀[ði]。

子音開頭用a	母音開頭用an
the student (the students) [ðə] 那個（些）學生	**the honest student(s)** [ði] 那個（些）誠實的學生
the polluted water [ðə] 那些被污染的水	**the unpolluted water** [ði] 那些未被污染的水

2. 冠詞的位置

(1) 在名詞片語中，冠詞一般放在最前面

不定冠詞	定冠詞
a dictionary 一本字典	**the last few days** 最後的日子
an old blue car 一輛藍色的舊車	**the owner of a shop** 某店的店主

(2) 名詞片語裡如果有：all, both, exactly, just, many, twice, half, quite, rather, such, what等詞，這類詞可放在冠詞之前

all the time	自始至終
both (the) sisters	姐妹兩都
exactly the wrong number	正是那錯誤的數字
It's just the right place.	就是這個地方了。
I've only done half the work.	我只做了一半的工作。
It's quite a problem.	這真是個難處理的問題。

(3) 和as, how, so, too 連用時，形容詞放在冠詞之前

He's not so big a fool as you think.	他沒你想的那麼傻。
She's as beautiful a girl as you can imagine.	你可以想像她有多漂亮。

It was too good a chance to be missed.	這是個好機會，不能錯過。

🚩 第二節：不定冠詞的用法

1. 基本用法

(1) 表示數量「一」（強調時用one）或「任何一個」

I bought a dictionary and two pens.
我買了一本字典和兩支鋼筆。（數量）

Give me a book. 給我一本書。
（泛指、無特定，意即隨便哪一本都行）

(2) 第一次提到或出現「某一個」，但並不特別指明具體情況

One day, an old woman went into a shop with her grandson.
有一天，一位老太太帶著孫子走進一家商店。

(3) 在作修飾語的名詞前加上不定冠詞，說明名詞所代表的東西（人或物）屬於哪一類

Dr. Peter Baker is an expert on DNA.
彼得・貝克博士是DNA方面的專家。

We all thought of him as a suitable person for the job.
我們都認為他是適合這項工作的人。

(4) 當某一單個的人或事物能說明整個類屬的特點時，可在這個名詞前加上不定冠詞來概括整體，例如：

A teacher must love his students. 老師應該要愛護學生。
(=Teachers must love their students.)

(5) 在表示價格、速度、比率等的名詞前表示「每一」

four times a day 每天四次
sixty miles an hour 每小時60英里

(6) 表示「相同尺寸、年齡」等

They are nearly of an age. 他們年紀相近。
These doors are of a size. 這些門尺寸一樣。

2. 慣用片語

all of a sudden 突然	as a matter of fact 事實上
as a result 結果	a little 一點、一些
a bit 一點	a great many 許多、大量
a great deal (of...) 許多	a lot (of...) 許多
have a cold 感冒	make a fool of 捉弄
go for a walk 去散步	have a good time 玩得很開心
be a waste of time 浪費時間	make a fuss 大驚小怪

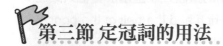 **第三節 定冠詞的用法**

1. 基本用法

有明確、限定、特指意義的名詞，就用 the，例如：

(1) 前面已提及的名詞，在後面提到時通常要加 the

The book is about farming and gardening.
該書是關於農事和園藝方面的。

(2) 談話雙方都知道的

Pass me the book, please.
請把書遞過來。（雙方都知道指的是哪本書）

The film is not just about love.
這部電影不只是愛情。（雙方都知道是哪部電影）

(3) 帶有某些限制性成分的名詞要加 the。這時名詞的詞義被縮小到一個特定的範圍內，這類的限制性成分包括：

(a) 形容詞

名詞	加上限制性成分的片語	中譯
days 日子	the good old days	從前美好的日子
class 班級	the same class	同一個班

(b) 有限定性質的形容詞子句

We will visit the factory which makes minibuses.
我們將參觀生產小型汽車的工廠。

(c) 介系詞片語

the ice sheet in Greenland 格陵蘭的冰層

(d) 分詞和分詞片語

The fire fighters arrived at the burning building.
消防人員趕到了著火的房子。

(3) 單數可數名詞前加 the 代表一類人或物的整體，以區別於其他人或物

This is America—the paradise of the rich and the hell of the poor.
這就是美國——富人的天堂，窮人的地獄。

The dead no longer need help. We must do something for the living.
死去的人已不需要什麼幫助了。我們應當為活著的人做點什麼。

此外還有 **the blind**（盲人）、**the deaf**（聾子）、**the old**（老人）、**the young**（年輕人）、**the impossible**（不可能的事）等等。

(4) 表示世界上獨一無二的名詞

the sun 太陽、the moon 月亮、the earth 地球、the east 東方

(5) 用在序數詞和形容詞最高級前

the first 第一、the best 最好

(6) 用在某些由普通名詞構成的國家名稱、機關團體、階級等專有名詞前。

the United States 美國

(7) 用在表示樂器的名詞之前。

the piano 鋼琴；the violin 小提琴

(8) 用在姓氏的複數名詞之前，表示一家人。

the Greens 格林一家人

2. 慣用片語

on the whole 總括來說	to tell the truth 說真話
on the left / right 在左邊/右邊	in the middle of 在……中間
go to the theatre (cinema) 看戲（電影）	in the day 在白天
the day after tomorrow 後天	the day before yesterday 前天
in the rain 在雨中	in the distance 在遠處
in the middle (of) 在～中間	by the way 順便說說

重點提示：必學文法小要點

在有些片語中，有冠詞和無冠詞意思不同，請注意使用上的區別：

無冠詞	有冠詞
in front of 在～前面	in the front of 在～範圍內的前部
in hospital （生病）住院	in the hospital 在醫院裡

第四節：專有名詞前冠詞的用法

大多數專有名詞不加冠詞，但有些根據習慣要用冠詞。

1. 不用冠詞的情況

人名	Hank 漢克	Joe 喬	Mark Twain 馬克·吐溫
地名	Taipei 台北	Asia 亞洲	Mediterranean 地中海
街道	Seventh Avenue 第七大道	Broadway 百老匯	Time square 時代廣場
其他	Sunday 星期天	May 五月	German 德語

2. 要用定冠詞的情況

the Pacific Ocean 太平洋	the Himalayas 喜馬拉雅山
the Philippine Island 菲律賓群島	the Sahara 薩哈拉沙漠
the Great Salt Lake 大鹽湖	the Lake of Geneva 日內瓦湖

the United Nations 聯合國	the State Department 國務院
the World Trade Centre 世界貿易中心	The Atlantic Pact 大西洋公約

3. 用不定冠詞的情況

不定冠詞表示「一」、「某一」，用於泛指。用於專有名詞前也產生同樣效果。

(1) 「一」、「某一」、「一類」

A Mr. Black called this morning.
一位叫布萊克的先生今天上午來過電話。

(2) 表示「類似……的一個」，相當於one like

Your son is an Edison. He likes to invent things.
你兒子真像個愛迪生，喜歡發明東西。

(3) 用於有修飾語修飾的專有名詞前說明某種屬性或特色

It was a hot August.
那是個炎熱的八月。

(4) 人名、商標前加不定冠詞可表示一件作品、產品

I bought a Van Gogh.
我買了一幅梵谷的畫。

4. 不加定冠詞和加了定冠詞

表示不同意義，例如：星期、月份、日期之前一般不用冠詞，但有時會加上定冠詞 the 表示特定的時間。

The winter here is quite warm.
這裡的冬天很暖和。

They completed the project in the summer of 2005.
他們在2005年夏天完成了該項目。

重點深度學： **Day 02** **進階挑戰**

　　若要表示某個大概的、不具體的時間，會用不定冠詞 a/an。例如：

He left on a Sunday of July.
他是在7月份的某個星期天離開的。

We had a terribly cold spring last year.
去年春天冷得要命。

第五節：不定冠詞和定冠詞的省略

　　為了文字簡潔、美觀，而在說、聽雙方確認對指涉對象無疑，可以將不定冠詞 a/ an和定冠詞 the 省略。例如：

Bus No. 1 was late. 一號公車誤點了。
(Bus No.1前省去了定冠詞 the，也可補上。)

Letter from Taiwan. 臺灣來信。
(Letter前省去了不定冠詞 a，可補上。)

　　最常出現的定冠詞與不定冠詞省略句式，大致有以下幾種：

(1) 避免重複，同等成分的後者常省略不定冠詞或定冠詞

例句	中譯	說明
At that moment a teacher and (a) student came in.	這時一位老師和一名學生進來了。	student前面省去了不定冠詞 a
Do you like the rose or (the) tulip of the flowers?	花朵中你喜歡玫瑰花還是鬱金香?	tulip 前省去了定冠詞 the

(2) 口語中，雙方都已明確，且不定冠詞或定冠詞位在句首時，往往可省略。

例句	中譯	說明
(A) Girl is waiting for you at the door.	大門口有位女孩在等你。	句首省去不定冠詞 a

例句	中譯	說明
(The) Class is over.	課結束了。	句首省略了定冠詞 the
It is raining hard. We need a raincoat and (an) umbrella.	雨下得很大。我們需要雨衣和雨傘。	umbrella前省去了不定冠詞 an
The short term and (the) long term loan are handled very differently by the bank.	銀行對長期與短期貸款的處理方式截然不同。	二者是同事物，long term前省去了定冠詞 the
(The) Football season begins next month.	足球賽季下個月開始。	句首省略了定冠詞 the

(3) 報紙標題

例句	中譯	說明
(A) Warm welcome to James Trudeau.	熱烈歡迎賈斯汀‧杜魯道。	句首省略了不定冠詞 a
(The) Canadian Commander in Chief in Shanghai.	加拿大總司令在上海。	句首省略了定冠詞 the

(4) 廣告

例句	中譯	說明
(The) Leather Jacket on Discount.	皮夾克正在打折。	句首省略了定冠詞 the
(A) Film *Into the Woods* on Show.	正在上演《魔法黑森林》電影。	句首省略了不定冠詞 a
(A) Tour Guide Wanted.	招聘導覽員。	句首省略了不定冠詞 a
(The) Time is up.	時間到了。	句首省略了定冠詞 the

(5) 書名、圖解、便條、日記、電子郵件中，為了醒目、簡潔、美觀而省去不定冠詞和定冠詞，例如：

Modern English Chinese Dictionary.《現代英漢詞典》

(6) 如果把並列名詞看作一個整體，後面的冠詞也可以省略

I'm an expert on illnesses of the ear, (the) nose and (the) throat.
我是一個耳鼻喉科專家。

A smile and (a) handshake show welcome.
微笑和握手表示歡迎。

She eats with a knife and (a) fork.
她用刀叉吃飯。

第六節：零冠詞的用法

用於專有名詞、抽象名詞和物質名詞前，而且還用於類名詞、集合名詞以及名詞化的各種詞類。特定對象跟泛指的對象都可以用。例如：

- **Disease may be aggravated by anxiety.**
  疾病會因焦慮而惡化。（抽象名詞，泛指對象）
- **Plane is the fastest mode of transport.**
  飛機是最快的運輸方式。（單數名詞，泛指對象）

有時候名詞前面加或不加冠詞，會代表不同的意思，例如：

表現抽象概念	表示具體去某地
go to sea 當水手	go to the sea 到海邊去
go to hospital 去看病	go to the hospital 去某醫院
be at table 在用餐	be at the table （坐）在桌子旁
in charge of 負責，主管	in the charge of 由……負責
in place of 代替	in the place of 在……地方

1. We visited _____ Smiths who live in _____ small town.
   A. the; the   B. the; a   C. a; the   D. a; a

2. _____ date of _____ year-end party has not been decided yet.
   A. A; a   B. The; the   C. A ; the   D. The; a

3. I wouldn't see _____ board clearly sitting in _____ back of the classroom.
   A. a; a   B. a; the   C. the; x   D. the; the

4. _____ Mt. Kilimanjaro is located in _____ East Africa.
   A. A; the   B. The; a   C. x; x   D. the; the

5. _____ Louvre is not open to _____ public when it's under renovation.
   A. A; the   B. The; a   C. x; the   D. the; the

6. The commercial is appealing to both _____ young and _____ old.
   A. the; the   B. the; a   C. a; a   D. x; x

7. Mr. White is not in the office at ____ moment. He is out of _____ town for business.
   A. the; the   B. the; a   C. a ; the   D. the; x

8. _____ Chapter II is about _____ use of nouns.
   A. The; the   B. x; the   C. The; x   D. x; x

9. He met _____ Queen when he visited London in _____ September of 2016.
   A. the; the   B. x; x   C. x; the   D. the; x

10. _____ Osaka is sleeted to host _____ World Fair in 2025.
    A. The; the   B. x ; the   C. the; x   D. x; x

1. 正解為(B)。此題當中Smiths是史密斯一家人，而小鎮未有明確的指涉對象，所以用不定冠詞 a。

2. 正解為(B)。兩個詞都是屬於可明確推知有特定指涉對象，而非泛指的用法，所以兩個空格中都要填定冠詞 the。

3. 正解為(D)。黑板應該是有特定指涉對象的用法，所以用定冠詞，而「in the back of the classroom」是固定用法，表示「在教室裡面的後方」。

4. 正解為(C)。句子當中的兩個專有名詞，習慣用法都是前面不加冠詞。

5. 正解為(D)。羅浮宮為專有名詞，慣用是前面有加定冠詞「the」，而「the public」是慣用法，表示「大眾」。

6. 正解為(A)。句子的意思是「這個廣告對年輕人和老人都有吸引力。」其中用到「the + 形容詞」代表某個族群的人。

7. 正解為(D)。句子當中，「at the moment」是在「目前、現在」，而「out of town」是「出城去」，是表示抽象概念，不加定冠詞，兩者都是習慣的用法。

8. 正解為(B)。第二章可以說是「the second chapter」或者「chapter two」，習慣用法是將數字放在後面時，前面不加定冠詞。「the use of nouns」是代表「名詞的用法」，表示抽象的概念，前面有加定冠詞。

9. 正解為(A)。「the Queen」是特定指「Queen Elizabeth」，而九月September本來前面是不用加定冠詞 the，但指某一年的九月時，前面要加定冠詞。

10.正解為(B)。大阪Osaka是專有名詞，慣用的用法是前面不會加定冠詞。「the World Fair」意思是「世界博覽會」，習慣的用法是前面會加定冠詞the。

Day

03

代名詞
Pronoun
Part1

Day 03 代名詞 Pronoun Part1

第一節：概述

代替名詞的詞叫做代名詞。代名詞可以分為以下九類：

1. 人稱代名詞	2. 所有代名詞	3. 反身代名詞
4. 指示代名詞	5. 相互代名詞	6. 疑問代名詞
7. 關係代名詞	8. 連接代名詞	9. 不定代名詞

第二節：人稱代名詞

人稱	數 格	單數		複數	
		主格	受格	主格	受格
第一人稱		I 我	me 我	we 我們	us 我們
第二人稱		you 你	you 你	you 你們	you 你們
第三人稱		he 他	him 他	they 他們	them 他們
		she 她	her 她	they 她們	them 她們
		it 它	it 它	they 它們	them 它們

1. 人稱代名詞主格的用法

(1) 人稱代名詞的主格主要當作句子的主詞

You should do as the teacher tells you to.
你應該照老師講的那樣去做。

You, she (he) and I all enjoy music.
你、她（他）和我都喜歡音樂。

(a) 表示月亮、船隻、國家、大地等的名詞常用she代替：

The moon is shining brightly tonight. She is like a round silvery plate.
今夜月光明亮。她好似一個銀色的圓盤。

(b) 主詞是動物或無生命的東西，需擬人化或表示說話者對它的情感時，常用he, she代替 it：

The elephant is proud of himself, for he has a big and strong body.
大象很自豪，因為他有龐大強壯的身體。

(c) you 究竟是表示單數「你」還是表示複數「你們」，往往要根據具體情況來確定：

Are you tired, Rick? 瑞克，你累了嗎？（you表示單數）
You are good boys, and I am proud of you.
你們真是好孩子，我為你們感到驕傲。（you表示複數）

(d) we, you有時用來泛指一般人：

We (You) never know what may happen in the future.
誰也不知道將來會發生什麼事。

(e) they也可用來泛指某些人：

They don't allow us to smoke here.
這裡不可以抽菸。（they代替誰不清楚）
They say that honesty is the best policy.
人們說誠實是上策。（they泛指人們）

(f) 第三人稱單數 it 常代表已提到過的一件事物：

I love swimming. It keeps me fit.
我喜歡游泳，它能使我保持健康。

(g) 當說話者不清楚、或沒必要知道說話物件的性別時，也可以用 it 指代：

It's a lovely baby, isn't it? 寶寶真可愛，不是嗎？
Is it a boy or a girl? 是男孩還是女孩？
There is someone knocking at the door. Who is it?
有人敲門。是誰呢？

(h) it 還可用來指代時間、距離、自然現象等。例如：

It is half past three now. 現在是三點半。
It is six miles to the nearest hospital from here.
離這裡最近的醫院，也有六英里的距離。

It is very cold in winter here. 這裡冬天很冷。

(i) it 有時沒有特定的指涉對象。例如：
How's it going with you? 你近況如何？

重點深度學： 進階挑戰

it 除了當作代名詞外，還可以作虛主詞、虛受詞，或用在強調結構。

(1) it 作虛主詞

例句	中譯	說明
It's no use crying.	哭是沒用的。	真正的主詞是crying
It is dangerous for you to swim in the river.	在這條河裡游泳是危險的。	真正的主詞是"for you to swim in the river"
It is a waste of time to talk to him.	跟他談話是白白浪費時間。	真正的主詞是"to talk to him"

(2) it 作虛受詞

例句	中譯	說明
We thought it no good telling him that.	我們認為把那件事告訴他絕沒有好處。	真正的受詞是"telling him that"
Don't take it for granted that he is honest.	別理所當然地認為他是誠實的。	真正的受詞是that引導的名詞子句

(3) it 用於強調結構

例句	中譯	說明
It was Madeleine who lost her necklace at the palace ball last night.	昨晚在皇宮舞會上丟了項鍊的是瑪德蓮。	強調主詞Madeleine
It was her necklace that Madeleine lost at the palace ball last night.	昨晚瑪德蓮在皇宮舞會上丟的是項鍊。	強調受詞necklace

| It was last night that Madeleine lost her necklace at the palace ball. | 瑪德蓮是昨晚在皇宮舞會上丟項鍊的。 | 強調時間last night |
| It was at the palace ball that Madeleine lost her necklace last night. | 昨晚瑪德蓮是在皇宮舞會上丟的項鍊。 | 強調地點 at the palace ball |

2. 人稱代名詞受格的用法

(1) 人稱代名詞受格一般當作受詞（包括直接受詞、間接受詞與介系詞受詞）

例句	中譯	說明
We often go to see her on Sundays.	我們常在星期天去看她。	直接受詞her
She gave me some water.	她給了我一些水。	間接受詞me
I don't want to go with them.	我不想跟他們一起走。	介系詞受詞them

(2) 人稱代名詞用於as和than之後，如果as和than是作介系詞，往往用受格；如果as 和than用作連接詞，則往往用主格

例句	中譯	說明
He is taller than me.	他比我高。	than 作介系詞
I am a good student as him.	我和他一樣是個好學生。	as 作介系詞
He is taller than I (am).	他比我高。	than 作連接詞
I am as tall as he is	我和他一樣高。	he 作連接詞

第三節：所有代名詞

代名詞的所有格，有形容詞性質的和所有代名詞兩種。

	我的	你的	他、她、它的	我們的	你們的	他們的
形容詞所有格	my	your	his, her, its	our	your	their
所有代名詞	mine	yours	his, hers, its	mine	yours	theirs

1. 代名詞的所有格

相當於形容詞，只能修飾後面的名詞。

my childhood 我的童年	his face 他的臉	our school 我們的學校
her baby 她的嬰兒	your parents 你的父母親	their family 他們的家

2. 所有代名詞的用法

所有代名詞相當於名詞，可用作主詞、補語和受詞，還可用「of+所有代名詞」結構作修飾語。

(1) 作主詞

例句	中譯	說明
His father is a driver; mine is a doctor.	他父親是司機；我父親是醫生。	mine代替my father
Our room is on the first floor and theirs (is) on the second.	我們的房間在二樓，他們的房間在三樓。	theirs代替their room

(2) 作句子中的主詞補語

This room is ours. That's yours. 這個房間是我們的。那間是你們的。

(3) 作受詞

My husband often writes letters to his parents, but he only sends postcards to mine.

我丈夫常寫信給他父母，但只會寄明信片給我父母。

(4) 與of連用構成雙重所有格作修飾語

He is a friend of mine. 他是我的一個朋友。

(5) 可當作禮貌用語

A Happy New Year to you and yours from me and mine.（mine 代替 my family）

我和我的全家祝你和你全家新年快樂！

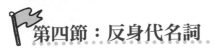

第四節：反身代名詞

反身代名詞在句中的用法：

(1) 作受格

She is too young to look after herself.
她年紀太小了，不能照顧自己。

(2) 作主詞補語

He will be himself again very soon. 他等一下就會好的。

(3) 作同位語時，表示某人「本人自己」或「親自」。

Life itself is a great school, and everything that inspires thought is a teacher.
生活本身就是一所巨大的學校，鼓舞思想的每種事物都是一位老師。

(4) 反身代名詞偶爾當作主詞。

Peter and myself know nothing about it.
彼得和我都對此事一無所知。

某些詞常和反身代名詞連用搭配成習慣用法，例如：
amuse oneself 自娛 excuse oneself 自我辯解
speak to oneself 自言自語 devote oneself to 獻身於
make oneself understood 讓別人懂自己的意思

重點深度學：Day 03 進階挑戰

另外有一些固定慣用語，需要特別記起來，例如：
＊by oneself 獨自地，單獨地
He lives there all by himself. 他一個人住那裡。
＊for oneself 替自己，為自己
He has a right to decide for himself. 他有權自己決定。
＊in oneself 本身，本質上
Nothing on earth is either good or bad in itself.
地球上的任何事物本身無善惡。

＊between ourselves 私下説的話（不可告訴別人）

All this is between ourselves.

這些都不能告訴別人。

＊among oneselves ……之間

They had a heated discussion among themselves.

他們之間進行了激烈的討論。

＊to oneself 供自己用

I do hope to have a room to myself. 我真希望有一個自己的房間。

第五節：指示代名詞

指示代名詞主要有: this（這個）、these（這些）、that（那個）、those（那些）。this的複數形式是these，指離説話人近的事物或人。that的複數形式是those，指離説話人遠的事物或人。

1. this / that / these / those 的用法

指示代名詞this，that，these，those在句中可以當作主詞、受詞、補語、修飾語、副詞等。

(1) 作主詞

This is my mother. 這是我媽媽。

Those are his books. 那些是他的書。

(2) 作受詞

Do you like these? 你喜歡這些嗎？

I will do that. 我願意做那件事。

(3) 作補語

What I want is that. 我想要的是那個。

My suggestion is this. 我的建議是這樣的。

(4) 作修飾語

These fast foods can be microwaved easily.
這些速食能方便地用微波爐加熱。

(5) 作副詞

this和that有時當作副詞，相當於so，表示程度，意為「這麼」和「那麼」。例如：

The tree is this high. 那棵樹有這麼高。

That book is that thick. 那本書有那麼厚。

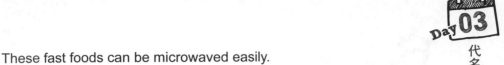

重點深度學：Day03 進階挑戰

(1) that 和 those 可以用來代替前面已提到過的名詞，以避免重複。例如：

The oil output in 2005 was much higher than that of 2000.
2005年的油產量比2000年的油產量高得多。

The machines made in this year are better than those made in last year.
今年生產的機器比去年生產的還要好。

(2) that 和 those 後面常會有一個修飾語（形容詞子句等等）。例如：

He was among those who passed the exam.
他是考試及格的人之一。

What's that hanging on the tree?
樹上掛的是什麼？

(3) 敘述事物時，that，those指前面整句話描述的狀況或事物，中文常用「這」來表示。

We don't have enough money to do it. That's our trouble.
我們資金不夠。這就是我們的問題。

What I want to tell you is this: English is very important.
我想要告訴你的是：英語十分重要。

第六節：相互代名詞

1. 受格形式

each other和one another都表示相互關係，一般認為one another較多用於較正式文體，而each other多用於非正式文體。相互代名詞只能作動詞或介系詞的受詞。例如：

They gave each other a present.
他們互相送禮物。

They write to each other/ one another every week.
他們每週都互相通信。

2. 所有格形式

相互代名詞的所有格形式（each other's 相互的，one another's 相互的）只能接在名詞前面使用。例如：

We are old friends and we know one another's liking.
我們是老朋友了，彼此知道各自的喜好。

People try to respect each other's privacy.
人們嘗試著尊重彼此的隱私。

第七節：疑問代名詞

疑問代名詞主要有：

1. who 誰（主格）	2. whom 誰（受格）	3. whose 誰的（所有格）
4. what 什麼（人、物）	5. which 哪一個，哪些（人、物）	

1. who, whom 的用法：

who 只能指人，在非正式英文和口語中，who 可以代替 whom，但介系詞後面要用 whom；whom 也指人，常當作受詞。例如：

Who did this? 誰做的？（主詞）　　Who is it? 是誰？（補語）

Who do you like best? 你最喜歡誰？（口語）

Whom do you like best? 你最喜歡誰？（較正式）

With whom did you go? 你和誰一起去的？

（口語中用 Who did you go with?）

2. whose 的用法：

whose 和所有代名詞一樣，具有名詞和形容詞性質，可作主詞、補語和修飾語。例如：

例句	中譯	說明
Whose is better? / Whose are better?	誰的比較好？	名詞性，作主詞，等於whose book / books等
Whose shirt is this?	這是誰的襯衫？	形容詞性，作修飾語
Whose is this?	這是誰的？	名詞性，作補語，等於whose book等

3. what 的用法：

what 表示「什麼（人或物）」，可當作單數和複數，具有名詞和形容詞性質，作主詞、受詞、補語、修飾語等。例如：

例句	中譯	說明
What happened?	發生了什麼事？	主詞
What are you doing?	你在做什麼？	主詞
What is happiness?	幸福是什麼？	補語
What question do you want to ask?	你想問什麼問題？	修飾語

4. which 的用法：

which 表示「在一定範圍內的哪一個（哪一些）人或物」，可當作單數和複數，具有名詞和形容詞的性質，當作主詞、修飾語、受詞等。例如：

例句	中譯	說明
Which are yours? / Which is yours?	哪些（哪個）是你的？	主詞
Which do you prefer?	你比較喜歡哪一個？	主詞
Which language is the most widely spoken in the world?	哪一種語言在世界上使用最廣泛？	修飾語

5. 疑問代名詞的用法比較

(1) who與what的區別：

who 多用來問姓名、關係等，what 多用來問職業、地位等等
—What is he? 他是做什麼的？
—He's a director. 他是導演。

(2) which和who、what的區別：

who、what用來泛指，而which是特指，表示「在一定範圍內的哪個或哪些人、事物」

例句	中譯	說明
Who is Tom?	湯姆是誰呀？	泛指
Which is Tom?	哪一位是湯姆？	特指
What sport do you like best?	你最喜歡什麼運動？	不限制範圍
Which sport do you like best?	你最喜歡哪一項運動？	限制在一定範圍內

(3) 同是就「某人」提問，who 指的是主詞，而 which 則有區別意義。

Which of you wants to join in the game?
你們當中誰想參加這個遊戲？

這裡一般不用who，因為要參加的人都在這裡，只是不知道是其中哪一位或哪幾位。

(4) 疑問代名詞作主詞時，後面的動詞可使用複數形式，也可使用單數形式，主要取決於所代表的是單數名詞還是複數名詞。如果不清楚指的是單數還是複數，多使用單數形式。

Who lives in this house? 誰住在這間房子裡？

What's in the classroom? 教室裡有什麼？

第八節：關係代名詞

　　關係代名詞常用來引導關係子句（又稱為形容詞子句）。關係代名詞一方面在關係子句中擔任一個成分，如主詞、受詞、補語或修飾語，另一方面又代表關係子句所修飾的那個名詞或代名詞（通常稱為先行詞）。主要關係代名詞有：

1. who 主格—某人	2. whose 所有格—某人的	3. whom 受格—某人
4. that 指事物/人	5. which 代表事物	6. as 用在「such ~as」結構中

1. who, whom, whose 的用法

　　who和whom代表人，在關係子句中作主詞時用who，作受詞時用whom，非正式場合有時也用who代替，但介系詞後面一定要用whom。例如：

例句	中譯	說明
The foreigner who visited our school yesterday is from Canada.	昨天來參觀我們學校的那位外賓是加拿大人。	who在子句中作主詞
The person to whom you just talk is Mr. Li.	剛才跟你談話的那個人是李先生。	whom在子句中作talk to的受詞，由於介系詞to提前，所以只能用whom而不用who

　　whose 代表「某個人的」，在子句中作修飾語：

The only true great man is the man whose heart is beating for all people.

心為所有人跳動的人，才是真正的偉人。

2. which 的用法

which 指物，在關係子句中作主詞和受詞。作受詞時，在限定關係子句中可以省略。例如：

例句	中譯	說明
They planted the trees which didn't need much water.	他們種了些不太需要水的樹。	which在關係子句中作主詞
The fish (which) we bought were not fresh.	我們買來的那條魚不新鮮了。	which在限定關係子句中作受詞
This is the story from which we learned a lot.	這就是那個故事，我們從中受益匪淺。	which作介系詞from的受詞

3. that 的用法

that 可以指人，也可以指物。在關係子句中作主詞、補語和受詞。指物時與 which 大致相同。例如：

例句	中譯	說明
He is no longer the man that he was.	他已經不是過去的他了。	作關係子句的補語
The girl (that / who / whom) we saw yesterday is Jim's sister.	我們昨天看到的那個女孩是吉姆的姐妹。	作關係子句的受詞
Have you seen the note that she left on your desk?	你看見她放在你桌上的便條了嗎？	作關係子句的受詞

4. 當關係代名詞指物時，常用 that 而不用 which 的情況

(1) 當先行詞是everything, nothing, something, anything, all, little, much等不定代名詞時

Everything that I have seen in the room is in good order.
我在屋裡看到的一切都擺放得井井有條。

(2) 先行詞被all, every, no, some, any, little, much等詞修飾時

There is little time that we can spare.
沒有可以抽出的時間了。

(3) 先行詞被序數詞或形容詞最高級所修飾時

This is the best hotel that I know.
這是我知道最好的旅館。

(4) 在there be句型引導的關係子句中

There is a seat in the corner that is still free.
角落裡仍有一個空位。

(5) 當先行詞既是人又是物，或兩個不同的人或物時

Scientists also developed new fuels and engines that allow us to travel without the fear of polluting the environment.
科學家還開發了新型燃料和引擎，使我們旅行時不必擔心會污染環境。

Robots can only respond to things and ways that have been programmed by humans.
機器人只能對由人設計的東西和方式作出反應。

5. 關係代名詞指代事物時，常用which而不用that的情況

(1) 在非限定關係子句中

In 1988, he wrote *A Brief History of Time*, which quickly became a best seller.
1988年，他寫了《時間簡史》，很快成為暢銷書。

(2) 關係代名詞前有介系詞時

The games in which the young men competed were difficult.
那些年輕人參加的比賽很艱難。

(3) 關係代名詞後有插入句時

This is the book which, as I have told you, will help you to improve your English.

這就是我跟你說過的，能幫你學好英語的那本書。

6. 關係代名詞指人時，常用who而不用that的情況

(1) 先行詞為one, ones, anyone或those時

Anyone who breaks the rules will be punished.
任何違反規章制度的人都要受處罰。

Those who work deserve to eat; those who do not work deserve to starve.
勞動者應該享受美食，不勞動者應該忍饑挨餓。

(2) 在以there be開頭的句子中

There is a man who wants to see you. 有位男士要見你。

7. 關係代名詞作關係子句的受詞

若介系詞前置，則不能用that，而且只能用whom指人，which指物；若介系詞後置則不受這種限制

The room (that / which) they live in is not large.

The room in which they live is not large.（介系詞前置）他們住的房子並不大。

8. 關係代名詞的省略

(1) 在限定關係子句中，如果關係代名詞在子句中作受詞，可以省略；但在非限定關係子句中不可省略

Football is a sport (that / which) he likes.
足球是他喜歡的一種運動。

The runner (who / that) you are asking about is over there.
你要找的那位賽跑選手在那邊。

This poem, which almost everybody knows, is written by Li Bai.（正確）

This poem, almost everybody knows, is written by Li Bai. （錯誤）
這首大多數人知道的詩，是李白寫的。

(2) 能在關係子句中作表語的只有that，可指人或物，通常可以省略

She is not a beautiful young girl (that) she was before.
她不再是過去那個年輕漂亮的女孩了。

但that作關係子句的主語時，不可省略：

A plane is a machine that can fly. 飛機是一種能飛的機器。

Day

04

代名詞
Pronoun
Part2

第九節：連接代名詞

連接代名詞可連接主句和子句，並在子句中充當一定的句子成分；有格的變化，和指人指物的區別。連接代名詞的形式如下表：

	指人	指物	
主格	who	which	what
受格	whom		
所有格	whose	whose	

1. 連接代名詞引導主語子句

例句	中譯	說明
What I want to talk about is this.	我想談的事情就是這個。	what引導的子句作整個句子的主語，是作主詞用的子句，what相當於the thing which
It is not decided who may go first.	誰可以先走還沒決定。	It是虛主詞，真正的主詞是who引導的子句

2. 連接代名詞引導的受詞子句

例句	中譯	說明
Do you know whose book it is?	你知道這是誰的書嗎？	whose引導的子句作know的受詞，是受詞子句
I can't tell which picture is more beautiful.	我說不出哪一張畫比較漂亮。	which引導的子句作tell的受詞，是受詞子句

3. 連接代名詞引導的補語子句

例句	中譯	說明
That's what we are going to do this evening.	這就是今晚我們要做的事。	what引導補語子句，what等於 the thing which
The problem is who(m) we should ask.	問題是我們應該問誰。	who / whom引導補語子句

4. 連接代名詞還可帶出子句作為插入語

例句	中譯	說明
She shouted loudly and, what was rare, ran wildly in the field.	她大聲叫喊，還狂亂地在田野裡奔跑，這是更少有的。	what引導的子句作插入語，what代表後面提到的情況

重點深度學： Day 04 進階挑戰

who(m)，which和what還可以與ever構成合成詞，用以引導各類子句，作為強調作用，有「一切、任何」這類意思。

Whoever breaks the rules will be punished.
凡是破壞規定的人都要受到懲罰。

Richer countries have a responsibility towards poorer countries and must do whatever they can to help others.
富國對於窮國負有責任，他們必須盡可能地幫助其他國家。

Call to who(m)ever you want.
你可以打電話給任何你想找的人。

第十節：不定代名詞

不定代名詞可分為肯定和否定兩類：

肯定	否定
all、everybody	no、nobody、none
both、either	neither
everything、some	nothing、none、no
somebody、someone	no one、nobody、none
something	nothing
a little、a few	little、few

不定代名詞可以在句子中扮演不同的角色：

主詞	Many have set off. 許多人已經出發了。 Much has been done to welcome the Olympics. 為迎接奧運已做了許多工作。 One must do one's duty. 人人都應盡責。
主詞補語	That's all I can do. 這就是我能做到的一切。 He is something of a scholar. 他滿有學問的。
同位語	They all agree to carry out the plan quickly. 他們都同意快點執行這項計畫。
受詞	This apple is not good. Please give me another. 這顆蘋果不好，請給我另外一顆。 Jasmine was always ready to help others. 茉莉總是樂於助人。
形容詞	Have you got any other different opinion? 你有沒有不同的意見？ This story is much more interesting than the other two. 這個故事比另外兩個有趣得多。
副詞	I spent some two hours doing my homework yesterday. 昨天我大約花了兩個小時做作業。 "I don't think there's anything about a haircut that could make me love you any less," said Jim. 吉姆說：「我想就算妳把頭髮剪掉，也不會使我對妳的愛有任何減少。」

下面分述不定代名詞的用法。

1. some的用法

(1) some通常表示不定數量「一些」，修飾或代替可數名詞複數或不可數名詞，既可指人，又可指物。常用在肯定句中

Some people like pop music, but some don't.
有些人喜歡流行音樂，但有些人不喜歡。

(2) some有時可修飾可數名詞單數，表示「某個」

He went to some place in Europe.
他到歐洲某個地方去了。

(3) some也可用在「請求、建議、反問」等含義的疑問句中，以期得到肯定的回答

Why don't you take some apples?
你何不帶些蘋果去呢？

(4) some也可修飾數詞，表示「大約」

It took me some twenty days to get there.
我大約花了二十天時間才到達那裡。

2. any 的用法

　　不定代名詞 any和some一樣表示不定數量「一些」，修飾和代替可數名詞複數和不可數名詞，既可指人又可指物。但一般用在否定句、疑問句、條件子句中

Do you have any questions? If you have any, don't hesitate to ask me.
你有什麼問題嗎？如果你有問題的話，儘管問我好了。

Let me know if you find any.
如果你找到了，就告訴我。

3. 合成不定代名詞的用法

　　不定代名詞 some，any，no 和 -one，-body，-thing可組成幾個合成不定代名詞：

someone, somebody 某人	something 某事	anyone, anybody 任何人
anything 任何事	no one, nobody 沒有人	nothing 沒有事

合成不定代名詞都表示單數概念，且修飾合成不定代名詞的對象應放在它們後面，例如：

someone (that) I know 我認識的人	something important 重要的事
anything worth doing 值得做的任何事	everything in hand 手邊有的每樣東西

4. one 的用法

one可以當作不定代名詞來指代「一個人或事物」。

指代人→所有格形式 one's和反身代名詞oneself

美國英語中常用his / her；himself / herself與前面的one 相對應。例如：

One should be strict with oneself. 一個人應對自己要求嚴格。

Sad movies always make one cry. 悲傷的電影常常使人落淚。

指代事物→代替上文中出現過的名詞，以避免重複。

有時可有複數形式ones，有時還有自己的修飾語或冠詞。例如：

The story he told is a very interesting one.
他講得是個非常有趣的故事。

5. none的用法

none只具有名詞性質，可以代替人和事物，表示「三者(以上)都不」，「沒有一個人（一件事物）……」。作主語時，如果談到的是所有人的情況，動詞多用複數形式；如果談到的是每個人的狀況，則多用單數形式。例如：

例句	中譯	說明
None of us like to swim in the polluted water.	我們誰都不會喜歡在受污染的水中游泳。	none作主詞

| None of them has a bike. | 他們誰也沒有自行車。 | none作主詞 |
| I like none of the films. | 這些電影我全不喜歡。 | none作受詞 |

6. each, every 和 everyone, everybody, everything

(1) each表示「各個，每一個」，強調人和事物的個別情況。**every**強調「每個都，個個都，人人都」，含**all**之意。

例句	中譯	說明
Every citizen has equal rights regardless of race, color or creed.	不論種族、膚色、信仰，每個公民都擁有平等的權利。	修飾語
They each sang a song at the party last night.	昨天的晚會上他們每人各自唱了一首歌。	同位語
The teacher handed out exercise books to each of the students.	老師把練習本發給每一位同學。	受詞
Each in our group knows what to do next.	我們組每一個人都知道下一步自己該做什麼。	主詞

另外，every 還可表示時間的間隔「每，每隔」，例如：

He comes every other day. (= He comes every two days.)
他每隔一天來一次。(=他每兩天來一次。)

The Olympic Games are held every four years.
奧林匹克運動會每四年舉行一次。

(2) everyone, everybody和everything

只具有名詞性質，一般作主詞、受詞和補語等

例句	中譯	說明
Everyone / Everybody likes the new teacher.	每個人都喜歡這位新老師。	主詞
We've asked everybody.	我們已經問過所有的人了。	受詞
Money isn't everything.	金錢不是一切。	補語

7. all 的用法

all表示整體概念「全部」，用於兩個以上的人或物，或者不可數的事物。all的位置較靈活，應注意。例如：

例句	中譯	說明
All are here.	大家都到了。	主詞，all指人
All want, all lose.	什麼都想要，什麼也得不到。	主詞，all指事物
Bill visited all of us.	比爾拜訪了我們所有的人。	受詞
That's all I know.	我所知道的就是這些。	補語
I know them all.	我認識他們所有人。	同位語
All men are mortal.	人生自古誰無死。	修飾語

重點深度學： **Day 04** 進階挑戰

all與否定詞連用表示部分否定。全部否定要用none或no one。例如：

All are not friends that speak us fair. (=Not all are friends that speak us fair.)
說我們好話的並不都是朋友。

He hasn't paid it all. (= He has paid some of the money.)
他還未付清全部款項。

None knows the weight of another's burden.
沒人知道別人肩上的壓力。

He has paid none.
他什麼都沒付。

另外，all還可用作副詞，類似completely, totally。例如：
That's all wrong. 那全錯了。
She was all wet. 她身上全濕了。

8. both, either 和 neither 的用法

(1) **both**表示「兩者都」，作主詞時動詞用複數。與否定詞連用時表示部分否定，全部否定用**neither**。

例句	中譯	說明
Both are very honest.	兩個人都很誠實。	主詞
Both of them didn't go there. (=Not both of them went there, though one of them did.)	他們兩個並沒有都去那裡。	主詞，部分否定
Life is dear. Love is dearer. Both can be given up for freedom.	生命誠可貴，愛情價更高；若為自由故，兩者皆可拋。	主詞
Both my sisters are tall.	我的兩個姐妹個子都很高。	修飾語
Neither of them went there.	他們兩人都沒去那裡。	全部否定
These two pictures are very beautiful. I like both.	這兩張畫很美，我（兩張）都喜歡。	受詞
Give us some bread. We both want to try a bit.	給我們一些麵包。我們都想嚐嚐。	同位語
All street signs, names of cities and places must be written in both languages.	所有街道標示、城市名及各種場所的名稱都必須用兩種語言書寫。	修飾語

(2) **either** 表示「兩個中的任何一個」，**neither**表示「兩個都不」。**either**和**neither**作主語時動詞用單數。若作修飾語，所修飾的名詞也用單數。

例句	中譯	說明
Either of them sings very well.	他們兩人唱歌都不錯。	主詞
Neither of them has come yet.	他們兩人都還沒來。	主詞
Here are two dictionaries. You may use either of them.	這裡有兩本字典。你用哪本都可以。	受詞
I agree with neither of you.	你們兩個人的話我都不同意。	受詞
There are shops on either side of the street.(= on both sides)	街道兩邊都有商店。	修飾語
Neither book is expensive.	兩本書都不貴。	修飾語

9. other(s), another 的用法

other(s)和another都具有名詞和形容詞性質，可作主語、受詞和修飾語。

其中another接單數名詞，但後面接數詞時，也可用複數名詞，表示「再……」。

例如：another three weeks 再三個星期、buy another five pens 再買五支筆。

other(s)不加冠詞表示泛指「另外一些」，加了定冠詞表示「另外那個」、「另外那些」，具體用法如下表：

例句	中譯	說明
This skirt is too long, Please show me another. (= Show me another one.)	這條裙子太長了，請再拿一條給我看看。	泛指，受詞
I agree with you, but others may not. (others =other people)	我同意你，但別人可能不同意。	泛指，主詞
In this world there are only two tragedies. One is not getting what one wants, and the other is getting it.	世間只有兩個悲劇。一個悲劇是得不到自己想要的東西，另一個悲劇是得到自己想要的東西。	(the other = the other tragedy)

10. 表示數量的不定代名詞

a little, little, much→不可數名詞
a few, few, many→可數名詞
a little, a few→表示「一些」
little, few →表示「幾乎沒有，很少」。

例句	中譯	說明
I know little about him.	我對他瞭解甚少。	受詞
I have a few friends, but my younger sister has very few.	我有一些朋友，但我妹妹幾乎沒有什麼朋友。	修飾語，受詞
Few (of us) can speak four foreign languages.	（我們當中）很少有人會說四種外語。	主詞

little, much, many, few等詞也作形容詞，它們有比較級（less, more, fewer）。

11. 一些固定用法

注意下列部分表示數量的不定代名詞以及其他片語的用法：

(1) 用於不可數名詞

much 許多	little 幾乎沒有	a little 一些
less 較少	a great amount of 大量	a small amount of 少量的

(2) 用於可數名詞

many 許多	few 幾乎沒有	a few 一些
several 幾個	a great (good) many 大量	a great number of 大量的

(3) 可數和不可數名詞都可以

a lot of 許多	lots of 許多	more 更多	a quantity of 大量的
most 大多數	plenty of 足夠的	some 一些	quantities of 大量的

1. When the member of Congress arrived at the airport, _____ was picked up and brought to five-star hotel.
   A. he   B. him   C. his   D. himself

2. Nancy would check the report _____ to make sure there are no mistakes in it.
   A. she   B. her   C. hers   D. herself

3. David will never believe in _____ that the corrupted politician says.
   A. something   B. anything   C. everything   D. nothing

4. _____ in the audience of this concert has got the special figurine of the singer.
   A. Anyone   B. Everyone   C. Whoever   D. Whichever

5. The twin sisters have been helping _____ since they were little.
   A. both   B. all   C. each other   D. one another

6. Everything _____ is sold in this auction is verified to be genuine.
   A. which   B. that   C. what   D. who

7. I know _____ about the history of the U.S., so I am unfamiliar with the origins of some holiday traditions in that country.
   A. few   B. little   C. a few   D. a little

8. Kevin proposed two plans to the client, but _____ of them were accepted.
   A. both   B. one   C. either   D. neither

9. It is _____ three weeks until the holidays.
   A. other   B. another   C. the other   D. others

10. The average temperature in June this year is higher than _____ of the last year.
    A. this   B. that   C. these   D. those

1. 正解為(A)。此題空格中要填的代名詞指涉對象是「member of congress」，代名詞在句子當中扮演的角色是主詞，所以用主格的he。

2. 正解為(D)。這句話的意思是「親自確認報告沒有任何錯誤」，自己去做某件事，會使用反身代名詞「oneself」來表達。

3. 正解為(B)。本題句子表示「大衛再也不會相信貪腐政客所說的話」，否定的句子當中使用的不定代名詞為「anything」。

4. 正解為(B)。句子的意思為「演唱會觀眾每個人都獲得這位歌手的公仔。」其中anyone 通常用於否定和疑問句，而若要用Whoever，題目的句子應改為「whoever is in the audience of this concert can get the special figurine of the singer.」才是正確。

5. 正解為(C)。本句意思是「雙胞胎姊妹從小就會互相幫助」，選項(C)和(D)都是相互代名詞，而twin sister 表明是兩人之間互相幫助，需選用each other作為受詞；one another 是三者以上的互相。

6. 正解為(B)。句子的意思是「在這場拍賣會出售的每樣東西都被驗證為真品。」，其中用「everything」與其他像是「everything、anything、nothing」這類複合詞，接續的關係代名詞習慣用that而不是which。

7. 正解為(B)。句子當中，「know little about ~」是指「對某件事情所知甚少」，為否定意味，而選項(C)和(D)都是有肯定的意味。且對於歷史的知識，屬於抽象的概念，為不可數名詞，會使用little而非few來代替。

8. 正解為(D)。句子的意思是「凱文提出了兩個計劃，但是兩者都沒有被客戶接受」。選項中，both表示「兩者皆是」，one表示「其中一個」，either表示「兩者任一」，neither表示「兩者皆不」，題目的後半句用but開頭，表示前面的提案沒被接受，所以選用neither最符合語意。

9. 正解為(B)。本句的意思是「再過三個星期才會放假」，其中「再過幾個小時／星期／幾個月」通常用「for another three hours / weeks / months」來表示。

10.正解為(B)。本題題目的意思是「今年六月的平均溫度比去年六月的平均溫度高」，句子後半會用到指定代名詞來代替「the average temperature in June」，通常用that 或 those 代替前面提到過的同類型名詞。而temperature是單數的指涉對象，所以用that。

Day

05

數詞
Numeral

Day 05 數詞 Numeral

第一節：概述

在英語中表示數目或順序的詞稱為數詞，其中表示數目的詞稱為基數詞，表示數目順序的詞稱為序數詞，還有以基數詞和序數詞合成的分數詞。

類別	句法功能	例詞
基數詞	主詞、主詞補語、受詞、形容詞、同位語	nine, twelve, one hundred
序數詞	主詞、主詞補語、受詞、形容詞、同位語、副詞	first, ninth, fortieth
分數詞	主詞、主詞補語、受詞、形容詞、同位語、副詞	three-fifths, thirty percent

第二節：基數詞

1. 基數詞的表示法

英語中表示數目多少的詞叫做基數詞，例如：one, two, three等；1-20對應的單字如下：

one	two	three	four	five
six	seven	eight	nine	ten
eleven	twelve	thirteen	fourteen	fifteen
sixteen	seventeen	eighteen	nineteen	twenty

二十以上的數字就以「幾十 + 個位數字」，中間接上連字號來表達，例如：

| 21 twenty-one | 25 twenty-five | 32 thirty-two |
| 118 one hundred and eighteen | 366 three hundred and sixty-six | 279 two hundred and seventy-nine |

2. 基數詞的用法

基數詞在句子的角色如下。

功能	例句	中譯
主詞	It was reported that more than 200 people had been killed in the fire.	據報導，那場大火燒死了200多人。
主詞補語	Britain is one of the member states of the European Union.	英國是歐盟成員國之一。
主詞補語	Six times six is thirty-six.	6乘6等於36。
受詞	The bison population is thought to have fallen from 60 million to just a few hundred.	據說美洲野牛的數量已從6,000萬頭下降到幾百頭了。
修飾語	There are five different time areas in the United States.	在美國有五個不同的時區。
受詞補語	We call five two and three.	五是二加三得來的。

3. 數量詞的特殊用法

dozen、thousand、million、billion以複數形式出現，後面常接of+名詞，表示不確定的數目。

In 1963, Martin Luther King made a speech to thousands of black people that immediately became world famous.
1963 年，馬丁‧路德‧金向成千上萬的黑人發表了一篇演說，這篇演說詞立即成為舉世聞名的名篇。

This is because each year millions of smokers die from the habit of smoking.
這是因為每年都有幾百萬吸菸者死於這種（抽菸的）習慣。

Hundreds of students took part in the composition competition.
數百名學生參加了作文比賽。

第三節：序數詞

英語中表示順序先後的數詞叫做序數詞，例如：first、second、third 等。

1. 序數詞的表示法

(1) 英語序數詞第1-19除了first, second與third有特殊形式外，其餘的都由基數詞後加上字尾th構成。

fifth→第五	eighth→第八
ninth→第九	twelfth→第十二

(2) 十位數的序數詞的構成方法

先把十位數的基數詞的詞尾ty中的y變為i，然後加上字尾eth

twentieth→ 20th	thirtieth →30th	fortieth →40th
fiftieth→ 50th	sixtieth→ 60th	seventieth→ 70th
eightieth→ 80th	ninetieth→ 90th	

(3) 十位數的序數詞如果含有1-9的個位數時，十位數用基數詞，個位數用序數詞，中間用連字元符號「-」

twenty-first→21st	thirty-second→ 32nd
forty-third→43rd	fifty-fourth→ 54th

(4) 百、千、萬等的序數詞由hundred, thousand, million等加字尾th

one hundredth →100th	one millionth →1,000,000th
one thousandth →1,000th	one billionth →1,000,000,000th

注意：序數詞前的one不可用a代替。

另外，多位數序數詞的後位數字如果含有 1-9 時，則後位數用序數詞，前位數用基數詞，中間出現零時，用and連接。例如：

two hundred and first →201th
three thousand four hundred (and) fifty-sixth→ 3456th

2. 序數詞的用法

序數詞在句子中可扮演下列的角色：

功能	例句	中譯
主詞	The first is that it has stored supplies of fat in its body during the summer and autumn.	第一是在夏秋兩季，它體內儲存了大量的脂肪。
主詞補語	Who was the first to summit Mount Everest in the world?	誰是世界上第一個登上聖母峰的人？
受詞	Annie was among the first to realize that blind people never know their hidden strength until they are treated like normal human beings.	雙目失明的人，只有受到同正常人一樣的待遇時，才會知道自己蘊藏的力量。而安妮正是最先認識到這一點的人之一。
修飾語	My family goes back 300 years, while his family goes back to the 15th century.	我的家族延續了300年，而他的家族可追溯到15世紀。
受詞補語	They nicknamed him "the third."	他們稱呼他為「老三」。
同位語	We will have a speech contest on Monday, the 28th this month.	我們將於本月28日星期一舉行演講比賽。
副詞	China ranks second, only next to the United States, with 32 gold medals at the Athens Olympic Games.	中國在雅典奧運會上獲32金，金牌總數列第二，僅次於美國。

第四節：倍數、分數、小數和百分數

1. 倍數

(1) 表示倍數的方法有多種

This room is three times as large as that one.
這個房間是那個房間的三倍大。

This room is three times larger than that one.
這個房間比那個房間大三倍。

(2) 用times表示倍數，一般只限於表示三倍或三倍以上的數

The population in and around San Francisco is now ten times more than it was in 1906.

現在在舊金山市市區和郊區的人口已是1906年的十倍以上了。

但表示兩倍（中文中的一倍實際上也指兩倍）時則用twice或double。例如：

He has worked twice as long as I have.

他參加工作的時間是我的兩倍。

Our total income of 1998 was double that of 1997.

我們1998年的總收入是1997年的兩倍。

(3) 表示增加多少倍也可用百分比

Population has increased by 200% in the past 25 years.

人口在過去25年內增加了200%。

注意：如果表示「增加」用times，英語要多說一倍，例如「增加了三倍」，要用four times。

2. 分數

(1) 分數是由基數詞和序數詞合成的。

分子用基數詞，分母用序數詞。分子是1時，分母（序數詞）用單數形式；分子大於1時，分母用複數形式，序數詞的字尾會加上s。例如：

| 1/3 | one third | 三分之一 |
| 2/3 | two thirds | 三分之二 |

重點深度學：**Day 05** 進階挑戰

(1) 分數的不同讀法

1/2→	a (one) half	one over two
1/4→	a (one) quarter	one over four
2/3→	two thirds	two over three

| 3/4→ | three fourths | three over four |

(2) 整數與分數之間必須用 and連接,再照著發音

　　3 1/2 three and a half 三又二分之一

(3) 小數的讀法是小數點(point)前的基數詞與前面所講的基數詞
讀法完全相同,小數點後則須將數字一一讀出。例如:

　　0.25 → zero point two five

　　1.34 → one point three four

(4) 百分數中的百分號「%」讀percent,無複數形式。

第五節:數詞的其他用法

1. 算式表示法

　　關於加、減、乘、除算式的讀法:

算式	讀法
1+2=3	One and two is / makes three.
50+48=98	Fifty plus forty-eight is / equals ninety-eight.
4-3=1	Three from four is / leaves one. Four minus three is / makes one.
94-40=54	Ninety-four minus forty is / equals fifty-four.
8×3=24	Three eights are twenty-four.
12×12=144	Twelve times twelve is / makes one hundred and forty-four.
36÷6=6	Six into thirty-six is / goes six. Thirty-six divided by six is six.

　　表示面積或體積常用by,介詞by在這裡表示「用⋯⋯去乘」的意思。例如:

　　We need to find a tanker about 30 centimeters(cm) by 30 cm by 50 cm.

　　我們需要找一個大約 30公分寬、30 公分高、50 公分長的水箱。

2. 編號表示法

編號可用序數詞或基數詞表示，序數詞位於名詞前面，並加定冠詞，基數詞位於名詞後面。例如：

the first part= part one 第一部分
the second chapter= chapter two 第二章
the tenth lesson= lesson ten 第十課

Take turns to offer each other the foods in Part Two in pairs.
兩人一組，輪流請對方吃第二部分列出的食品。

如果數位較長，一般情況用基數詞。例如：

page 403	page four o three	第403頁
Bus (No.) 532	bus number five three two	第532路公車
Tel No. 2341801	telephone number two three four one eight o one	電話號碼2341801

3. 年、月、日表示法和讀法

(1) 年份的表示法和讀法

年份通常用阿拉伯數字表示，用基數詞讀。
西元前用BC表示，西元用AD表示。
AD一般用於西元1年到西元999年之間的年份。例如：
776 BC 西元前776年（英語讀作：seven seven six BC）
in 1949 在1949年（英語讀作：in nineteen forty-nine）
1900 年讀作nineteen hundred
1999 年讀作nineteen ninety-nine

(2) 年代表示法和讀法

年代用年份的阿拉伯數字加's或s表示。例如：

in the 1990's (1990s)→在20世紀90年代 (in the nineteen nineties)

Many of the streets in Disneyland are built to look like streets in the USA in the 1890s.
迪士尼樂園裡有許多街道，修建得像 19 世紀 90 年代的美國街道。
(1890s也可寫作1890's，讀作eighteen nineties)

初期、中期、末期分別用early, mid-和late表示，例如：
20 世紀 90 年代初期→ the early 1990's

20 世紀 90 年代中期→ the mid-1990's
20 世紀 90 年代末期→ the late 1990's

(3) 月、日的表示法和讀法

表示月、日既可以先寫「月」再寫「日」，也可以先寫「日」再寫「月」。例如：

June 1→June the first / 1 June→ the first of June

表示年、月、日，要將年份放在最後，用逗號和月、日隔開，例如：

2006年5月 31日→May 31, 2006 / 31 May, 2006。

4. 時刻表示法

(1) 十二小時計時制

使用十二小時計時制，為了避免午前、午後時刻的混淆，有時要在時刻後面加 A.M. / AM / a.m. 或P.M. / PM / p.m. 以示區別。例如：

six o'clock	six	六點
nine fifteen	a quarter past nine	九點一刻
eleven o five	five past eleven	十一點零五分
five twenty-five	twenty-five past five	五點二十五分
six forty-five	a quarter to seven	六點四十五分
ten fifty	ten to eleven	十點五十分

(2) 二十四小時計時制

使用二十四小時制，書寫時用四位元數字。例如：

14:15→ fourteen fifteen = 2:15 pm
20:50→ twenty fifty = 8:50 pm
24:00→ twenty-four hundred hours = midnight

5. 幾十歲表示法

說「幾十歲」時，應該用複數形式，並且在前面加上in one's...

Mr. Franklin started his own business and established his enterprise in his early forties.

富蘭克林先生在他四十幾歲的時候創業並且建立自己的公司。

1. Joe plans to go on a grand tour in Europe in her _____.
   A. twenty   B. twentieth   C. twenties   D. early twenty

2. His mansion is _____ large as my cottage.
   A. two times   B. twice as   C. two time   D. as twice

3. According to the report, there are _____ protesters in front of the municipal government building.
   A. a thousand of   B. ten thousands
   C. thousands of   D. two thousands

4. Approximately _____ the students in the class passed the final exam.
   A. one-three of   B. one-third of
   C. one on three   D. one for three

5. The archeologist pointed out that the palace was built during the _____ century.
   A. twelve   B. twelvth   C. twelves   D. twelfth

6. It is said that the electric car with AI-assisted driving system costs _____ dollars.
   A. one million   B. a million of   C. some millions   D. two millions

7. The house price nowadays is _____ that of the early nineteen-nineties.
   A. two time   B. double   C. scales of   D. little higher

8. The movie starts at _____.
   A. twelve five   B. twelve O-five
   C. twelve-fifteen   D. five-to-twelve

9. The author gives briefly described the history of Roman Empire in _____ of the book .
   A. second chapter   B. two chapter
   C. chapter second   D. Chapter Two

10. The survey indicates _____ the citizens support the policy for limits on single-use plastics.
    A. fifty percent   B. fifty percents
    C. a fifty percent   D. fifty percent of

1. 正解為(C)。此題空格中要表達的意思是「在她二十幾歲時」，慣用說法為「in her twenties」。如果是說「在二十出頭左右」，要說「in her early twenties」，選項(D)應改為複數。

2. 正解為(B)。這句話的意思是「他家豪宅是我家小屋的兩倍大」，兩倍可以說是「twice as large as」，三倍以上的數目就會使用「數字＋times＋as large as」來表達。

3. 正解為(C)。本題句子表示「據報導，在市政府大樓前面有數千名抗議者」，要表達「數千人」的概念，可在thousand 加上複數s，但如果thousand前面有明確的數字表達到底有多少千人的時候，thousand 後面不會加複數的s，也不會加of。

4. 正解為(B)。句子的意思為「這個班大約三分之一的學生通過期末考試。」這題考的是分數的寫法，可以說「one-third of the students」或者「one out of three students」來表示。

5. 正解為(D)。本題題目的意思是「考古學家指出這個皇宮是在十二世紀所建立的」，考的是十二的序數拼法。

6. 正解為(A)。句子的意思是「據說這台有人工智慧輔助駕駛系統的電動車要價一百萬。」一百萬可以說 one/a million dollars如果有明確數字「one」或者「several」修飾，就不會加複數的s。

7. 正解為(B)。句子的意思是「現在的房價是一九九零年代初期的兩倍。」要表達「兩倍」，可以用twice 或者double。如果要表達房價「高了一點」，可以說「a little higher than that」。

8. 正解為(B)。句子的意思是「電影在十二點零五分開演。」這題在考的是時間的唸法，要表達12:05，要說「twelve O-five」，如果說「five to twelve」是「再過五分鐘就十二點」也就是「11:55」，但是中間不用加連字號，所以選項(D)不是正確的寫法。

9. 正解為(D)。本句的意思是「作者在這本書的第二章簡短描述了羅馬帝國的歷史」，其中「第二章」可以說「the second chapter of the book」或是「Chapter Two of the book」。

10. 正解為(D)。本題題目的意思是「問卷調查顯示，有百分之五十的市民支持限制一次性塑膠製品的政策」，其中「fifty percent of」表示「百分之五十」，percent 不用加複數的s，而後面要加of再接名詞。

Day

06

形容詞
Adjective

Day 06 形容詞 Adjective

第一節：概述

形容詞是用來描寫或修飾名詞（或代名詞）的詞。

1. 形容詞的主要語法特徵

(1) 通常放在所修飾的名詞之前

The sudden cold weather brought on his fever again.
天氣突然變冷，引起他再次發燒。

(2) 多數形容詞具有比較級和最高級

Disney's greatest wish was to be a famous artist.
迪士尼最大的願望就是成為一位著名的藝術家。

(3) 有獨特的字尾

字尾	範例單字
-able	comfortable 舒適的，輕鬆自在的、valuable 值錢的，貴重的
-al	agricultural 農業的，農學的、industrial 工業的
-ant, -ent	important 重要的、excellent 極好的，優秀的
-ary, -ory	elementary 基本的、contradictory 矛盾的
-ful	doubtful 懷疑的、merciful 仁慈，寬大的
-ic	electronic 電子的、heroic 英勇的
-ive	active 積極的、主動的、radioactive 放射性的
-less	endless 無止境的，沒完沒了的、priceless 無價的
-ous	dangerous 危險的、famous 著名的
-y	dirty 骯髒的、funny 有趣的，可笑的

另外，還有否定字首。例如：

字尾	範例單字
in-	incomplete 不完全的、indifferent 不關心的
un-	uncertain 不確定的、unequal 不相等的

2. 簡單形容詞和複合形容詞

(1) 簡單形容詞由一個單字構成，例如：

certain 某種，一定的	correct 正確的，對的
free 免費的	fresh 新鮮的

有些形容詞由現在分詞或過去分詞構成。例如：

delighted 感到開心的	disappointed 失望的
encouraging 鼓舞人心的	flaming 火紅的，火焰般的

(2) 複合形容詞由一個以上的詞構成

good-looking 好看的	heart-breaking 令人傷心的
low-lying 地勢低窪的	duty-free 免稅的

有些片語也可構成形容詞。例如：a face-to-face talk 面對面的談判

3. 形容詞根據其與所修飾名詞的關係分為限制性形容詞和描述性形容詞

(1) 限制性形容詞表示事物的本質，它的位置緊靠它所修飾的名詞。

a Chinese dish 中式菜餚	a Catholic church 天主教教堂

(2) 描述性形容詞又叫非限制性形容詞，它只有描述的作用，位置可在限制性形容詞之前。

a delicious Chinese dish 一道味道鮮美的中式菜餚

an impressive Catholic church 一座氣勢宏偉的天主教教堂

🚩 第二節：形容詞在句中的作用

1. 作形容詞

The apartment has a very reasonable design.
那間公寓的設計相當合理。

Corn is a useful plant that can be eaten by both people and animal.
玉米是人畜都能吃的有用植物。

2. 作主詞補語

The house was found empty. 房子發現是空的。

It's going to be dry and sunny for the next two days.
接下來兩天將是乾燥、晴朗的天氣。

It's hard to try to make ends meet with the money I get paid.
我得到的酬金很難做到收支相抵。

重點提示：必學文法小要點

　　有些形容詞只能作主詞補語用，常見的有ill, well以及以字母 a 開頭的afraid, alike, awake, aware, ashamed, alone, alive 等。例如：

The baby is asleep now. 現在嬰兒睡著了。

He has been ill recently. 最近他病了。

3. 作受詞補語

We found the film quite instructive. 我們發現那部電影很有教育意義。

The Internet also makes it easier for companies to keep in touch with customers and companies in other countries.
網際網路也讓公司能更便利地聯絡國外的客戶和公司。

4. 作主詞或受詞

這有一定的限制，主要是指「定冠詞 + 某些形容詞」，表示一類人或事物，這種形容詞已名詞化。例如：

例句	中譯	說明
The rich and the poor live in separate sections of London.	在倫敦富人和窮人住在不同的地區。	作主詞
We should respect the old and love the young.	我們要尊老愛幼。	作受詞

第三節：形容詞的位置

幾個形容詞並列作形容詞時，一般說來與中心詞（即被修飾的詞）關係更密切的修飾詞，要更靠近中心詞。

一般排列順序是這樣的：

8	7	6	5	4	3	2	1	
冠詞或反身代名詞、指示代名詞、不定代名詞	數詞	物體大小、長短、高低及形狀的形容詞	一般的描繪性形容詞	年齡大小、長幼、新舊的形容詞	顏色的形容詞	國籍的形容詞	物質材料、類別、用途的形容詞	中心詞
例：those	two	big	nice	old	yellow	British	wooden	tables

Jane wore a pretty purple silk dress.
珍妮穿著一件漂亮的紫色真絲衣服。（描述+顏色+材質）

She has a very valuable big gold watch.
她有一隻很珍貴的大金錶。（程度＋描述＋大小＋材質）

形容詞與其他詞語構成片語作形容詞時，要放在中心詞後面，如：
Chinese is a language difficult to master.
（中文是一門不易精通的語言。）

有些通常作主詞補語用的形容詞作形容詞時，要放在中心詞後面，
如：They're the happiest children alive.（他們是當代最幸福的孩子。）

在修飾something, everything, anything, nothing等不定代名詞時，形容詞應放 在這些詞的後面，如：

She did everything possible to make him happy.
（她做了所有她能做的事情，只為了讓他高興。）

第四節：形容詞的比較級和最高級

1. 形容詞等級的構成形式

(1) 規則變化

單音節詞和少數雙音節詞，詞尾加-er, -est來構成比較級和最高級。

構成法	原級	比較級	最高級
一般單音節詞末尾加-er, -est	tall（高的） great（巨大的）	taller greater	tallest greatest
以不發音的e結尾的單音節詞和少數以-le結尾的雙音節詞只加-r, -st	nice（好的） large（大的） able（有能力的）	nicer larger abler	nicest largest ablest
以一個子音結尾的閉音節單音節詞，重複結尾的字母，再加-er, -est	big（大的） hot（熱的） fat（胖的）	bigger hotter fatter	biggest hottest fattest
「子音字母+y」結尾的雙音節詞，變y為i，再加-er, -est	easy（容易的） busy（忙的）	easier busier	easiest busiest
少數以-er, -ow結尾的雙音節詞末尾加-er, -est	clever（聰明的） narrow（窄的）	cleverer narrower	cleverest narrowest

其他雙音節詞和多音節詞，在前面加more, most來構成比較級和最高級。

原級	比較級	最高級
important（重要的）	more important	most important
beautiful（漂亮的）	more beautiful	most beautiful

(2) 不規則變化

原級	比較級	最高級
good （好的）well （健康的）	better	best
bad （壞的）ill （有病的）	worse	worst

old （老的）	older elder	oldest eldest
many （多的） much （多的）	more	most
little （少的）	less	least
far（遠的）	farther further	farthest furthest

2. 形容詞原級的用法

表示「和……一樣」時，要用原級。例如：

Tom is as tall as Jack. 湯姆和傑克一樣高。

A contrivance as simple as the envelope did not come into use until 1839.

像信封這樣簡單的發明，一直到1839年才開始使用。

3. 形容詞的比較級的用法

(1) 形容詞的比較級是用來把彼此獨立的事和人進行比較，表示「比……更……一些」的意思，通常用一個由從屬連接詞than引導的副詞子句來表示和什麼相比。

There was a certain mineral which was even more radioactive than uranium.

有一種礦物，它具有的放射性甚至比鈾還強。

Prevention is better than cure.

預防勝於治療。

有時副詞子句可以省略。例如：

If the hurricane had happened during the daytime, there would have been more deaths.

如果颶風發生在白天，死亡人數會更多。

重點深度學：Day 06 進階挑戰

有時比較級前可以用many, much, far, even, a little, still, yet, a bit, a lot, completely等表示程度的狀語。例如：

An even bigger earthquake will hit the area around San Francisco.

舊金山市周圍地區還會發生更大的地震。

> It is much cheaper to post or email a long report than to fax it.
> 透過郵寄或電子郵件的方式寄送一個長篇的報告比用傳真便宜得多。
>
> Things are no better than before.
> 情況並不比以前好。

(2) 在作否定的比較時，可以用not as...as...，not so...as...，也可以 less...than...， 在現代英語中，三者都可使用。例如：

The length of your life is less important than its depth.
人生的長度不及深度重要。

(a) 在這一結構中，有時也可以用just, almost, nearly, half等表示程度的副詞。例如：

The Atlantic Ocean is only half as big as the Pacific.
大西洋的面積只有太平洋的一半。

(b)「as...as...」結構和「the same...as」結構一樣。例如：

In area Australia is about the same size as the USA (without Alaska), which has more than thirteen times as many people.
從面積上講，澳洲大致上相當於美國（阿拉斯加除外），而美國的人口卻比澳洲的 13 倍還多。

(c) 形容詞比較級在特定的上下文中，暗含最高級的意思。例如：

As a foreign language, no other language is more widely studied or used than English.
作為外語，英語是被學得最多、用得最廣的語言。

(3) 形容詞的比較級還可用在下列句型中

(a)「雙重比較」的結構後面不可接than引導的子句。例如：

After the year 1986, more and more countries joined in the Olympic Games.
1986年以後，越來越多的國家參加了奧林匹克運動會。

Computers are getting smaller and smaller, and computing faster and faster.
電腦變得越來越小，而計算速度卻越來越快。

(b) 表示兩個變化是一起發生的，可以把比較級形式和the一起用，表示「越……，就越……」的意思。例如：

The more we study, the more we discover our ignorance.
一個人懂得越多，就越發現自己無知。

(c) the more..., the less...表示「越……就越不……」。例如：

The more you learn, the less you will feel you know.
你學習的越多，越會感到自己學識不夠。

從結構上説，第一個「the + 比較級…」是表示比較的副詞子句，第二個「the + 比較級…」是主句。這裡的兩個the不是冠詞，而是副詞。有時，在上下文很清楚的情況下，可以省略動詞。例如：The sooner, the better.（越快越好。）

(d) more (less) than 表示「不僅，不止，多過，不到，少於」的意思。例如：

Gandhi was much more than a clever lawyer, a fine speaker, a determined fighter for human rights and a political leader.
甘地遠不只是一位聰明的律師、優秀的演説家、堅定的人權戰士和政治領導人。

其他的用法：

all the more...	因而更加……
more or less	大體上，或多或少
so much the better (worse)	就更好，就更糟
had better	最好

(4) 形容詞比較級的特殊情況

(a) 「too + 原級」和「原級 + for短語」也可以表示比較級。例如：

He is too old for the job. 他太老了，不適合做這項工作。

The coat is a bit too small for me.
這件上衣太小了一點，我穿不合適。

He is brave for his age. 就他那樣的年齡來説，他是勇敢的。

(b) 原本就帶有比較級意思的單字superior, inferior, senior, junior, prior, major, minor：

He is three years senior to me.
他比我大三歲。

This computer is superior in many respects to that.
這台電腦在很多方面比那台要好。

(c) 有些固定用比較級的表達法。例如：

younger generation 年輕一代

higher education 高等教育

3. 形容詞的最高級的用法

(1) 形容詞最高級的前面通常要加定冠詞the，且會有一個相對照的限定範圍

People think that Charlie Chaplin is one of the greatest and funniest actors in film making.
人們認為查理‧卓別林是電影史上最偉大、最逗趣的演員之一。

The earliest coins in the West were made of gold mixed with silver.
西方最早的硬幣是用金和銀的合金製成的。

(2) 有時在形容詞最高級前可以有序數詞以及much, by far, nearly, by no means, almost等

This is about the earliest computer ever manufactured in China.
這大概是中國最早製作的電腦了。

Shanghai is by far the largest industrial city in China.
上海是中國最大的工業城市。

(3) 在作補語的形容詞最高級前，如果不是和別的人（物、事）相比較，可以不加定冠詞

Fruits are best when they are fresh.
水果新鮮的時候最好。

The air pollution was most serious in this area.
這個地區的空氣污染最嚴重。

(4) 有時最高級形式後面可以不跟名詞

Today, Abraham Lincoln is still considered as one of the greatest of all American presidents.

直到現在，亞伯拉罕・林肯仍然被認為是美國最偉大的總統之一。

Lake Baikal in Asia was once the cleanest in the world, with over 700 different kinds of plant and animal life.

亞洲的貝加爾湖曾經是世界上最乾淨的湖，湖裡有700多種不同的植物和動物。

第五節：名詞化的形容詞

英語中有些形容詞可以加上定冠詞the來代表整個類別的人，或代表其抽象概念，這些形容詞具有名詞的性質。當作名詞的形容詞就叫名詞化的形容詞。

1. 泛指用法

泛指一類人，作主詞時動詞要用複數形式。例如：

All the wounded have been sent to hospital.
所有傷患都已送去醫院了。

The difference between the impossible and the possible lies in a person's determination. —Tommy Lasorda.
不可能和可能之間的區別，在於人的決心。—湯米・拉沙德

2. 抽象用法

形容詞代表抽象事物作主詞時，動詞要用單數形式。例如：

The beautiful can never die. 美是不朽的。

The true is to be distinguished from the false. 真偽要辨明。

類似的還有：

the good 好的東西	the new 新的東西
the ordinary 普普通通的東西	the unusual 不尋常的東西

3. 固定片語

名詞化的形容詞有時出現在一些固定的片語中。

at best 充其量	at large 一般的	at the latest 最遲
at least 至少	at most 至多、最多	do one's best 盡力

文法實戰演練

1. Taking the High Speed Rail is _____ way to go from Taipei to Kaohsiung.
   A. faster   B. fastest   C. the faster   D. the fastest

2. We all consider him one of the _____ actors in this industry.
   A. greatest B. fast   C. fresher   D. same

3. Aaron plans to go to Europe for _____ studies after graduating from high school.
   A. far   B. farther   C. further   D. furthest

4. It's _____ to set off to work earlier. Traffic is very heavy during the rush hours.
   A. the good B. the better C. best   D. the best

5. It's a preconceived notion that some races are _____ others.
   A. superior to B. better to   C. superior   D. better

6. Your plan sounds _____ than his.
   A. as good   B. much practical
   C. a lot practical   D. much more practical

7. You can get access to _____ news by visiting the website of CNN.
   A. the late B. the latest C. the later   D. the latter

8. My _____ sister often read the martial arts fictions in her free time.
   A. elder   B. older   C. the older   D. the elder

9. The Minister of Education announced a new policy to improve the quality of _____ education. He hopes to see more innovation in college courses.
   A. high   B. higher
   C. the higher   D. the highest

10. Roughly speaking, a Mercedes-Benz is three times _____ a Toyota.
    A. most expensive   B. more expensive
    C. higher the price   D. as expensive as

1. 正解為(D)。此題題目的意思是「從台北到高雄最快的方式是搭高鐵」，考的是「fast」的最高級。如果是說「the faster」通常會表示「兩者當比較快的那一個」，此題沒有明確把比較的範圍所小到兩個項目，所以會用the fastest。

2. 正解為 (A)。此題考的是形容詞最高級的用法，意為「我們都認為他是這個產業最傑出的男演員之一」，故選 (A)。

3. 正解為(C)。本題句子表示「亞倫計畫高中畢業之後要去歐洲深造」，「去深造」有固定的說法「further studies」，其中far的比較級有兩種，farther 是指距離上更遠，而further指的是更進一步，所以留學深造要用further。

4. 正解為(C)。句子的意思為「最好早一點出發去上班。尖峰時刻交通很繁忙。」如果沒有明確和別的東西比較的意思，「It's best to~」其實就代表「It's wise to ~」，不需要加上定冠詞the。

5. 正解為(A)。本題題目的意思是「某些種族優於其他種族是一個毫無根據的想法」，其中「superior to」是單字當中原本就帶有比較級意味的用法，superior 後面固定會接 to，如果要用better，後面就會接than。

6. 正解為(D)。句子的意思是「你的計畫聽起來比他的計畫實際多了。」其中「much more practical」也可以說是「a lot more practical」，是以much more 來修飾比較級差別程度的用法。

7. 正解為(B)。這句話的意思是「你可以上CNN的網站上去看到最近的新聞。」其中選項(A)的the late 後面接表示人的名詞表示「已故的」，選項(C)的the later 是比較晚的，選項(D)的the latter 是指「後者」。

8. 正解為(A)。句子的意思是「我的姊姊常在空閒時間閱讀武俠小說。」表示年紀較長可以用「older than」，但如果還有輩份較長的意思，就要用「the elder」，兄姊會用elder brother 及 elder sister 表示。

9. 正解為(B)。本句的意思是「教育部長宣布新政策，要改善高等教育品質。他希望看到大學課程有更多創新。」，其中「高等教育」是固定用法，用「higher education」表達。

10. 正解為(D)。本題題目的意思是「大約來說，賓士車的價格是豐田車的三倍」，要表達「價格是三倍」可以說「three times as expensive as~」。但如果說是「three times more expensive than」就表示價差是豐田車價格的三倍，也就是賓士車的價格變成豐田車的四倍，這種細微的意思差異，在使用句型時要加以留意喔。

Day

07

副詞
Adverb

Day 07 副詞 Adverb

第一節：概述

1. 副詞的定義

　　用來修飾動詞、形容詞、其他副詞 以及全句的詞，即稱為副詞，用來表示時間、地點、程度、方式等概念。

2. 副詞的特徵

(1) 一般表示方式的副詞是由形容詞加-ly構成

gradually 逐漸地	differently 不同地	firmly 牢牢地
hardly 幾乎不、簡直不	possibly 可能地、也許	fortunately 幸運地
cheaply 廉價地	probably 很可能、大概	separately各自地

(2) 有些副詞與形容詞的形式相同

early 早的、早早地	lively 活潑的、活潑地
highly 高的、高高地	daily 日常的、每天

3. 有些副詞除與形容詞的形式相同外，又有加-ly的形式

loud（大聲地）—loudly（吵鬧地）	slow（慢）—slowly（慢）
quick（快）—quickly（快）	right（正確地）—rightly（主觀認為正確地）

4. 有些副詞沒有特殊詞尾

meanwhile 同時	now 現在	nowhere 任何地方都不
seldom 很少、不常	forward 將來、今後	thus 這樣、因而

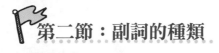

第二節：副詞的種類

1. 一般副詞

大部分都是由一個形容詞加字尾ly構成。

(1) 方式副詞

calmly 冷靜地	carefully 仔細地	carelessly 粗心地
patiently 耐心地	politely 禮貌地	proudly 自豪地
properly 適當地	quickly 快速地	rapidly 迅速地
suddenly 突然	successfully 成功地	willingly 情願地
warmly 熱情地	awkwardly 笨拙地	anxiously 急切地

(2) 地點副詞，包括表示地點的副詞和表示位置關係、方向的副詞

here 這裡	there 那裡	upstairs 樓上
downstairs 樓下	anywhere 任何地方	above 在上方
up 上面	down 下面	east 向東
west 向西	inside 裡面	outside 外面

(3) 時間副詞

類型	舉例
表示確定時間	yesterday 昨天，today 今天，tomorrow 明天
表示不確定時間	recently 最近，nowadays 現今，still 仍然，already 已經，immediately 立刻， just 剛剛
表示時間順序	now 現在，then 然後，first 首先，next 其次，later 後來，before 以前
表示時間頻率	always 總是，often 常常，usually 通常，seldom 很少，never 從不， sometimes 有時

(4) 程度副詞

用來回答how much這類問題，可用來修飾形容詞、副詞，有的還可用來修飾動詞、介詞片語、名詞、代名詞和子句等

a bit 有點	very 很	quite 十分	rather 頗
much 很	just 正好	only 僅僅	somewhat 有點

以下副詞一般位於它所修飾的詞的前面。例如：

例句	中譯	說明
If you don't try, you will never succeed.	你如果不嘗試，就絕不會成功。	修飾動詞succeed
It looks a bit ugly as it is.	它現在這樣子很難看。	修飾形容詞ugly
So what exactly are you suggesting?	那麼，你到底在暗示什麼呢？	修飾句子

2. 疑問副詞

疑問副詞有：

疑問副詞	例句	中譯
How（如何）	How are you getting on with your French lessons?	你的法語課學得怎麼樣？
When（何時）	When do you take your next exam?	你什麼時候參加下次考試？
Where（何地）	Where did you last see it?	你最後一次看到這東西時是在什麼地方呢？
Why（為什麼）	Why not read some English news?	為什麼不讀些英語新聞呢？

3. 關係副詞

關係副詞有：

關係副詞	例句	中譯
when	Childhood is a time when we solidify our personalities.	童年是我們形成個性的時期。
where	An estuary is the body of water where a river meets the ocean.	河口是河流與海洋會合的水域。

| why | This is the reason why he was late. | 這就是他遲到的理由。 |

4. 連接副詞

連接副詞用來把主要子句和從屬子句連接起來，包括：

連接副詞	例句	中譯
when	When it will be finished depends on the weather.	什麼時候能完成視天氣而定。
why	That is why Einstein and his family left Europe for the USA in 1933.	這就是愛因斯坦和他的家人於1933年離開歐洲去美國的原因。
how	This is how we conducted the experiment.	這就是我們做實驗的方式。
where	I don't know where we are going to have this meeting.	我不知道這個會在哪裡開。
whenever	Whenever we found an unknown plant, we had to describe it in our notebooks.	我們無論什麼時候發現一種不認識的植物，就要記在筆記本上。
wherever	Sit wherever you like.	你隨便坐哪裡都行。
however	He will never succeed, however hard he tries.	無論他如何努力嘗試，他都不會成功。

5. 句首副詞

用來連接句子、分句或子句，表示前後子句之間因果、條列、舉例的關係

表示因果	therefore 因此、accordingly 從而
表示條列	besides 此外、moreover 再者
表示對比	however 不管怎樣、nevertheless 然而
表示條件	otherwise 否則
表示順序	then 然後，lastly 最後
表示舉例	e.g. (=for example) 例如、for example 例如、i.e.(=that is) 那就是

第三節：副詞在句中的用法

副詞在句子中主要用來修飾動詞、形容詞、副詞和全句。

副詞作用	例句	中譯
修飾動詞	Advertisements appear everywhere in modern society.	廣告在現代社會無處不在。
修飾形容詞	Training by yourself in a gym can be highly dangerous.	在體育館自主訓練是非常危險的。
修飾副詞	You walked seriously fast.	你走得誇張地快。
修飾全句	You are obviously a person of great courage.	顯然你是個極有勇氣的人。

還有些其他的用法：

例句	中譯	說明
Now the computer has touched the lives of everyone, even people in faraway villages.	現在電腦已經觸及每個人的生活，甚至是遙遠鄉村人們的生活。	even修飾名詞 people
The fire has been out for half an hour.	火已熄滅半小時了。	副詞作補語
I went to see him only to find him out.	我去看他，不料他不在家。	副詞作受詞補語
Don't put off until tomorrow what should be done today.	今日事今日畢。	副詞作介詞的受詞
I hope you'll enjoy your stay here.	希望你在這裡過得愉快。	副詞作修飾語

第四節：副詞的比較級和最高級

英語中副詞和形容詞一樣有三個等級，即原級、比較級和最高級。

1. 副詞比較級和最高級的結構

副詞的比較級和最高級的形式大多數都加more和most構成，如：

quickly 快地	more quickly 更快地	most quickly 最快地

少數副詞用er和est構成比較級和 最高級：

fast 快地	faster更快地	fastest最快地
hard 努力地	harder 更努力地	hardest 最努力地
late 晚地	later 更晚地	latest 最晚地
loud 大聲地	louder 更大聲地	loudest 最大聲地
early 早	earlier 更早	earliest 最早

不規則變化：

原級	比較級	最高級
badly	worse	worst
far	farther/further	farthest/furthest
little	less	least
much	more	most
well	better	best

2. 副詞比較級和最高級的基本用法

英語中副詞和形容詞一樣有三個等級，即原級、比較級和最高級。副詞的比較級和最高級的形式大多數都加more和most構成，只有少數單音節的副詞（例如：fast, hard, late, long, slow, soon, loud, quick等）和early

同樣用er和est構成比較級和最高級。另外有幾個副詞比較級和最高級的變化是不規則的，例如：badly, worse, worst；far, farther / further, farthest / furthest；little, less, least；much, more, most；well, better, best 等。

(1) 原級

常用於as...as和not so (as)...as結構。

as...as可用於肯定句、否定句和疑問句，而so...as則只能用於否定句
Things didn't go so (as) smoothly as we had expected.
事情發展沒有我們預期的那樣順利。

(2) 比較級常用於「比較級 + than結構，有時than引導的比較副詞子句可以省略，比較級前可加上表示程度的副詞，例如：

many, much, far, a bit, a little, a great (deal), a lot, completely, even, still, yet等。
Could you talk a bit more quietly? 你們說話小聲點好嗎？

(3) 用最高級時，常常有一個片語說明比較的範圍。
Mary runs fastest among the girls. 瑪麗是女生中跑得最快的。

3. 副詞比較級和最高級的其他用法

(1) 表示「越來越……」用「比較級 + and + 比較級」結構或「more and more + 原級」，後面不可than 引導的比較副詞子句

As his work had become dominant, the rest had seemed to matter less and less.
由於他的工作占了主要地位，別的事似乎越來越無關緊要了。

He runs faster and faster when he is near the finishing line.
快到終點線時，他跑得越來越快。

(2) 表示 越……，越……」用「the + 副詞比較級，the + 副詞比較級」結構

The earlier you start, the sooner you will complete the task.
你越早著手進行，就越早完成任務。

(3) 可以用**much, far, a lot, a great deal, still, even, a bit (little)**或者名詞
（數詞）片語等來修飾形容詞和副詞的比較級：

You can read even better if you try.
如果你努力的話，還可以念得更好。

第五節：副詞的位置和排列順序

1. 副詞的位置

副詞在句中的位置比較靈活。

(1) 放在動詞後面或受詞後面

Sometimes many people talked together without anyone stopping them. 有時好些人一起聊天，也沒有人阻止他們。

I must be leaving now. 我現在該走了。

First, read a chapter quickly to get a general idea.
第一，快速閱讀一章，以便掌握中心思想。

重點提示：必學文法小要點

有些地點副詞例如：away, down, in, on, off, out, up等也可以放在動詞和受詞之間，但受詞如果是人稱代名詞，副詞只能放在受詞的後面。例如：

Turn on the radio.（或：Turn the radio on. / Turn it on.）
打開收音機。

---

(2) 頻率副詞通常放在動詞前面。如果句子中有助動詞或 be動詞，就放在這類動詞的後面。

He is seldom late for work. 他上班很少遲到。

The international oil crisis has greatly affected the internal economy.
國際石油危機嚴重地影響了國內的經濟。

這類副詞有：almost, already, always, frequently, hardly, nearly, occasionally, often, sometimes, usually, never, seldom等。

(3) yet, once, just, really, soon, surely等也是動詞前面、助動詞或 be動詞的後面。例如：

Fish soon goes bad in hot weather.（天氣熱魚很快就變質了。）

但有的副詞有時放在動詞後面。例如：

Do you come here often?（你常到這裡來嗎？）

(4) 疑問副詞、連接副詞、關係副詞和一些修飾整個句子的副詞，通常放在句子（或子句）的開頭。例如：

Actually 事實上	Fortunately 幸運地	Unfortunately 不幸地
Of course 當然	First 首先	At first 一開始
Secondly 第二	Surely 確定地	Perhaps 或許
Probably 可能	Certainly 當然	Consequently 因此

Perhaps we're going to have a storm. 可能有暴風雨要來了。

Surely you don't think she's beautiful? 你一定覺得她不漂亮吧？

有些時間副詞和頻率副詞也可放在句首，例如：

Yesterday 昨天	Tomorrow 明天	last night 昨晚
Finally 最後	at last 最後	Soon 很快地
Once 有一次	Occasionally 偶爾	Usually 通常

Occasionally I try to write poems. 我偶爾也試著寫幾首詩。

Finally, he demanded an end to the British rule over India and independence for his country.

最後，他要求結束英國對印度的統治，要求國家的獨立。

(4) 程度副詞一般放在其所修飾的詞的前面

After all, this ball is very important.

這次舞會畢竟還是很重要的。

My poor mother, your hair has gone quite white!
可憐的媽媽，妳的頭髮全都變白了！

重點深度學： Day 07 進階挑戰

enough要放在它所修飾的形容詞或副詞之後。例如：

He is smart enough for this work.
他很機靈，足以勝任這項工作。

A long life may not be good enough, but a good life is long enough.
漫長的人生未必是好的人生，但好的人生必然是地久天長的。

1. A: _____ do you feel today?
   B: I feel much better after taking enough rest.
   A. How   B. Why   C. When   D. Where

2. The tour guide speaks _____ and enunciates every word so that the foreign tourists could understand him.
   A. quick   B. quickly   C. clear   D. clearly

3. She could never sing _____ as the professional opera singer.
   A. good   B. well   C. as good   D. as well

4. I thought I worked pretty hard, but I realized that Jenny worked ____.
   A. even harder   B. somewhat hard   C. as hard as   D. the harder

5. _____, the negotiation between the employer and labor union broke down.
   A. Currently   B. Unfortunately   C. Secondly   D. Perhaps

6. I am disappointed with your performance. You could have done _____ if you work harder.
   A. good   B. better   C. bad   D. worse

7. The secretary is very meticulous with the documents. She _____ make mistakes like misspelling words.
   A. usually   B. often   C. occasionally   D. seldom

8. The cafeteria at the street corner is a place of memories for me. It's _____ I met my first girlfriend.
   A. how   B. when   C. where   D. why

9. He is not behaving _____. His attitude toward work and life leaves a lot to be improved.
   A. enough maturely   B. maturely enough
   C. enough mature   D. mature enough

10. Please mix the butter and the flour. _____, I can preheat the oven and prepare the other ingredients.
    A. Meanwhile   B. Probably   C. Suddenly   D. Especially

 **文法實戰解析**

1. 正解為(A)。此題題目中A講的意思是「你今天覺得如何？」，考的是疑問副詞，B的回答中沒有時間、地點或理由，所以知道是要選「how」。

2. 正解為(D)。這句話的意思是「導遊很清楚地講話並且把每個字發音清楚好讓外國旅客聽懂他說的話。」這題當中的要用副詞「clearly」去修飾動詞speak 以符合上下文情境。

3. 正解為(D)。本題句子表示「她永遠無法唱得像那位專業歌劇演唱者一樣好」，要用副詞修飾動詞sing，空格後面的有標示相等程度的介系詞as，要用as well as 的結構。

4. 正解為(A)。句子的意思為「我以為我已經很用功，但我發現珍妮比我還要更用功。」這題考的是修飾副詞比較級的程度詞，「work even harder」代表「甚至更用功」，符合上下文語意。

5. 正解為(B)。本題題目的意思是「不幸地，雇主和工會之間的協商失敗了」，這題要考的是放在句首的副詞，選項(A)是「目前」、選項(C)是「第二」、選項(D)是「或許」，都不符合上下文的意思。

6. 正解為(B)。句子的意思是「我對你的表現很失望。如果你更努力的話，本來可以做得更好的。」要選出修飾動詞「do」的副詞比較級，根據語意會選擇better 而非 worse。

7. 正解為(D)。這句話的意思是「秘書處理文件很小心。她很少會有拼錯字這類的錯誤。」這題考的是頻率副詞的意思，依據前面一句的意思，應選擇「很少、幾乎沒有」的seldom。

8. 正解為(C)。句子的意思是「街角的咖啡店對我來說是充滿回憶的地方。那是我認識初戀女友的地方。」這題考的是連接副詞的用法，代表地點，要選「where」。

9. 正解為(B)。本句的意思是「他行為不夠成熟。他對工作和生活的態度還有很多要改進的地方。」這題要用副詞maturely修飾動詞behave，而enough要放在maturely之後表示程度。

10. 正解為(A)。本題題目的意思是「請把奶油和麵粉混合。同時，我會預熱烤箱並且準備其他的材料。」這題在考的是放在句首的副詞用法，選項(B)表示「可能」、選項(C)表示「突然」、選項(D)表示「特別」，這些與上下文的意思不符合。

Day

08

介系詞
Preposition

介系詞 Preposition

第一節：概述

　　介系詞是一種虛詞，都是搭配其他的詞來表示種種不同的意思，因此掌握好介系詞是學好英語的關鍵之一。

第二節：介系詞的用法

(1) 介系詞後面一定會接一個名詞、代名詞、動名詞、數詞等作為受詞。

受詞類型	例句	中譯
名詞	I wandered round the orchard.	我在果園裡晃來晃去。
名詞子句	This will give you some idea of what relativity means.	這會使你對相對論的意義有所瞭解。
代名詞	There's a girl standing in front of me.	我前面站著一個女孩。
數詞	When we went in we found his room at sixes and sevens.	我們走進去的時候發現他屋裡亂七八糟。
動名詞	On arriving in Venice, we knew that it was a city of water.	我們一到威尼斯就知道它是一座水城。
動名詞片語	He entered the chemistry lab without being permitted.	他未經允許就進入化學實驗室。
副詞	Until then, I knew nothing at all about it.	在那以前，我對此一無所知。
子句	I am thinking of what I shall say at the meeting.	我在想我在會議上該說些什麼。

| 不定詞片語 | In one of his books, Marx gave some advice on how to learn a foreign language. | 馬克思在他的一本書裡，針對如何學習外語提出了一些建議。 |

(2) 介系詞的意思

意思	舉例
表示地點	about, above, across, after, against, along, among, around, at, before, behind, below, beneath, beside, between, beyond, by, down, from, in, inside, into, near, off, on, over, past, round, through, throughout, to, towards, under, up, upon, with, within, without, at the back / front / side / top / bottom of, at the beginning of, at the end of, away from, far from, in front of等。
表示時間	about, after, around, as, at, before, behind, between, by, during, for, from, in, into, of, on, over, past, since, through, throughout, till / until, to, towards, within, at the beginning / end of, at the time of, in the middle / midst of等。
表示除外	besides, but, except等。
表示比較	as, like, above, over等。
表示反對	against, with等。
表示原因、目的	for, from, with等。
表示結果	to, with, without等。
表手段、方式	by, in, with等。
表示所屬	of, with等。
表示條件	on, considering, without等。
表示讓步	despite, in spite of等。
表示關於	about, concerning, regarding, with regard to, as for, as to等。
表示對於	at, for, over, to, with等。
表示根據	on, according to等。
表示其他	for（贊成）, without（沒有）等。

113

常用來表示位置的介系詞可摘要如下圖：

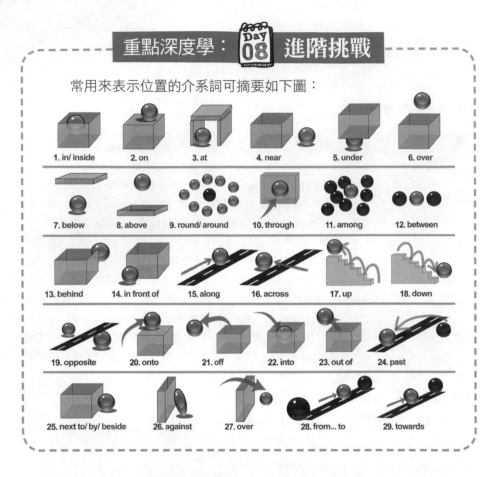

1. in/ inside　2. on　3. at　4. near　5. under　6. over

7. below　8. above　9. round/ around　10. through　11. among　12. between

13. behind　14. in front of　15. along　16. across　17. up　18. down

19. opposite　20. onto　21. off　22. into　23. out of　24. past

25. next to/ by/ beside　26. against　27. over　28. from... to　29. towards

(3) 介系詞片語在句子當中的作用

句中作用	例句	中譯
主詞	From Taipei to Tainan is two hours by High Speed Rail.	從台北到台南坐高鐵需要兩小時。
修飾語	Many cities along the coast are open to foreign trade.	許多沿海城市對外開放。
副詞	Because of the traffic, I was late for class.	由於交通堵塞，我上課遲到了。
主詞補語	His explanation cannot be accepted as being satisfactory.	他的解釋不是很令人滿意。
受詞補語	He soon found himself in harmony with his new co-workers.	他很快便發現自己能與新同事和睦相處。

(4) 介系詞與其他詞類的搭配

接續的詞	例子	
接名詞	at home 在家	at the cinema 在電影院
	by the door 在門口	in the city 在城裡
	on time 按時，準時	contribution to 對……貢獻
	acquaintance with 與……相識	devotion to 獻身於
	independence of 獨立於	effect / influence on 對……的影響
	sympathy with 對……同情	
接動詞	account for 說明	arrive at 到達
	depart from 離開	cooperate with 與……合作
	laugh at 取笑，嘲笑	specialize in 專攻
接形容詞	absent from 不在	anxious for 急需，渴求
	clever at 善於	different from 與……不同
	opposite to 與……對面	afraid of 對……害怕

重點深度學：Day 08 進階挑戰

(1) 詞根或詞源相同的名詞、動詞和形容詞一般共用一個介系詞。例如：

depend / dependent / dependence on 依賴，依靠

independent / independence of 獨立（於）

interest / interested in 對……感興趣

responsible / responsibility for 負責

skill / skilled / skillful at 熟練，善於

succeed / success / successful in 在……上取得成功

sympathy/sympathize/sympathetic with 同情

(2) 一個名詞、動詞或形容詞往往可以和一個以上的介系詞搭配。例如：

look for（尋找）	look at（看）

compare with（與……相比）	compare to（把……比作）
popular with（受……歡迎）	popular among（受……歡迎）
originate in（起源於，產生於）	originate from（起源於，產生於）

第三節：常用的介系詞

1. in

用法	表示地點	表示時間
in	表示「在……內」，例如： in the room 在房間裡 in a small village 在一個小村子裡 in the north of China 在中國北方 in space 在空中（太空） in Hong Kong 在香港 in the street 在街上 in the tree 在樹上 in the sky 在天空中 in the sun 在陽光下	表示在一段時間內，例如： in an hour 在1小時內 in half an hour 在半小時內 in the past fifty years 在過去50年裡 in spring 在春天 in February, 2007 在2007年2月 in the morning 在上午 in the winter of 2006 在2006年的冬天 in the 1990's 在20世紀90年代
	in English (Chinese...) 用英語（中文等） in order to 為了…… in surprise 驚訝地 in front of 在……前面 in battle 在戰鬥中 in a minute 立刻 in (great) need of （迫切）需要 in place of 代替 join in 參與 hit sb. in the face 打在某人臉上 in fact 事實上 in class 在上課 in hospital 在醫院 in trouble 遇上麻煩	

in	in a hurry 匆忙地 in one's own words 用某人自己的話 in prison 坐牢 do well in 在某方面學得好 be strict in (sth.) 嚴格對待某事 in time 及時

2. on

on	on time 準時 on (the) radio 在收音機上，透過無線電廣播 spend...on... 在……上花費…… depend on 依靠 on line 線上 on one's way to... 在去……的路上 on duty 值日 on the left (right) 在左（右）邊 (be) on show 在展出

3. at

(1) 表示地點：在……

　　Please enter at the front door. 請從前門進入。

(2) 表示時間：在……（時刻）；在……歲（時）

　　At the age of twelve (=At twelve), Edison began selling newspapers on the train.

　　愛迪生十二歲時開始在火車上賣報紙。

(3) 表示狀態：在……中；進行（某種活動）

　　The two countries are at war. 這兩個國家在交戰。

(4) 表示價格、速度：以……

　　The train runs at seventy kilometers an hour.
　　火車以每小時七十公里的速度行駛。

(5) 表示引起某種情緒的原因：因為；由於

We were greatly surprised at their failure.
我們對他們的失敗感到非常驚訝。

(6) 表示動作方向：朝，向

He threw a stone at the dog. 他朝狗扔了一塊石頭。

(7) 在（某方面）

He is clever at drawing. 他擅長畫畫。

(8) 其他常用片語

at first 首先	at once 立刻	at the same time 同時
be good at 擅長	look at 看著	arrive at 到達
at last 最後	at work 在上班	shout at 對著……大叫
throw at 對著……扔	knock at 敲……	at the age of 在……歲時
at first 起先；開始的時候	at least 至少	at home 在家，無拘束
at present 現在；目前	at the same time 同時	at breakfast 在吃早餐

4. about

意義	例句	中譯
關於；有關	Don't feel bad about it.	別難過。
在周圍	He likes travelling about the world.	他喜歡環遊世界。
大約	We left there about eight o'clock that morning.	那天早上我們是大約八點鐘離開那裡的。
特殊片語	What about meeting outside the theatre?	在劇場外見面怎麼樣？

5. above

意義	例句	中譯
表示在……以上	Many birds are flying above the woods.	許多鳥在樹林上空飛。
表示超出……之外	The temperature tonight should be above freezing.	今晚的氣溫應該在零度以上。

6. across

意義	例句	中譯
表示動作方向、位置：穿過，橫過	Let's help push the car across the bridge.	我們幫忙把車子推過橋吧。
表示地點：在……對面	The post office is just across the road.	郵局就在馬路對面。

7. after

意義	例句	中譯
表示時間或位置：在……之後	It is easy to be wise after the event.	後見之明是容易的。（諺語）
按照，仿照	Johnson is named after his father John.	強森是依他的父親約翰命名的。
探求；追	A policeman is running after a thief.	一個員警在追一個小偷。

8. against

意義	例句	中譯
表示位置：倚著，靠著；撞擊	The ladder was against the wall.	梯子靠牆放著。
反對	Are you for my proposal or against it?	你是贊成還是反對我的建議？

9. along 沿著

They walked together along the river. 他們一起沿著河走。

10. among 在……中間；在……之中（在三者或三者以上之中）

Shelly is among the greatest poets in the world.
雪萊是世界上最偉大的詩人之一。

11. around

意義	例句	中譯
表示位置：在……周圍；環繞	The earth moves around the sun.	地球繞太陽轉。
在……範圍內	They travelled for a month around Europe.	他們在歐洲旅行了一個月。
表示數目：大約	He came here around three o'clock.	他大約三點鐘來到這裡。

12. before

意義	例句	中譯
表示時間：在……以前	Pride goes before a fall.	驕者必敗。
表示位置：在……前面	We will never bow before difficulties.	我們絕不向困難低頭。

13. behind

意義	例句	中譯
表示位置：在……後面	He never looked behind him.	他從不向後看。
表示時間：比……晚，遲於；引申意義：落後於……，不如……	The train is behind time.	火車誤點了。

14. below

意義	例句	中譯
表示位置：在……下面	Our classroom is below theirs.	我們教室在他們的下面。
表示數量、程度、年齡、能力等：低於；在……以下	The temperature is 5 ℃ below zero.	氣溫是攝氏零下五度。

15. beside 在……旁邊

She sat beside me at supper. 吃晚飯時她坐在我旁邊。

besides 除……以外（還有）

What other languages do you know besides English?
除了英語以外，你還懂其他什麼語言？

16. between

在（兩者）之間（有時也可用於三者及其以上之間）

Would you come between eight and nine o'clock?
你在八、九點之間來好嗎？

17. beyond

意義	例句	中譯
表示位置：在……外邊；在……那邊	The lake is beyond the hill.	湖在小山那邊。
表示範圍、限度：超出；高於	Good advice is beyond price.	好忠告是無價寶。（諺語）

18. but 除了……；除……之外

I haven't told anybody but you. 除了你我誰也沒說。

19. by

意義	例句	中譯
表示地點：在……旁邊；從……旁邊	Come here and stand by me.	到這裡來，站在我旁邊。
表示方式、手段：用；靠；透過；根據；由（某人做的）	It was done by hand, not by machine.	這是手工做的，不是機器做的。
表示時間：到……的時候；到……為止	By the end of last term, we had learned 2,000 English words.	到上學期期末，我們已學了兩千個英語單字。
表示（增減）程度、尺寸、數量等：按；以	The cotton crop this year has increased by 25% over last year.	今年的棉花收成比去年增加了25%。

20. down

表示動作方向

Tears were rolling down his cheeks.
眼淚順著他的臉頰滾下來。

21. during 在……期間

During the summer season, all the hotels are full.
整個夏季所有的旅店都客滿。

22. except 除……以外

（與全肯定或全否定詞連用，表示排除關係）

He has not changed at all except that he is no longer so talkative.
他一點也沒變，只是不像以前那樣愛說話了。

23. for

意義	例句	中譯
表示目的、物件：為……；對於……	What did you go there for?	你為什麼去那裡？
表示一段時間或距離：達到	We haven't seen each other for a long time.	我們很久沒有見面了。
表示方向、目標：向；去；往	He got on the next plane for San Francisco.	他上了前往舊金山市的下一班飛機。
表示原因：因為	I'm sorry for being late.	對不起，我來晚了。
表示用途：給……的；供……用的	Here is a letter for you.	這裡有你的一封信。
表示同意或贊成	I'm for your idea.	我贊成你的意見。
就……而言	He is tall for his age.	就他的年齡而言，他的個子算高了。
當做；作為	It was selected as the site for the coming Olympic Games.	它被選為下一屆奧運會的地點
引導片語表示不定詞 to V 的邏輯主詞	It's time for us to study hard.	該是我們努力學習的時候了。

24. from

意義	例句	中譯
表示來源、起點	We are very busy from morning till evening.	我們從早到晚都很忙。
表示原因、動機	He did so from a sense of duty.	他出於責任感才這樣做的。
表示距離、間隔：離開	Far from eye, far from heart.	眼不見，心不想。（諺語）
表示原材料	Steel is made from iron.	鋼是生鐵煉成的。

25. into

意義	例句	中譯
表示時間或動作的方向：	They often work far into the night.	他們常常工作到深夜。
表示變化或進入某種狀態	Please put the following sentences into Chinese.	請把下列句子譯成中文。

26. like

意義	例句	中譯
像……一樣	Don't treat me like a guest.	別把我當客人。
是什麼樣子	What was the weather like yesterday?	昨天天氣怎麼樣？

27. near 表示時間或空間：靠近；接近；在……附近

A group of students were standing near the entrance.
一群學生站在靠近入口的地方。

28. of

意義	例句	中譯
表示所屬關係	I don't remember the name of the street.	我想不起這條街的名字。

表示具有某種性質、內容、狀況等	The meeting was of great importance.	這場會議很重要。
表示數量或種類	Perhaps the three of you can walk around a bit.	或許你們三個人可以到處走走。
表示同位關係	He came here in the month of May.	他是五月份來這裡的。
表示動詞與受詞關係	To buy this kind of computer is a waste of money.	買這種電腦是浪費錢。

29. since 從（某時間）起，自……以來

It's a long time since we last met. 從我們上次見面以來已經很久了。

30. till (until) 直到（某時間）為止

We didn't get there till (until) dark. 我們直到天黑才到達那裡。

31. over

意義	例句	中譯
在……上方	There is a bridge over the river.	河上有一座橋。
表示數目、程度：在……以上；超過	She spoke for over an hour at the meeting.	她在會議上講了一個多小時。
越過……；從……邊緣上往下	The thief jumped over the wall and ran away.	小偷翻牆逃跑了。
在……期間；直到……過完	Great changes have taken place in the world over the past few years.	過去幾年裡世界發生了巨大變化。

Over也用於某些固定搭配：

over again 重新開始	over all 全面地	over there 在那裡
over the telephone 透過電話	all over the world 全世界	all over the country 全國
over the radio 透過無線電	be over 結束	go over 檢查；複習；看一看

32. past

意義	例句	中譯
表示動作方向：從……旁經過	He walked past me.	他從我身旁走過。
表示時間、年齡、數量等超過……	The recorder is past repair.	這台錄音機已經無法修理了。

33. round/around

意義	例句	中譯
圍繞著……	The earth goes round/around the sun.	地球繞太陽轉。
表示時間：橫貫過；在……前後	She'll be back round Christmas.	她將在聖誕節前後回來。

34. through

意義	例句	中譯
穿過；通過	The train passed through a tunnel.	列車通過了隧道。
從頭到尾經過 從～開始到結束	Sometimes he works through the night.	他有時會通宵工作。
表示方式、手段、原因等	He learned Japanese through TV.	他從電視上學習日語。

35. to

意義	例句	中譯
表示方向、距離：到；向；往	It is ten kilometers to the station.	這裡離車站有10公里。
表示時間、程度：直到……為止	We'll fight to the end.	我們將戰鬥到底。
表示間接關係：給……；於……	John is the person to whom you should write.	約翰是你應該寫封信的對象。

| 表示目的：為了 | Let's drink to our health! | 為了我們的健康喝一杯! |
| 表示比較：比 | I prefer football to basketball. | 比起籃球，我更喜歡足球。 |

36. toward(s)

意義	例句	中譯
表示方向：朝；向	The house faces toward the south.	這間房子朝南。
表示對於	What's his attitude towards his work?	他的工作態度怎麼樣？
表示時間：接近；左右	They left here towards ten o'clock.	他們離開時將近十點了。

37. under

意義	例句	中譯
表示位置：在……下	Everyone ran under the trees when it started to rain.	開始下雨時，大家都跑到樹底下。
表示在……領導下	England was under Charles II then.	英國當時是在查理二世的統治下。
表示少於；不足	These children are all under the age of twelve.	這些孩子年齡都不足十二歲。
表示在某種過程或狀態之中	The railway is under construction.	鐵路正在修建中。

38. until

意義	例句	中譯
直到	We will go on working until next week.	我們將繼續工作到下星期。
（用於否定句）直到……才	Not until eleven o'clock yesterday did I go to bed.	我昨天直到晚上十一點才去睡覺。

39. with

意義	例句	中譯
表示共同關係：和……一起；	Can you come and stay with us for a time?	你能來和我們住一段時間嗎？
表示客體關係：對；對於	Our teacher is strict with us.	我們老師對我們很嚴格。
表示工具、手段等：被；用	He wrote a letter with a pencil.	他用鉛筆寫了一封信。
表示從屬關係：具有；帶有；在……身邊	Have you any money with you?	你身邊有帶錢嗎？
表示原因	The little boy is trembling with cold.	那小男孩正冷得發抖。
就……來說	Is everything going well with you?	你們一切都進展得順利嗎？

40. within

意義	例句	中譯
表示位置、地點：在……之內；在……裡	The ticket gives students unlimited free travel within the UK.	這種票讓學生在英國國內不受任何限制地免費旅遊。
表示時間：在……以內；不到……	He will come back within half an hour.	他半小時內就回來。

41. without 不；沒有

He came here without being asked. 他未被邀請就來這裡了。

1. The professor requests that we should submit the final report _____ Friday.
   A. within   B. by   C. until   D. along

2. The Net celebrity is very popular _____ teenagers.
   A. above   B. across   C. from   D. among

3. He has nothing _____ you. He is just trying to give you some advice.
   A. across   B. behind   C. against   D. without

4. The magnificence of the Louvre is _____ description.
   A. past   B. under   C. above   D. beyond

5. The main stadium for the upcoming Olympic Games is still _____ construction.
   A. beside   B. between   C. under   D. until

6. We spend thirty minutes to figure out the solution _____ the math problem.
   A. from   B. to   C. with   D. by

7. The birth rate in the country dropped drastically _____ the past few decades.
   A. above   B. round   C. through   D. over

8. When the train was moving _____ full speed, the passengers saw objects outside the window flew by.
   A. on   B. to   C. at   D. of

9. His test scores were _____ the threshold for admission by the prestigious university, so he decided to apply for the community college.
   A. above   B. below   C. under   D. over

10. The conversation between the chairpersons from the two electronic magnates was _____ the record. What they talked about was not revealed to the public.
    A. at   B. in   C. with   D. off

1. 正解為(B)。這句話的意思是「教授要求我們要在星期五以前繳交期末報告」。表示「在……之前」用介系詞by。

2. 正解為(D)。這句話的意思是「這位網紅很受年輕人的歡迎。」這句話中的「受～歡迎」可以用「be popular among / with」來表示。

3. 正解為(C)。本題句子表示「他沒有反對你的意思。他只是要給你意見。」選項(A)是「穿越」或「對面」的意思、選項(B)是後面、選項(C)是「反對」或「緊靠著」的意思、選項(D)是「沒有」的意思。

4. 正解為(D)。句子的意思為「羅浮宮的富麗堂皇無法用言語形容。」其中，「言語無法形容」可以說是「beyond words」或「beyond description」。

5. 正解為(C)。本題題目的意思是「即將到來的奧運比賽主場館仍在興建中」，這題要考的用在「興建中」這個片語中要用的介系詞「under construction」，類似的用法還有「under renovation」是「裝修中」的意思。

6. 正解為(B)。句子的意思是「我們花了三十分鐘找出那個數學問題的解法。」這題考的是「the solution to the math problem」（數學問題的解決方法）這個慣用說法，會使用介系詞to，類似的說法還有「the answer to the question」（這個問題的答案）。

7. 正解為(D)。這句話的意思是「該國的出生率在過去幾十年大幅降低。」在「過去幾十年」可以說是over the past decades、throughout the past decades、during the past decades、in the past few decades 等等。

8. 正解為(C)。句子的意思是「火車以全速前進時，乘客看見窗外的物體一閃而過。」這題考的是「at full speed（全速）」這個片語，也可以說是「the train is in full speed」。

9. 正解為(B)。本句的意思是「他的考試分數未達到著名大學的入學門檻。」表示「未達標準（below the threshold）」、「未達平均（below average）」會使用below這個介系詞。

10. 正解為(D)。本題題目的意思是「這兩家電子業巨擘總裁，他們之間的對話是保密的。他們討論的事情未對外公開。」這題在考的是「並未對外公開」的片語「off the record」。

Day

09

連接詞
Conjunction

Day09 連接詞 Conjunction

🚩 第一節：概述

連接詞是連接單字、片語、子句或句子的一種虛詞。根據其性質可分為兩大類：「對等連接詞」和「從屬連接詞」。

🚩 第二節：對等連接詞

對等連接詞用來連接並列的詞、片語、子句或句子。常見的對等連接詞有：

and	but	or	for
as well as	neither...nor	either...or	both...and
yet	so	not only...but also	

1. 表示轉折意思的對等連接詞

連接詞	例句	中譯
but	Science knows no national boundaries, but a scientist has his motherland.	科學沒有國界，但科學家有祖國。
but	The true value of life is not in what we get, but in what we give.——Edison	人生的真正價值不在於我們得到什麼，而在於我們奉獻什麼。一（美）愛迪生
yet	One strange animal lays eggs, yet feeds its young on its milk.	有一種怪獸會產卵，然而又給幼兒哺乳。
yet	Time covers up everything, yet it also reveals everything.	時間遮蓋一切，可也顯現一切。（德國諺語）

	We have not yet won; however, we shall keep trying.	我們還沒勝利。然而，我們必須繼續努力。
however	However, his struggle had already changed the whole society in the USA.	然而，他的鬥爭已經改變了整個美國社會。
nevertheless	There was no news; nevertheless, she went on hoping.	目前還沒有消息，然而她繼續抱持希望。

2. 表示因果關係的對等連接詞

連接詞	例句	中譯
for	You must get rid of carelessness, for it often leads to errors.	你一定要克服粗心大意，因為粗心大意常常造成錯誤。
so	The trees in the forests can keep rain drops from hitting the soil directly, so soil is not easily washed away.	森林裡的樹木能夠防止雨滴直接衝擊土壤，因此土壤也就不容易被沖走了。
therefore	The whale therefore has to look for the squid using sound waves.	因此巨頭鯨必須用聲波去搜尋魷魚。

3. 其他的對等連接詞

連接詞	例句	中譯
and	Dinosaurs lived on the earth for more than 150 million years, and then disappeared about 65 million years ago.	恐龍在地球上生活1億5千萬年以上，後來大約在6千5百萬年以前消失。
or	Have an aim in life, or your energies will all be wasted.	人生要有目標，否則你的精力會白白浪費。
either... or...	You can contact us either by phone, by email, or by letter.	你可以透過電話、電子郵件或者來信聯繫我們。
neither... nor...	He wants neither fame nor wealth.	他既不求名，也不求利。
not only... but also...	Drunk driving can not only cause traffic accidents, but also endanger the lives of pedestrians.	酒後駕車不僅會造成交通事故，而且會危害到行人的生命。

| both...
and... | They surf three times a day if possible, in both winter and summer. | 無論冬夏，只要有可能，他們一天都要衝浪三次。 |
| as well as | Future agriculture should depend on high technology as well as traditional methods. | 將來的農業不但要依靠傳統的方法，也要依靠高科技。 |

第三節：從屬連接詞

從屬連接詞主要用來引導子句。常見的從屬連接詞有：

after	although	as	as if
as soon as	as long as	as...as	if
as well as	before	because	even if
in case	in order that	now that	once
on condition that	since	so that	so...that
such...that	so...as	till	though
than	unless	until	when

1. 引導時間副詞子句的從屬連接詞

連接詞	例句	中譯
after	After the work was done, we sat down to sum up experience.	工作結束後，我們坐下來總結經驗。
as	As the sun sinks lower and lower, it looks like a great fiery ball.	當太陽越沉越低的時候，它看上去像一個大火球。
as soon as	As soon as the reporters know what to write about, they get down to work.	記者們一旦知道他們所要寫的新聞，就著手開始工作。
before	All things are difficult before they are easy.—Thomas Fuller	萬事先難後易。—（英）湯瑪斯·富勒
when	Westerners expect people to look at each other in the eyes when they talk	西方人談話時希望互相看著對方的眼睛。

while	Boards are laid down to protect the precious painted stones while the repair work is going on.	在進行修復工作的時候，為了保護這些繪有花紋的珍貴石頭，在它們上面鋪上木板。
since	It's just a week since we arrived here.	我們到這裡剛好一個星期了。
till / until	No man has learned the art of life till he has been well tempted.	經歷過各種誘惑的人才能學會生活的藝術。
once	Once you choose your way of life, be brave to stick it out and never return.	一旦選定生活的道路，就要勇敢地走到底，絕不回頭。

重點提示：必學文法小要點

while 還可作並列連接詞，引導並列分句，表示對比，意為「然而」。例如：

★He likes music while I'm fond of sports.
他喜歡音樂，然而我愛好體育。

★when有時表示「如果」，相當於「if」。例如：
I can't help you when you don't listen to me.
如果你不聽我的話，我無法幫助你。

2. 引導原因副詞子句的從屬連接詞

連接詞	例句	中譯
as	As the oceans are the sources of life on earth, the estuaries are our planet's nurseries.	由於海洋是地球上生命的泉源，河流的入海口就是我們這個星球上的生長溫床。
because	Radioactive matter is dangerous to work with because it has a bad effect on the blood.	從事放射性工作是危險的，因為它對血液有不良影響。
since	People come to his lecture since his word are always inspiring.	因為他說話總是很具啟發性，人們會來聽他的演講。
now that	Now that you are well again, you can work with them.	既然你已經康復了，你就可以跟他們一起工作。

3. 引導條件副詞子句的從屬連接詞

連接詞	例句	中譯
if	If a person is thirsty of knowledge, there lies in front of him a way to success.	如果一個人渴望知識，那麼成功之路就在他腳下。
unless	Victory won't come to me unless I go to it.	勝利是不會向我走來的，我必須自己走向勝利。
as / so long as	You may borrow this book as long as you keep it clean.	我可以借給你這本書，只要你不把它弄髒。
in case	You'd better take an umbrella in case it rains.	你最好帶把雨傘去，以防下雨。

4. 引導讓步副詞子句的從屬連接詞

連接詞	例句	中譯
although / though	Although a man may be born clever, his intelligence also needs to be further developed.	雖然一個人也許生來聰明，但他的智力仍需進一步開發。
even if / even though	Even though we have made great achievements, we should not be proud.	即使我們有了很好的成就，也不應該驕傲。
while	While there are many different interpretations of our body language, some gestures seem to be universal.	雖然對於手勢語的解釋各有不同，但某些手勢似乎是全球通用的。

5. 引導目的副詞子句的從屬連接詞

連接詞	例句	中譯
so that	He told the BBC that he wanted 17 hours of nonstop TV time so that both concerts could be shown on television.	他要求英國廣播公司提供17個小時的連續電視節目時間，以便播放這兩場音樂會的節目。

6. 引導結果副詞子句的從屬連接詞

連接詞	例句	中譯
so... that...	The film was so interesting that I went to see it several times.	這部電影十分有趣，所以我去看過好幾次。
such... that...	He made such rapid progress that before long he began to write articles in English for an American newspaper.	他進步得非常快，不久他就開始用英文替一家美國報紙寫文章了。

7. 引導比較副詞子句的從屬連接詞

連接詞	例句	中譯
as / so...as...	The work is not so easy as you imagine.	這工作絕不像你想像得那麼簡單。
than	He who can take advice is sometimes wiser than he who gives it.	能夠接受忠告的人有時候比提出忠告的人更加高明。

8. 引導主詞子句、補語子句、受詞子句等的從屬連接詞

連接詞	例句	中譯	說明
if	I wonder if he will accept the invitation.	我不知道他是否會接受這個邀請。	引導的子句作受詞
that	Current trends indicate that transportation is becoming cleaner, faster and safer.	當前的趨勢表明，交通正在變得更加乾淨、快捷和安全。	引導的子句作受詞
that	That she's still alive is a sheer luck.	她還活著真是幸運。	引導的子句作主詞
that	Your trouble is that you are absent-minded.	你的問題在於你太心不在焉了。	引導的子句作補語
whether	Whether John will go still remains a question.	約翰是否會去還是個問題。	引導的子句作主詞
whether	The question is whether the president will agree to the proposal.	問題在於主席是否會同意這項建議。	引導的子句作補語
whether	I asked Tom whether he was coming to the party.	我問湯姆是否來參加聚會。	引導的子句作受詞

1. _____ he was not very talented, he made lots of efforts and worked his way up to become a senior manager.
   A. Although   B. Unless   C. As long as   D. As soon as

2. Some farmers support using pesticides on crops, _____ others stick to the organic farming method.
   A. because   B. while   C. if   D. for

3. He won't give up _____ he is confronted with many obstacles; he will persist and solve all the problems.
   A. unless   B. even if   C. that   D. now that

4. It matters a lot _____ we can keep the African Swine Fever out of Taiwan.
   A. while   B. whether   C. so that   D. in case

5. The production line can work more efficiently _____ we have the new manufacturing machine.
   A. yet   B. but   C. so that   D. now that

6. _____ you have tasted the bitterest of the bitter, you will become the greatest of the great.
   A. Unless   B. Even though   C. If   D. In case

7. _____ the going gets tough, the tough gets going.
   A. When   B. For   C. Unless   D. Even if

8. It wasn't _____ the day before the deadline that he submitted the report.
   A. before   B. after   C. until   D. while

9. The research indicates _____ overusing smartphone and addiction to social media network may make people emotional and irritable.
   A. that   B. whether   C. than   D. as

10. The supervisor will offer you any possible support _____ you can complete the task on time.
    A. as long as   B. as well as   C. as much as   D. as to

1. 正解為(A)。這句話的意思是「雖然他不是很有才華的人，他還是努力在公司往上爬成為資深經理」。這句考的是讓步子句的連接詞Although。

2. 正解為(B)。這句話的意思是「有些農民支持使用殺蟲劑，但是其他農民堅持用有機栽種。」這句話前後子句是對比的意思，用「while」來連接。

3. 正解為(B)。本題句子表示「即使他遇到很多的阻礙，他也不會放棄；他會堅持下去並且解決所有的問題。」選項(A)是「除非」的意思，若套用，和後半句的句意不符；選項(B)是即使；選項(C)是引導出名詞子句的連接詞；選項(D)是「既然」的意思。

4. 正解為(B)。句子的意思為「我們是否能將非洲豬瘟隔離在台灣之外是相當中重要的事。」選項(A)是「然而」，選項(B)是「是否」，選項(C)是「為了、以便於」，選項(D)是「萬一、假如」。

5. 正解為(D)。本題題目的意思是「既然我們有了新的製造機器，生產線將可以更有效率地運作」，這題要考「既然」這個意思的連接詞。選項(A)是「但是」，選項(B)也是「但是」，這兩個都是對等連接詞，選項(C)表示「為了」，前面接手段，後面接目的，但是這一句是前半為結果、後半為原因，所以選now that。

6. 正解為(C)。句子的意思是「吃得苦中苦，方為人上人。」這題考的是表示條件的子句，前面所使用的連接詞「If」在這邊是「如果」，表示前半句的條件程例，後半句描述的事情才會成真。

7. 正解為(A)。這句話的意思是「當情況越發困難時，堅強的人會更勇於面對挑戰。」這句話的前半句是屬於描述條件與狀況的從屬子句。選項(B)表示「因為」，是對等連接詞；選項(C)是「除非」的意思，選項(D)是「即使」。

8. 正解為(C)。句子的意思是「直到期限前一天，他才繳交報告。」這題考的是「It's not until ~ that ~（直到～才～）」這個句型，這句也可以說「He didn't submit the report until the day before the deadline.」。

9. 正解為(A)。本句意思是「研究指出，過度使用智慧型手機，以及對社群網路上癮會使人變得情緒化且易怒。」空格當中要填的是引出作為句子受詞的名詞子句連接詞，就語意來說是肯定的，所以不會選whether（是否）而會用that。

10. 正解為(A)。本題題目的意思是「主管會給你所有可能的資源，只要你能準時完成任務。」這題在考的是「as long as（只要）」這個可以用於表示條件的連接詞。

Day

10

感嘆詞
Interjection

感嘆詞 Interjection
Day 10

第一節：概述

　　感嘆詞用來表示喜怒哀樂等感情或情緒，後面的句子常常說明產生這種感情或情緒的性質、原因等。

　　在感嘆的情緒較強時，後面通常會接感嘆號，如果不強，後面則接逗號。例如：

Oh! What a coincidence! 喔！好巧啊！

Oh, is that so? 啊，是這樣嗎？

　　感嘆詞有時也可以放在句中。例如：

The old man, alas, isn't out of danger yet.
那位老人，唉，還沒脫離危險。

第二節：一些常用的感嘆詞

例句	中譯	說明
Ah, here is the thing I'm after!	啊，這才是我要找的東西！	表示高興
Ah! I have never heard of such things before.	喲！我從來沒聽說過這樣的事。	表示驚訝
Aha, our team won!	啊哈，我們隊贏了。	aha 表示勝利或滿意
Oh! What a wonder!	哇！真是奇蹟！	表示驚訝
Oh, Mummy! Will you come here, please?	哦，媽媽！你過來好嗎？	表示恐懼
Oh! What a naughty boy!	唉！這個男孩真淘氣！	表示生氣

Oh Henry, what are you doing over there?	嗳，亨利，你在那裡做什麼呀？	表示不耐煩
Oh! What a fine day today!	啊！今天天氣真好！	表示高興
Oh! We are too careless!	唉！我們太粗心了！	表示後悔
Well, who would have thought about it?	唉，誰會想到這樣呢？	表示無奈
Well, here we are at last.	好了，我們終於到了。	表示寬慰
Well, there is nothing we can do about it.	唉，我們是無能為力的了。	表示無奈
Very well, then, we'll talk it over again tomorrow.	很好，那麼我們明天再談一談吧。	表示同意
Well, you may be right.	好吧，也許你是對的。	表示讓步
Here! Don't cry!	好了，別哭了。	用來引起別人的注意
Come, come, no time for such things.	得啦，得啦，沒有時間談這些事了。	表示不耐煩
Come, come, it isn't as bad as that.	好了，好了，並不是那樣糟糕。	表示鼓勵
Come, come, Alice, you must be patient.	好了，愛麗絲，你得忍耐點。	表示勸導
Come, tell me all about it.	喂，把這件事全告訴我吧。	表示促使注意
Why, even a child knows that!	哎呀，這連小孩子都知道！	表示不耐煩
Why, what's the harm?	哎，這有什麼害處呢？	表示抗議
Why, of course, I'll do it.	噢，當然，我要做的。	表示贊成
Why, yes, I think so.	呃，對的，我是這樣想的。	表示猶豫
Hello! How are you?	嘿，你好？	用來招呼人
Oh dear! Why should you be so cross!	哎呀！你怎麼生這麼大的氣！	表示驚奇、傷心
Say, haven't I seen you somewhere before?	哎呀，我以前是不是在什麼地方見過你？	表示驚奇
Nonsense! I do not believe it.	胡說，我不相信。	表示抗議

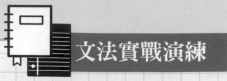

1. _____! What a surprise.
   A. Oh   B. Alas   C. Hey   D. Here

2. _____! The project didn't go well.
   A. Here   B. Hey   C. Here   D. Alas

3. _____. Don't be so sad. Things will get better.
   A. Alas   B. Say   C. Hi   D. Here

4. _____, then, we can continue the discussion tomorrow.
   A. Why   B. Alas   C. Well   D. Come

5. _____! This is the most stupid thing that I have ever done.
   A. Ah   B. Oh   C. Aha   D. Why

6. _____! Are there anything wrong?
   A. Why   B. Aha   C. Here   D. Hello

7. _____! We got into the final round of the contest.
   A. Aha   B. Why   C. Alas   D. Hello

8. _____! I have showed you the principles, and you still can't do it right.
   A. Aha   B. Well   C. Why   D. Come

9. _____, none of us expected this.
   A. Well   B. Why   C. Here   D. Come

10. _____! He wouldn't lie to me.
   A. Aha   B. Hello   C. Nonsense   D. Say

 **文法實戰解析**

1. 正解為(A)。這句話有驚訝、感嘆的意思,所以用Oh來表示。

2. 正解為(D)。這句話的意思是「唉!計畫進行得不順利。」這句話有感嘆的意思,所以用Alas。

3. 正解為(D)。這題表示安慰的意思,所以用Here比較適當。

4. 正解為(C)。句子的意思為「好吧。我們可以明天繼續討論。」這裡用的感嘆詞是表示同意,所以用Well。

5. 正解為(B)。本題的句子是「噢,這是我做過最愚蠢的事情了。」使用驚訝又有點懊悔意味的感嘆詞Oh。

6. 正解為(A)。句子的意思是「哎呀。有什麼問題嗎?」這裡表示的是有點驚訝或抗議意味的感嘆詞。

7. 正解為(A)。這句話的意思是「我們進入決賽了」這句話要選用表示開心驚訝的感嘆詞,所以使用Aha。

8. 正解為(C)。句子的意思是「我已經告訴過你原則了,而你還是無法正確做好事情。」這句會使用比較不耐煩的感嘆詞why。

9. 正解為(A)。本句意思是「我們沒人預期到會有這樣的結果。」選用表示無奈的感嘆詞Well比較適當。

10.正解為(C)。本題題目的意思是「他不會對我說謊的。」這句選用 Nonsense 表示抗議的意味。

Day

11

動詞
Verb

Day 11 動詞 Verb

第一節：概述

動詞主要表示動作，其次表示狀態或性質，有時態、語態、語氣等形式的變化。動詞一般包括以下：

分類依據	類型
句中的角色	及物動詞、不及物動詞
動詞的作用	助動詞、一般動詞
動詞變化方式	規則動詞、不規則動詞
動詞的構成	單字、動詞片語（動詞+介詞）、動詞片語（動詞+副詞）

1. 及物動詞與不及物動詞

及物動詞後需接有直接受詞。例如：

I want to introduce my friend, Jane. 我想介紹一下我的朋友，珍。

及物動詞可以有一個或兩個受詞。例如：

例句	中譯	說明
"You speak English very well." she said.	她說：「你英語講得很好。」	一個受詞
Can you lend me some money?	你能借我一些錢嗎？	雙受詞：some money是直接受詞，me是間接受詞

不及物動詞後不接受詞。例如：

例句	中譯	說明
He has travelled all over the world.	他曾在世界各地旅行。	travel 為不及物動詞，後面可接地點副詞

很多的動詞既可作及物動詞，又可作不及物動詞。例如：

例句	中譯	說明
I wish you play well in Singapore!	祝你在新加坡玩得愉快！	不及物動詞
Let's go to play football!	我們去踢足球吧！	及物動詞

及物動詞有動作的承受者，才會有被動語態，而不及物動詞只有主動語態，沒有被動語態。

例句	中譯	說明
A new company has been started.	一家新的公司已經被創立。	start為及物動詞，可使用被動語態
The sun rises in the east.	太陽在東方升起。	rise是不及物動詞，不能改成被動語態

2. 連綴動詞

連綴動詞是一個表示句子主要動詞關係的動詞，後面會接主詞補語。連綴動詞有以下類型：

類型	例句	中譯
基本的連綴動詞 be	Suffering is the teacher of life. —Balzac	苦難是人生的老師。—（法）巴爾扎克
	Ability and wisdom are mental weapons for man.	能力與智慧是人的精神武器。
與狀態呈現或改變有關的連綴動詞	During the 1990s, American country music has become more and more popular.	20世紀90年代，美國鄉村音樂變得越來越流行。
	A monkey remains a monkey, though dressed in silk.	猴子依然是猴子，儘管穿上絲綢的衣服。
	The sky is getting darker and darker.	天空越來越暗了。
	The theater appeared old and abandoned.	劇場看起來老舊又荒廢。
	You seemed unhappy.	你看起來不開心。
	Let's stay healthy together.	我們一起維持健康吧！

149

	We should keep it in good condition.	我們應該將它保持在良好狀態。
	The grass grew greener.	草地變得越來越翠綠了。
	His health condition gets better.	他的健康狀況變好了。
	The competition turned fierce.	比賽變得激烈了。
	I was in the kitchen cooking something and I felt the floor move.	我在廚房正煮飯時，感覺地板動了。
表示感覺和知覺	It sounded like a train that was going under my house.	聽起來像一輛正在我家房子底下行駛著的火車發出的聲音。
	The restaurant smelt bad.	餐廳聞起來很糟糕。
	The garden looks grandiose.	這座花園看起來很華麗。
	This dish tastes awful.	這道料理很難吃。

3. 一般動詞和助動詞

(1) 主動詞就是句子的主要動詞，例如：

When do you take your next exam?
你什麼時候參加下次考試？

I watched all the glasses that were on the table fall off onto the floor.
我看到在桌子上的所有玻璃杯掉落到地板上。

(2) 助動詞本身無辭彙意義，不能單獨用作句子主要動詞。

助動詞分為三類：

類型	例句	中譯	說明
基本助動詞	Your letter has been received.	你的來信已經收到。	用於現在完成式
	The Pacific plate is moving very slowly—at 5.3 centimeters a year.	太平洋板塊移動得很慢— 每年才移動5.3公分。	用於現在進行式
	The cars will be supplied to people all over the country.	這些汽車將向全國各地的人供應。	用於被動語態

	How many different time zones do you have in the U.S.?	在美國你們有幾個不同的時區？	用於疑問結構
	You don't need anything special.	你不需要什麼特別的東西。	用於否定結構
情態助動詞	I should have noticed the mistake.	我應該要注意到這個錯誤的。	放在主要動詞之前。
	The garbage must have been taken away.	垃圾一定是被拿走了。	被動用法。
	I cannot go until he comes.	直到他來了我才能離開。	否定句用法
	Do you think that would help?	你認為這會有幫助嗎？	疑問句用法
	You might not be able to buy your ticket now.	你現在應該買不到票。	否定句用法
	There will be an end to slavery. Slaves will finally have their freedom back.	奴隸制必將結束。奴隸們終將重獲自由。	表示一種堅定的願景
	Shall we go now?	我們該走了嗎？	疑問句用法
	You may have it if you want.	你要的話，你可以擁有這個。	表示允許

4. 規則動詞和不規則動詞

　　大多數動詞的過去式和過去分詞都是在原形後加字尾ed構成，稱為規則動詞，例如：

原型	過去式	過去分詞
work	worked	worked
study	studied	studied
stop	stopped	stopped

另一些動詞變化是不規則的，稱為不規則動詞：

原型	過去式	過去分詞
lie	laid	lain

build	built	built
begin	began	begun

這些不規則動詞可分為三類：

(1) 第一類不規則動詞的三態同型，亦即原形，過去式，過去分詞同形，如：

原型	過去式	過去分詞
burst	burst	burst
cast	cast	cast

(2) 第二類不規則動詞的過去式與過去分詞同形，如：

原型	過去式	過去分詞
bend	bent	bent
bring	brought	brought

(3) 第三類不規則動詞的原形、過去式和過去分詞都不相同，如：

原型	過去式	過去分詞
arise	arose	arisen
awake	awoke/awaked	awoken/ awaked

(4) 此外還有少數不規則動詞的過去分詞與原形相同，如：

原型	過去式	過去分詞
come	came	come
become	became	become
run	ran	run

第二節：動詞的基本形式

英語動詞有五種基本形式，即動詞原形、第三人稱單數現在式、過去式、過去分詞、以及現在分詞。例如：

原型	第三人稱單數	過去式	過去分詞	現在分詞
study	studies	studied	studied	studying
do	does	did	done	doing
have	has	had	had	having
learn	learns	learned/ learnt	learned/ learnt	learning

1. 原形動詞

各詞典中所列的動詞形式都是原形，也就是前面沒有to的形式。例如：go、come、carry、catch等。

2. 第三人稱單數現在式

當主語是第三人稱單數，動詞用的時態是一般現在式。例如：My dad works for him.（我爸爸替他工作。）

第三人稱單數現在式一般由動詞原形後加s或es構成。其變化規則如下：

情況	變化	規則例詞
一般情況	-s	works, learns, comes, eats, plays, says, wants, needs
結尾為ss, x, sh, ch或o	-es	passes, discusses, washes, pushes, teaches, watches, boxes, fixes, goes
結尾為「子音字母+y」	變y為i再加-es	carry—carries, cry—cries, study—studies, hurry—hurries, fly—flies, try—tries

註：動詞be和have的第三人稱單數現在式分別是is和has。

3. 過去式與過去分詞

其構成有規則的和不規則的兩種，其變化規則和讀音如下：

規則\讀音	在動詞後加ed	在以e結尾的動詞後加d	以「子音字母+y」結尾的動詞，先將y變為i再加ed	以短母音或r音節結尾，而末尾只有一個子音字母時，須重複這個子音字母再加ed

153

在無聲子音後讀/t/	looked clashed	hoped liked		stopped mapped
在母音和有聲子音後讀/d/	stayed entered bowed called	named disguised believed	studied tried copied carried	planned inferred preferred referred
在子音/t, d/後讀/id/	expected rested needed			admitted omitted permitted

4. 現在分詞

現在分詞的結構一般是在動詞原形後加ing。其規則列表如下：

情況	加法	例詞
一般情況	-ing	doing, looking, studying,
以不發音的e結尾動詞	去e再加ing	having, taking, writing
以重讀閉音節結尾，且末尾只有一個子音字母	重複該字母再加ing	sitting, planning, swimming

第三節：動詞假設語氣

到目前為止，我們已經理解了動詞的基本意義和變化，接著便可以進階學習假設語氣。在英語中，隨著講話者的意圖不同，動詞就需要用不同的形式。

1.

條件句分真實條件句與非真實條件句兩種。真實條件句所表的假設是可能發生或實現的，句中的條件子句與結果主句皆用直陳語氣，且這種句子主句是一般將來式時，子句則要用一般現在式表示將來式。例如：

You'll be late for class if you don't hurry.
如果你不快一點，上課就要遲到了。

If winter comes, can spring be far behind?
如果冬天到了，春天還會遠嗎？

而非真實條件句所表的假設是指不可能或不大可能發生或實現的，句中的條件子句與結果主句都得用假設語氣，還可細分成下列三種：

a. 表示與現在事實相反的假設

　　其基本結構是：條件句中動詞用過去式（be的過去式用were），主句中用「would / should / could / might + 動詞原形」，用來表示與現在事實相反或現在發生的可能性不大。例如：

If I were you, I wouldn't do it like that.	假如我是你的話，我就不會這樣做。
We could ask him if he were here.	如果他現在在這裡，我們就能問他了。
If I knew his telephone number, I would ring him up.	如果我知道他的電話號碼，我就可以打電話給他了。

b. 表示與過去事實相反的非真實條件句

　　其基本結構是：條件句動詞用「had + 過去分詞」，而主句動詞用「would / should / could / might + have + 過去分詞」。例如：

If we had known that she was to arrive yesterday, we could have met her at the station.

如果我們知道她昨天到，就可以到車站接她了。

（事實是：我們不知道她昨天到，所以我們沒能到車站去接她）

c. 表示與將來事實相反的情況

　　基本結構有三種：(1) 條件句動詞用過去式（be的過去式一般用were），主句用「should / would / could / might + 動詞原形」；(2) 條件子句的動詞用「should + 動詞原形」，主句用「should / would / could / might +動詞原形」；(3) 條件子句的動詞用「were to + 動詞原形」，主句與上面相同。例如：

例句	中譯	釋義
If it rained tomorrow, our plan would be put off.	假如明天下雨，我們的計畫就得推遲。（最近天氣很好。）	條件子句中的動詞用過去式，表示說話人認為「下雨」的可能性不大；而如果用一般現在式的話，則表示說話人認為「下雨」的可能性很大。

If he should see me, he would tell me.	假如他看見我，就會告訴我。	用「should + 動詞原形」強調一種有偶然實現的可能性，其實現性比用「were to + 動詞原形」大，比「過去式」小
If he were to come, what should we say to him?	假如他來了，我們對他說什麼呢？	用「were to + 動詞原形」比較正式，多用於書面語中，表示實現的可能性很小
If the sea were to rise 500 feet, India would become an island.	如果海洋水面上升500英尺，印度就將變為一個孤島了。	

2. 省掉if的條件子句的用法

如果子句中有should，had，were時，則可以省去if，把這些詞提到句首，用倒裝來表達假設條件。例如：

Were I you, I would get up early every morning.
如果我是你，我每天早晨就早起。（這是一種勸人做某事的委婉說法）

Should she come tomorrow, I should give her the book.
假如她明天來，我就給她這本書。

3. 虛擬語氣在名詞性子句中的用法

a. 動詞wish後的受詞子句中，動詞的主要形式。

適用情況	受詞子句動詞形式	例句
現在	動詞過去式（be動詞用were）	I wish I were a bird. 我但願是隻小鳥。
過去	had + 過去分詞	He wished he had known the answer at that time. 他希望當時知道答案。
未來	would（should, could, might） + 動詞原形	I wish that she could go with us tomorrow. 我希望她明天能和我們一起去。

b. 在**would rather / had rather / would sooner / prefer**等後面的受詞子句中，動詞的主要形式。

適用情況	受詞子句動詞形式	例句
現在	過去式	I'd rather (I prefer) you helped me. 我寧願你幫助我。
過去	過去式	I'd rather you came tomorrow. 我寧願你明天來。
未來	過去完成式	I'd rather you had come yesterday. 我寧願你昨天來。

c. 表示要求、建議、命令、讚許、氣憤、驚奇、不滿等語氣

這些動詞是：advise（勸告）、suggest（建議）、propose（建議）、insist（堅持要、主張）、request（請求）、demand（要求）、recommend（建議）等。注意，有些可以用名詞的形式來表達。

例句	中譯
My father suggested that we (should) do the job at once.	我父親建議我們立刻做這項工作。
The suggestion that the sports meet (should) be put off was rejected.	延遲運動會的建議被否決了。
The nurse proposes that he undergo a surgery.	護士建議他動手術。
She recommends that he watch the play.	她建議他去看那齣劇。
I insist that everyone be served whole-heartedly.	我堅持每個人受到最好的服務。

重點提示：必學文法小要點

suggest作為「表明、暗示」解釋時，不用假設語氣，所以必須先判斷好語意。例如：

The smile on his face suggested that he was satisfied.
他臉上的微笑表明他是滿意的。

1. He _____ satisfied with the proposed plan.
   A. does   B. can   C. appears   D. keeps

2. You _____ ask Laura when you have any questions.
   A. does   B. seem   C. could   D. are

3. How _____ they complete the difficult task yesterday?
   A. does   B. did   C. do   D. will

4. Hank _____ computer engineering every day, for he is interested in this field.
   A. study   B. studies   C. studied   D. studying

5. Jerry _____ as an accountant in that company before, but now he has his own company.
   A. was   B. works   C. was working   D. used to work

6. The Palace Museum _____ between 1964 and 1965.
   A. built   B. was built   C. building   D. was building

7. The loud noise from the street _____ the baby last night.
   A. awake   B. awaking   C. awoke   D. awokened

8. I am planning to _____ several European countries during summer vacation.
   A. travel   B. go   C. move   D. visit

9. Keven _____.
   A. sent me a postcard   B. sent a postcard me
   C. send a postcard for me   D. send a postcard to me

10. Just tell her the truth. She _____ understand.
    A. used to   B. appears   C. will   D. is going

1. 正解為(C)。這句考的是連綴動詞「似乎（appear）」的用法。空格中也可以填用seems（似乎）、look（看起來）。

2. 正解為(C)。空格後面接的是一個一般動詞，可知空格有一個助動詞，其中does適用於第三人稱單數的主詞，而seem和語意不符，are後面會接現在分詞，由此可知，空格應該填could。

3. 正解為(B)。本題考的是助動詞的時態，句尾有時間副詞yesterday，可知應用過去式的did。

4. 正解為(B)。本題考第三人稱單數現在式的動詞形式，應使用studies。

5. 正解為(D)。本題的句子是「傑瑞以前在那家公司做會計，現在他自己經營公司。」表示過去時間的動作，空格中可以填入worked或者used to work。

6. 正解為(B)。句子的意思是「故宮是在1964到1965年建立的。」動詞要使用過去式的被動，所以使用was built。

7. 正解為(C)。這句話的意思是「昨晚街上的噪音吵醒了這個小寶寶。」這邊要使用awake（喚醒）的過去式，空格應填入awoke。

8. 正解為(D)。「我計劃暑假時拜訪幾個歐洲的國家。」空格之後直接接了受詞several European countries，需要填入一個及物動詞，而travel、go、和move都是不及物動詞，所以不選。

9. 正解為(A)。本句意思是「凱文寄給我一張明信片。」選項(B)和選項(C)應改為「sent a postcard to me」，當中加在間接受詞之前的介系詞不對。選項(D)應注意動詞，可改為過去式或在send加上表示第三人稱單數的s。

10. 正解為(C)。本題題目的意思是「告訴她事實吧。她會理解的。」這句話也可以填上半助動詞be going to 表示「將會」的意思。

Day

12

動詞的時態
Verb Tense
Part1

動詞的時態 Verb Tense Part1

第一節：概述

動詞的時態可分為現在簡單式、過去簡單式、未來簡單式、現在進行式、過去進行式、未來進行式、現在完成式、過去完成式、未來完成式、現在完成進行式、過去完成進行式、未來完成進行式等共12種：

	簡單	進行	完成	完成進行
現在	write / writes	am /is / are writing	has / have written	has / have been writing
過去	wrote	was/ were writing	had written	had been writing
未來	will write	will be writing	will have written	will have been writing

第二節：現在簡單式

1. 構成

主要由動詞原形表示。主詞是第三人稱單數時，用現在時第三人稱單數形式（見動詞基本形式），be和have動詞有特殊的人稱形式。疑問式一般在句首加助動詞do或does構成，第三人稱單數用does，其餘人稱用do，這時主要動詞一律用原形；動詞be只需與主詞的位置互換即可。否定式一般在動詞前加do（或does）not 構成，動詞be則在後面加not。

2. 用法

用法	例句	中譯	說明
表示現狀、性質、狀態和經常的或習慣性的動作	Nature is always beautiful.—Rodin	自然總是美的。—（法）羅丹	這些動詞常與頻率副詞連用，即與 always, ever, frequently, hardly ever, never, occasionally, often, rarely, seldom, sometimes, usually, every day, now, once a week, on Sundays等時間
	Every day I work from dawn till dark.	每天我從早工作到晚。	
	On this special day Americans always have the traditional dinner of turkey, sweet potatoes and pumpkin pies.	在這個特別的日子裡，美國人總是舉行傳統宴會，吃火雞、甜薯和南瓜餡餅。	
表示客觀事實或普遍真理	Water boils at 100˚C.	水在攝氏一百度時沸騰。	說話者確定是普世共同認定的事實，就會用現在簡單式表達
	The Earth goes around the Sun.	地球繞太陽轉。	
表示將來確定會發生的動作	Your future is bright.	你的前途是光明的。	常用動詞 go, come, leave, start, arrive, be, sail等等，後面接時間副詞
	The next train leaves at 9:15.	下趟火車九點十五分開。	
條件子句中，可用現在簡單式代替未來簡單式	If a person loses one third of his / her blood, he / she may die.	如果一個人流血超過其血量的三分之一，他（她）可能會死。	子句由when, which, before, after, until, as soon as等引導的時間狀語子句和由連詞 if 和unless引導
	If your brother passes the exam, he will be enrolled.	如果你弟弟考試及格了，他就會被錄取。	

that 子句 用現在簡 單式表示 未來式	I hope that you have a good time.	我希望你玩得很愉快。	用在句型I hope，I bet 等後面的 that…子句中和句型see (to it) / make sure / make certain + that…子句
	Make sure that the guests have a good rest.	務必使客人們好好休息。	
現在簡單 式動詞表 示現在發 生的動作	"Now watch, here are three bottles," he said.	他説:「現在看仔細，這裡有三個瓶子。」	使用在某些以here, there開頭的句子中
	Here comes the English teacher!	英語老師來了。	

第三節:過去簡單式

1. 構成

　　動詞改為加-ed或者過去式的型態，後面通常會接過去式時間副詞。常見的過去式時間副詞如:two hours ago, the day before yesterday, last month, in 1898, just now, during the night, in those days等等。

2. 用法

用法	例句	中譯	説明
過去的動作或 狀態	I often played hide-and-seek when I was a child.	我小時候經常玩捉迷藏。	與表示過去的時間副詞連用
	Another earthquake shook San Francisco on October 17th, 1989.	1989年10月17日地震又一次襲擊了舊金山市。	説明過去某一特定時間地點發生的事件。
用在want, wonder, think, hope 等動詞後 面	We thought he was an honest man.	我們原本以為他是個老實人。	表示婉轉口氣

用在It's time..., I wish..., I'd rather...等結構後面的that子句中	It's time you went to bed.	你（現在）該去睡覺了。	表示與現在事實相反或者表示對將來事態的主觀設想
	I wish you lived close to us.	我真希望你和我們住得近一些。	
	I'd rather that my brother took the bigger orange.	我倒寧願我兄弟拿那一顆較大的橘子。	

🚩 第四節：未來簡單式

1. 構成

句型	用法
shall / will + 動詞原形	Space stations and bases on the moon will serve as stepping stones to Mars and other heavenly bodies. 月球上的太空站和基地將成為到達火星和其他天體的橋樑。
be going to + 不定式	Look at these black clouds—it is going to rain. 看這些烏雲一 天就要下雨了。
be to + 不定式	We are to meet at the school gate. 我們約定在校門口碰頭。
be about + 不定式 / be on the point of + 名詞／動名詞	The plane is on the point of taking off. 這架飛機快要起飛了。

2. 用法

用法	例句	中譯
表示意願	I will tell you all about it.	我願意把全部情況告訴你。
表示承諾	I will give you an honest answer.	我會給你一個誠實的答案。
表示決心	I will not stop my fight against slavery until all slaves are free.	我不會停止反對奴隸制的鬥爭，一直到所有的奴隸都自由為止。

| 徵詢意見 | Shall we talk about it when I get back from my holiday? | 等我渡假回來後,我們再來談論這件事,好嗎? |

第五節：現在進行式

進行式所表示的動作具有持續性、暫時性和未完成性。

1. 構成

is (am, are) + 現在分詞（動詞 + ing）

2. 用法

意義	例句	中譯
説話時正在發生或進行著的動作	We'll have to take a roundabout course, for the road is being repaired.	我們得要繞遠路走了，因為這條路正在修理。
表示按計劃安排近期內即將發生的動作，常用於come, go, leave, start, arrive	I must be leaving now.	我現在該走了。
	I'm changing my hotel.	我就要換旅館了。
表示反覆出現的或習慣性的動作，常與always, continually, really, actually, only, simply, merely, constantly, for ever, all the time等副詞連用	John is constantly complaining that he is poorly paid.	約翰總是抱怨他薪水低。
表示剛剛過去的動作，常與ask, tell, talk, say, exaggerate 等動詞連用	You don't believe it? You know I'm telling the truth.	你不相信？你要知道我說的可都是實話。
表示客氣的口氣，常和hope, wonder 等 動詞連用	I'm hoping you'll give us some advice.	我希望你能給我們提些建議。

Day 12

動詞的時態 Verb Tense Part1

重點提示：必學文法小要點

★現在進行式表示將來時間的用法還常見於某些時間副詞子句和條件副詞子句中。例如：

When you are travelling, you should take care of your health.
旅行時，你應該注意身體健康。

★現在進行式的用法與一般現在式的區別在於後者只是説明事實，而前者則往往帶有説話人的感情色彩，如讚揚、遺憾、討厭或不滿等。比較：

例句	中譯	說明
Jack comes late for school.	傑克上學遲到。	只説明事實
Jack is always coming late for school.	傑克上學老是遲到。	表示説話人對Jack的不滿
Mary does fine work at school.	瑪麗在學校成績優秀。	只説明事實
Mary is constantly doing fine work at school.	瑪麗在學校總是成績優秀。	表示説話人對Mary的讚揚

第六節：過去進行式

過去進行式表示過去某個時間點正在進行中的動作。

1. 構成

第一人稱單數和第三人稱單數用「was+v-ing」，其餘都用「were+v-ing」。

2. 用法

用法	例句	中譯
過去某時正在發生的動作，常與when / while引出的時間狀語子句連用	When Prof White came into the classroom, the students were doing their homework.	當懷特教授走進教室時，學生們正在做作業。
	What was he doing at this time last week?	上個星期的這個時候他在做什麼？
	While we were having supper, all the lights went out.	我們吃飯的時候，所有的燈都滅了。
過去某段時間內持續進行的動作	They were expecting you yesterday.	他們昨天一直在等你。
	In those years, I was studying at middle school.	那些年，我在中學讀書。
來為一個或一系列動作的發生提供背景，使形象逼真、生動	Smoke was coming from the chimney of the farm house. The farmer's children were playing with the dog and the farmer himself was leaning on his gate.	煙從那農舍的煙囪冒出來，農民的孩子正在和小狗玩耍，農夫靠在自己家的門上。
與always, constantly, continually, forever等副詞連用表示不同的感情色彩	He was continually asking questions.	他老是在問問題。（帶有厭煩情緒）
	The two brothers were frequently quarrelling.	兩兄弟常吵架。（帶有不滿情緒）
hope, want, wonder, think等動詞的過去進行式還可用來表示有禮貌的請求	I was hoping you could lend me some books.	我希望你能借我一些書。
	I was wondering if you could help me.	我不知道你能否幫我一下。

| 表示在過去預計、安排未來要發生的動作 | He told us over the phone that he was coming to see us the next day. | 他在電話裡告訴我們，他第二天要來看我們。 |

第七節：未來進行式

1. 構成

shall / will + be + 現在分詞

2. 用法

用法	例句	中譯
表示未來某時正在進行的動作	We will be seeing a fashion show this time tomorrow afternoon.	明天下午的這時候我們將在看一場時裝表演。
	I'll be taking my holidays soon.	我不久將要渡假了。
	The bus will be leaving in a second.	公車馬上就要開了。
表示推測	They will be watching football game now.	他們現在大概在觀看足球賽呢。
	It's Sunday. She won't be studying now.	今天是星期天，她不會在讀書的。
表示婉轉口氣	Will you be needing anything else?	你還需要什麼嗎？
	When will you be coming to see me?	你什麼時候會來看我？

1. The anchor _____ for a mistake he made on the live report yesterday.
   A. apologize   B. is apologize   C. apologizing   D. apologizes

2. We _____ a meeting when you come to our office tomorrow.
   A. will be having   B. have   C. had   D. are having

3. He _____ a letter to his aunt in English every month.
   A. writes   B. writing   C. write   D. written

4. I have to clean the guestroom in my house now because Aunt Stacy _____ with us this weekend.
   A. stay   B. stays   C. stayed   D. is staying

5. It _____ them three years to build the luxurious hotel. Now it houses hundreds of travelers per day.
   A. take   B. took   C. is taking   D. will take

6. Language _____. Many new terms are created every year.
   A. change   B. changing
   C. is always changing   D. changed

7. The NBA star James LeBorn _____ us how to shoot a three pointer this afternoon.
   A. is showing   B. shows   C. showed   D. was showing

8. The department store _____ its twelfth anniversary now. It's having a sale this weekend.
   A. celebrated   B. will celebrate
   C. celebrate   D. is celebrating

9. The machine _____ when the government inspector came to our factory.
   A. was repairing   B. repaired
   C. was being repaired   D. is repaired

10. If the boss _____ our proposal on the meeting tomorrow, we will go ahead and carry out the plan.
    A. won't oppose   B. doesn't oppose
    C. opposes   D. will oppose

文法實戰解析

1. 正解為(D)。這句話的意思是「主播為他昨天在做現場報導時的錯誤道歉。」可以使用現在進行式、現在簡單式、未來式的動詞，選項(A)、(C)、(D)的形式都不對，而使用apologizes用現在是強調描述節目表演現況的用法。

2. 正解為(A)。本題意思是「你明天來我們辦公室的時候，我們將是正在開會的狀態。」這裡用一個when開頭的時間副詞子句標明一個未來特定的時間，所以用未來進行式表示在那個時間點的動作和狀態。

3. 正解為(A)。這題要選出正確的動詞形式，句子當中有時間副詞every month表示習慣、常態的動作，所以用現在簡單式writes。

4. 正解為(D)。這句話的意思是「我得要打掃客房，因為史黛西阿姨這個週末或住在我們家。」這裡用現在進行式表示即將發生、計畫將要進行的動作，空格填is staying最適合。

5. 正解為(B)。本題的句子是「這座旅館花了三年的時間建造。現在它每天提供好幾百名旅客住宿。」。這句話後半段暗示旅館的建造已經完成，所以是過去的動作，空格中應該填took。

6. 正解為(C)。句子的意思是「語言總是在變化。」表示習慣，可以說「Language changes all the time.」在這邊用現在進行式強調動作的持續進行，空格填is always changing才符合語意。

7. 正解為(A)。這句話的意思是「NBA球星詹姆士·勒布朗下午會告訴我們投出三分球的方法。」這邊使用現在進行式表示未來會發生的動作，空格填is showing。

8. 正解為(D)。這句話是說「這家百貨公司正在慶祝十二年週年慶。它這週末有拍賣活動。」空格之後接了表示現在的時間副詞now，所以用現在進行式。

9. 正解為(C)。本句意思是「政府的檢查人員來我們工廠的時候，機器正在被修理。」句子當中有限制過去某個時間點正在發生的動作或狀態，所以用過去進行式的被動語態表示，空格填was being repaired。

10. 正解為(B)。本題題目的意思是「如果老闆明天會議上沒有反對我們的提案，我們就會著手實行這項計畫。」if開頭的條件子句當中用現在式代替未來式，所以空格會填上 doesn't oppose。

Day

13

動詞的時態
Verb Tense
Part2

🚩 第八節：現在完成式

現在完成式所涵蓋的意思包括：

A. 說話之前已經完成的動作，而且這個動作的結果對現在仍有影響。

例：I have had breakfast.（我已經吃過早餐。）
　→現在不會餓、不用再吃東西了。

B. 表示過去已經開始而持續到現在的動作或狀態。

例：She has worked here for ten years.（她已經在這裡工作十年了。）
　→在這裡工作這件事情從十年前持續到現在。

1. 句子構成

> have (has) + 過去分詞

2. 用法

(1) 現在完成式常和過去式不同。過去式只強調過去的動作本身，而現在完成式會強調動作與現在結果之間的關係：

例句	中譯	說明
He has given up drinking.	他已經戒酒了。	他在一個過去時間戒了酒，現在已經不喝酒了
He gave up drinking last month.	他上個月戒了酒。	只表示過去的動作

He has been ill for two weeks.	他病了兩週了。	病也許還沒好
He was ill for two weeks.	他病了兩週。	指過去病了兩週，現已痊癒
We have bought a new computer.	我們已經買了一台新電腦	表示現在已經有電腦了，接下來都有電腦可以使用。
We bought a new computer yesterday.	昨天我們買了一台新電腦。	單純表示昨天的一個動作。

重點提示：必學文法小要點

have / has gone to 和 have / has been to 在意義上的區別：

● She has gone to Vancouver. 她已經到溫哥華去了。
→ 她已前往溫哥華，或在途中，或已到達。現在人不在這裡。

● She has been to Vancouver. 她曾到過溫哥華。
→ 她以前去過溫哥華。表示一種經歷，說話時她還在這裡。

(2) 現在完成式通常不會接明確指出時間的副詞

例如：last week, yesterday, in 1949, a minute ago, just now, when I came in 等。

但現在完成式可以接一個不明確指出時間的副詞

例如：just, already, yet, sometimes, always, often, before, lately, recently, once, twice, ever, never等。

現在完成式後面也可以接一個包括現在在內的時間副詞

例如：this morning, today, now, this week, this month等。

例句	中譯	說明
"I've always been interested in geography," he said.	他說：「我一直對地理感興趣。」	用always 表示這個狀態一直持續到現在
It has been cold this winter.	今年冬天一直很冷。	說話時仍是冬天

第九節：過去完成式

過去完成式表示在過去某一時間之前，或在過去某一動作發生之前，已經發生或完成了的動作。

1. 句子構成

> had + 過去分詞

可以注意的是，過去完成式多使用在某一過去時間以前（即：by / before + 過去時間）或過去事件之前（即：when/ before/ than副詞子句內的一般過去式）已發生並完成的動作或存在的狀態，這一動作可以是一直持續到過去這一時刻或將繼續下去。或者，也可搭配在一種未實現的願望或想法，以及假設語氣中。

2. 用法

例句	中譯	說明
He suddenly remembered that he had left his key in the lab.	他突然想起他把鑰匙丟在實驗室了。	表示在過去某時間之前發生的動作或狀態。
We had learned 2,000 English words by the end of last term.	到上學期期末為止，我們學了2,000個英語單字。	表示從過去某時間點起一直延續到過去這一時間的動作或狀態。

That was the second time he had visited our school.	那是他第二次造訪我們學校。	表示到過去某時間為止，某動作或狀態的總結或總和。
No sooner had he arrived home than he was asked to start on another journey.	他剛到家就又得要開始另一次旅行。	在No sooner...than...; Hardly(Scarcely)...when... 的結構中，前面的動詞多用過去完成式。
If I had seen him this morning, I would have asked him about it.	今天早晨我要是見到他，我會問起他那件事的。	使用與過去事實相反的假設語氣，If 開頭的子句中，使用過去完成式。
He had intended to speak, but time did not permit.	他本想發言，可是時間不允許。	表示過去的某一願望或意圖。

🚩 第十節：未來完成式

此時態主要表示將來某時之前已經完成的動作，並往往對將來某一時間產生影響。它常與表示未來的時間狀語「by / before + 未來時間或條件狀語子句」連用。

1. 句子構成

> will + have +過去分詞

2. 用法

例句	中譯	說明
By the end of this month we will have finished this project.	我們將在本月底前完成這項工程。	表示將來某時之前已經完成的動作。

例句	中譯	說明
You will have received an invitation to the wedding then.	你到時候會收到參加婚禮的請帖的。	表示說話人對某一已完成的動作或事態的推測,主要用於第二、第三人稱主詞。

第十一節:現在完成進行式

現在完成進行式表示某個動作持續到現在,且強調現在仍在進行中。

1. 句子構成

> have + been +Ving

2. 用法

例句	中譯	說明
I have been waiting for you for two hours!	我已經等你兩個小時!	表示等待的動作一直持續到說話的當下。
She has been working on this project for three months.	她已經進行這個計畫三個月了。	表示進行計畫的動作一直持續到說話的當下,而且應該會持續下去。

第十二節:過去完成進行式

過去完成進行式表示某個動作持續到過去某時間點的當下。

1. 句子構成

> had + been +現在分詞

2. 用法

例句	中譯	說明
He had been investigating the case for a while when you asked him about it.	你詢問他這件事情的時候，他已經調查這件事好一陣子了。	強調在「詢問這件事」的時間點之前，就有進行調查。
She had been studying computer coding since she was little.	她從小就一直在學電腦程式編碼。	強調一直到說話者提到的某個過去時間為止，持續進行中的動作。

第十三節：未來完成進行式

未來完成進行式主要表示動作從某一時間開始一直延續到將來某一時間。這一動作可能是已經完成，也可能還要繼續下去。它常和表示將來某一時間的副詞連用。

1. 句子構成

> will + have been +現在分詞

2. 用法

例句	中譯	說明
I will have been studying English for twelve years by the end of the year.	到今年年底，我將學習英語十二年了。	強調未來某個時間點會已經持續一段時間且持續進行的動作。
If we don't hurry up the train will have been leaving before we get there.	我們如果不快一點，等我們到那裡，火車就會開走了。	強調未來某個時間點會正在進行中的動作。

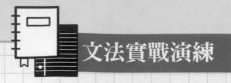

1. The company _____ a new smartphone for three months.
   A. developed   B. develops   C. had develops   D. has developed

2. If I _____ her the truth, she would not have been so angry.
   A. tell   B. told   C. have told   D. had told

3. We _____ with the professor about the topic of our final report by this time tomorrow.
   A. will discuss   B. will have discussed
   C. discussed   D. had discussed

4. I _____ for the test for a while when you come to my house tomorrow.
   A. study   B. will be study
   C. will have been studying   D. would have studied

5. Mike _____ of becoming a lawyer since he was a child. Now he is studying in the law school.
   A. dreams   B. is dreaming
   C. has been dreaming   D. had dreamed

6. We were late. The movie _____ when we arrived at the theater.
   A. had started   B. has started
   C. has been starting   D. will have been started

7. Gary _____ a baseball fan. He never misses any MLB game.
   A. has always been   B. was once
   C. had been   D. will have been

8. Mr. and Mrs. Smith _____ for twenty years by this December.
   A. had married   B. have married
   C. will have been marrying   D. will have been married

9. Mr. Benson _____ Japan for a business conference this morning. He won't be back until next week.
   A. has been to   B. have left for
   C. had gone to   D. have been leaving for

10. Jenny _____ the Netherlands several times. She really likes the scenery there.
    A. has been to   B. has left for
    C. had gone to   D. have been leaving for

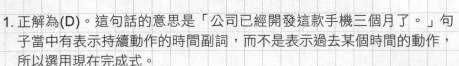

1. 正解為(D)。這句話的意思是「公司已經開發這款手機三個月了。」句子當中有表示持續動作的時間副詞，而不是表示過去某個時間的動作，所以選用現在完成式。

2. 正解為(D)。本題意思是「如果我當時有告訴她實話，她就不會那麼生氣了。」句型是與過去事實相反的假設語氣，if 開頭的條件子句應用過去完成式的動詞時態。

3. 正解為(B)。這題意思是「到了明天這個時候，我們將會已經和教授討論過報告的題目了」這裡的時間副詞為「by this time tomorrow」表示到未來某個時間點會已經進行過的動作，所以使用未來完成式。

4. 正解為(C)。這句話的意思是「明天你來到我家的時候，我已經念書準備考試一段時間了。」這裡用未來完成進行式表示到時候某個動作已經持續一段時間、且會繼續進行的意思。

5. 正解為(C)。本題的句子是「麥可從小就夢想成為一位律師。現在他在法學院就讀。」這句話表示動作從以前一直持續到現在，而且持續進行中，所以使用現在完成進行式。

6. 正解為(A)。句子的意思是「我們遲到了。我們到達戲院的時候，電影已經開始了。」表這句話強調過去某個時間點之前，start這個動作就已經完成，所以動詞時態用過去完成式。

7. 正解為(A)。這句話的意思是「蓋瑞一直是個棒球迷。他從來不會錯過大聯盟的比賽。」作為棒球迷的狀態影響一直持續到現在，所以使用現在完成式的動詞時態。

8. 正解為(D)。這句話是說「到今年十二月為止，史密斯夫婦將會已經結婚二十年了。」表示到未來某個時間，某個狀態會已經維持多久的時間，用未來完成式的時態。

9. 正解為(C)。本句意思是「班森先生今天早上已經去日本參加商業研討會了。他下星期才會回來。」如果人已經前往某處，現在不在，則用 has gone to 來表達。

10.正解為(A)。本題題目的意思是「珍妮去過荷蘭好幾次。她很喜歡那邊的風景。」如果表示曾經去過，而沒有特別強調句子當中的人目前在那個地方，則用 has been to。

Day

14

動詞被動語態
Passive Voice

動詞被動語態 Passive Voice
Day 14

🚩 第一節：概述

1. 英語動詞有兩種語態

主動語態和被動語態。主動語態表示主詞是動作的執行者；被動語態表示主詞是動作的承受者。例如：

主動語態			被動語態		
The people	make	history.	History	is made	by people.
人民創造歷史。			歷史是人民創造的。		
執行者	動作	承受者	承受者	動作	執行者

2. 被動語態的基本結構

被動語態以 be 動詞 + 動詞過去分詞表達，依時態又可分為以下形式：

	簡單	進行	完成
現在	I am cured.	I am being cured.	I have been cured.
過去	I was cured.	I was being cured.	I had been cured.
未來	I will be cured.		I will have been cured

History is made by people. 歷史是由人民創造的。

Nature would not cheat us; we are often cheated by ourselves.
大自然不會欺騙我們，欺騙我們的往往是自己。

In 2020, the 32nd Olympic Games will be held in Tokyo.
2020年，第32屆奧運會將在東京舉行。

The term "Information Highway" was coined a few years ago.
「資訊高速公路」這個術語是幾年前創造出來的。

Many international conferences are held in Geneva.
許多國際會議在日內瓦舉行。

Modernism was invented in the 1920s by a group of architects who wanted to change society with buildings that went against people's feeling of beauty.

現代主義是20世紀20年代一群建築師們所創立的，他們想用背離人們審美標準的建築來改變社會。

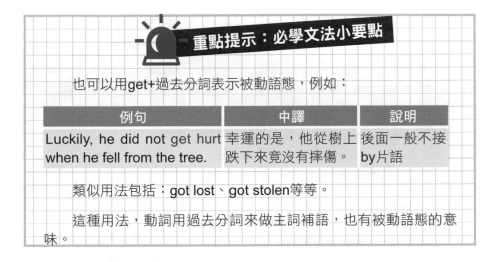

重點提示：必學文法小要點

也可以用get+過去分詞表示被動語態，例如：

例句	中譯	說明
Luckily, he did not get hurt when he fell from the tree.	幸運的是，他從樹上跌下來竟沒有摔傷。	後面一般不接by片語

類似用法包括：got lost、got stolen等等。

這種用法，動詞用過去分詞來做主詞補語，也有被動語態的意味。

3. 動詞片語的被動語態

原則上，英語中只有及物動詞才有被動語態，但是有些動詞片語常用作及物動詞，因此它們也有被動語態。但應注意：動詞片語是一個不可分割的整體，在變為被動語態時，不可省略構成短語動詞的介系詞或副詞。例如：

We have brought down the price.（主動）我們已經削減了價格。

The price has been brought down.（被動）價格已被削減。

They will put up a notice on the wall.（主動）他們將在牆上張貼佈告。

A notice will be put up on the wall.（被動）佈告將被張貼在牆上。

A new training centre will be set up.（被動）將成立一個新的培訓中心。

He was praised for his hard work.（被動）他因工作努力受到了表揚。

Manmade satellites have been sent up into space by many countries.
許多國家都曾經向太空發射了人造衛星。

The soil is made from the dead leaves of the trees above.
那裡的土壤是由上面的枯葉腐爛而成的。

重點深度學：Day 14 進階挑戰

某些動詞（例如：give, send, pay, tell, buy, lend, offer, throw, hand, bring, get, make, leave等）有時帶兩個受詞，變成被動語態時，有形成兩種結構的可能：

- Someone gave me a book. 有人給我一本書。
- I was given a book (by someone).
- A book was given to me. (by someone).

- He bought me a present. 他買了一樣禮物給我。
- I was bought a present (by him).
- A present was bought for me (by him).

第二節：被動語態的用法

1. 強調或突出動作的承受者

例句	中譯	說明
New Zealand wine is of high quality and is sold all over the world.	紐西蘭葡萄酒品質很高，行銷全世界。	重點不是在於誰賣，而是被賣出的酒品。
Modern cellphones are more than just phones—they are being used as cameras and radios, and to send email or surf the Internet.	現代手機不僅僅是電話一它們也當作照相機和收音機使用，還可以發送電子郵件或上網。	重點不是在於誰用，而是在被使用的手機。

2. 不知道或無須說出動作的執行者（不用接by片語）

例句	中譯	說明
In the USA 1.5 million copies Taylor's new album were sold in the first fortnight.	在美國，泰勒的新專輯發行首兩週就銷售了150萬張唱片。	執行動作的人不明。
Credit cards are mainly used to make purchases.	信用卡主要用於購物。	執行動作的人太多，不需指名。

3. 為了使更簡潔、或與上下文連貫，使用被動語態

例句	中譯	說明
By the end of the year, the total money collected had come to over 92 million dollars, all of which were sent to Africa.	到年底，集資總數已超過 9,200 萬美元，這些錢全都送往非洲。	用形容詞子句補充說明募款的流向。
She appeared on the stage and was warmly applauded by the audience.	她出現在臺上，觀眾熱烈鼓掌。	共用主詞 she，是appear這個動詞的句型者，applaud這個動詞的承受者。

4. 學術文獻或新聞報導中，為了表示客觀，常使用被動語態

例句	中譯	說明
Electricity can now be made from the water rushing through the base of the dam.	現在可以利用穿過壩基的急流來發電。	比説「We can make electricity from the water rushing through the base of the dam.」客觀。
Fifteen million trees had been blown down by the high winds.	一千五百萬棵樹被強風刮倒。	比説「The high winds have blown down fifteen million trees.」客觀。

5. 被動語態的慣用語

慣用語	例句	中譯
be born 出生	When and where were you born?	你何時何地出生的呢？
be called 被稱作	The people of northern Canada are called Inuit, who came from Asia and settled in Canada about 4,000 years ago.	北部的加拿大人被稱為是因紐特人，這些人來自亞洲，約於4,000年前定居於加拿大。
be considered 被認為是	This book was considered to be an important summary of the knowledge of farming.	這本書被認為是農業知識的重要總結。
be made up of 由……組成	The UK is made up of four countries.	英國是由四部分國土組成的。
be done 完成	It's done!	完成啦！

重點提示：必學文法小要點

★被動結構可以用much來修飾，例如：

The driver was much agitated by the young man's death in the car accident.
在這次車禍中，那個年輕人的死，使司機深感不安。

★有些靜態的動詞，不會使用被動語態，例如：belong（屬於）、exist（存在）、fit（適合）、seem（似乎）、appear（出現）、disappear（消失）、last（持續）、happen（發生）等。

第三節：特殊的被動結構

在英語中，及物動詞的被動語態是表示被動意義的主要方法，但還有其他一些也表示被動意義的結構。

1. 主動結構表被動含義的動詞

某些由及物動詞轉化來的不及物動詞，例如：read, write, clean, wash, iron, burn, draw, cook, keep, cut, open, blow, peel, sell, act等，常和副詞well, easily, smoothly等連用，且通常用主動結構表示被動含義，例如：

This pen writes smoothly. 這支筆寫起來很流暢。

In hot weather meat won't keep long. 熱天，肉不能長時間存放。

2. 動詞 need... + V-ing 結構表被動含義

動詞如 need, require, want, deserve, be worth 後續 v-ing 的主動結構常表被動含義。例如：

My watch can't work, it needs repairing (=needs to be repaired). 我的手錶不會走了，需要修了。

This film is really worth seeing (= to be seen). 這部電影的確值得看。

3. 「連綴動詞 + 形容詞」結構表被動含義

某些連綴動詞，如 feel, prove, smell, taste, sound, look等加上形容詞，也可用主動語態表示被動意義。

How sweet these flowers smell! 這些花聞起來多香啊！

The music sounds very familiar to me. 這音樂我聽起來很耳熟。

The food tastes delicious. 這食物很美味。

Your suggestion proved quite effective. 你的建議已證明是很有效的。

1. The patient was _____ by the medical professionals.
   A. taking care of　　B. taken care of　　C. look after　　D. looking after

2. _____ in the experiment that the new machine is more energy-efficient.
   A. He observes　　　　　　　　B. He is observed
   C. It is observed　　　　　　　D. It is observing

3. Carrots _____ a good source of several vitamins and minerals.
   A. are thought as　　　　　　　B. are thought of
   C. are considered　　　　　　　D. considered as

4. The visitors _____ by the curator of the museum.
   A. welcomed warmly　　　　　　B. were warmly welcomed
   C. was warmly welcomed　　　　D. were welcoming warmly

5. The tip of her index finger _____ when she touched the prick of the rose.
   A. hurt　　　　　B. hurts　　　　　C. got hurt　　　　D. got hurting

6. The victim of the accident _____ to the hospital as soon as the rescuers got him off the wrecks of the car.
   A. sends　　　　B. sent　　　　C. was sending　　　　D. was sent

7. Donald proposed several innovative ideas after he _____ as the president of student association.
   A. got elected　　　　　　　　B. got electing
   C. has elected　　　　　　　　D. have been elected

8. _____ that the criminals have fled to Thailand.
   A. It is believed　　　　　　　B. It is reporting
   C. People are believed　　　　D. It has reported

9. Stronger measures _____, or the global warming effect would get even worse.
   A. are taking　　　　　　　　　B. have taken
   C. has been taken　　　　　　　D. should be taken

10. Chemotherapy _____ for cancer treatment.
    A. has used　　　　　　　　　　B. have been used
    C. is being used　　　　　　　　D. have used

文法實戰解析

1. 正解為(B)。這句話的意思是「病人被醫護人員照顧著。」選項當中「take care of」和「look after」都是照顧的意思，而被動語態應用be taken care of 或looked after。

2. 正解為(C)。本題意思是「實驗中觀察到，新的機器更加高效節能。」為了表示客觀，句子當中的觀察這個動詞用被動態表示，所以用It is observed 加在that子句之前。

3. 正解為(C)。這題意思是「紅蘿蔔被認為是好幾種維他命和礦物質的極佳來源。」其中「被認為」可以用「be considered (to be)」或者「be thought of as」來表示。

4. 正解為(B)。這句話的意思是「來訪者受到博物館館長溫暖的歡迎。」這裡由句子當中的by+動作執行者這個片語可看出是用被動語態，所以用was warmly welcomed。

5. 正解為(C)。本題的句子是「當她碰到玫瑰花上的刺，食指的指尖就受傷了。」hurt這個字主動的用法是「感覺到痛」，像是「My legs are hurting.」。被動可以跟injure這個字互換使用。例如「我腳趾受傷了。」可以說「My toe was injured/hurt.」

6. 正解為(D)。句子的意思是「救難人員將車禍受害者從車子的殘骸中救出來之後，他就被送往醫院。」這句話的時態是用過去式，而傷患應是被送往醫院而不是將別人送往醫院，用被動語態was sent。

7. 正解為(A)。這句話的意思是「唐納獲選為學生會長之後，提出了好幾項創新的想法。」這裏「被選為」可以說是「was elected as」或「got elected as」。

8. 正解為(A)。這句話是說「據信這些罪犯已經逃到泰國。」要表示「據報導、據信」可以說「It is believed/reported that」用被動語態表示客觀的說法。

9. 正解為(D)。本句意思是「應該要採取更強烈的措施，否則溫室效應將會加劇。」這句當中stronger measures 是動作的承受者作為句子主詞，應是採用被動語態，所以空格會填should be taken。

10. 正解為(C)。本題題目的意思是「化療被用在癌症治療上。」選項(B)和選項(D)都是被動語態，但是應選用單數的動詞，所以空格選填 is being used。

Day

15

動詞不定式
Infinitive

Day 15 動詞不定式 Infinitive

第一節：概述

不定詞通常以 to V 的型態呈現，在句子當中不能當作主要動詞。它的特徵包括：

(1) 無人稱和數的變化

(2) 有時態和語態的變化

(3) 不能單獨作動詞

(4) 有自己的受詞和副詞

(5) 在句中可以作主詞、主詞補語、受詞、受詞補語、形容詞和副詞

不定詞的構成：

類型	構成	例子
肯定式	to + 動詞原形	to go, to say
否定式	not to + 動詞原形 never to + 動詞原形	not to go never to say
不定詞片語	to + 動詞原形 + 受詞（主詞補語、副詞）	to have a look, to be a teacher

不定詞的時態與語態：

	主動語態	被動語態
簡單式	to do	to be done
完成式	to have done	to have been done
進行式	to be doing	

第二節：不定詞的用法

　　不定詞有動詞的性質，也有名詞的性質，在句子當中可以扮演不同的角色。

例句	中譯	說明
To see is to believe.	眼見為憑。	作句子的主詞
This suit doesn't seem to fit me.	這衣服似乎不適合我穿。	作主詞補語
She wanted to see which shops offered the best service.	她想看看哪些商店提供最好的服務。	作受詞
Please tell him to come here tomorrow.	請告訴他明天來這裡。	作受詞補語
She has a wish to become a singer.	她有一個成為歌唱家的願望。	作形容詞
He went there to see what would happen.	他去那裡是想看看會出什麼事。	作副詞（表示目的）

1. 不定詞作主詞

　　當不定式作主詞時，常用下列句型：

(1) It is+adj.+to do...

　　常用形容詞有：easy, hard, difficult, important, possible, impossible, comfortable, necessary, better, the first, the next, the last, the best, too much, too little, not enough等。

例句	中譯	說明
It is important to learn English well.	學好英語很重要。	原本為「To learn English well is important.」
It is easy to do it well.	做好這件事很容易。	原本為「To do it well is easy.」

(2) It takes/costs/makes +n.+to do...

例句	中譯	說明
It took us three hours to walk there.	我們花了三個小時走到那裡。	可以說「To walk there took us three hours.」
It made me happy to meet you here.	我很高興在這裡見到你。	可以說「To meet you here made me happy.」

2. 不定詞作主詞補語

例句	中譯	說明
His job is to keep the street clean.	他的工作是保持街道乾淨。	不定詞修飾「his job」
The best way of expanding my social circle is to join several student clubs.	我拓展社交圈最好的方式就是參加好幾個社團。	不定詞修飾「The best way of expanding my social circle」

3. 不定詞作受詞

下列詞語常用不定式作受詞：afford, promise, refuse, expect, hope, learn, offer, wish, want, fail, plan, agree, forget, like, prefer, decide, manage, try, arrange, determine, desire等。

例句	中譯	說明
Some students failed to pass the test.	有一些學生沒有通過考試。	「to pass the test」是「fail」的受詞
He refused to accept the gifts.	他拒絕接受禮物。	「to accept the gifts」是「refuse」的受詞

下列動詞後可接「疑問詞+不定式」：teach, decide, wonder, show, learn, forget, ask, find out, advise, discuss等。

例句	中譯	說明
He hasn't decided where to go on holidays.	他還沒決定要去那裡度假。	「where to go」是 decide 的受詞
She is learning how to make the Italian dessert, Tiramisu.	她正在學習如何製作義大利點心提拉米酥。	「how to make」是 learn 的受詞

4. 不定詞作受詞補語

動詞：see, watch, notice, hear, listen to, observe, feel, taste, smell, make, let, have等的受詞補語用動詞原形，變被動時要加to，此時的不定式就是主詞補語。

例句	中譯	說明
She was found to use a fake ID.	她被發現在使用假的身份證。	「to use」修飾主詞「she」。原本句子為「Someone found her using a fake ID.」
He was observed to do the experiment.	他被看到在做這個實驗。	「to do」修飾主詞「He」。原本句子為「Someone observed him doing the experiment.」

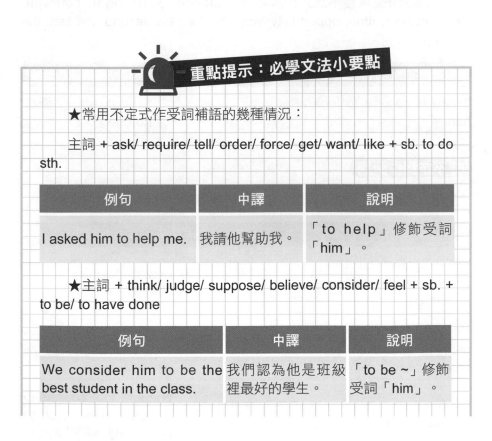

重點提示：必學文法小要點

★常用不定式作受詞補語的幾種情況：

主詞 + ask/ require/ tell/ order/ force/ get/ want/ like + sb. to do sth.

例句	中譯	說明
I asked him to help me.	我請他幫助我。	「to help」修飾受詞「him」。

★主詞 + think/ judge/ suppose/ believe/ consider/ feel + sb. + to be/ to have done

例句	中譯	說明
We consider him to be the best student in the class.	我們認為他是班級裡最好的學生。	「to be ~」修飾受詞「him」。

★主詞 + call on/ upon/ depend on/ wait for/ ask for+sb. + to do sth.

例句	中譯	說明
We are waiting for him to come.	我們正在等他來。	「to come」修飾受詞「him」。

5. 不定詞作形容詞

下列詞語後常接不定式作形容詞：chance, wish, right, courage, need, promise, time, opportunity, way, the first, the second, the last, the only等。

例句	中譯	說明
There is no one to look after her.	沒有人照顧她。	「to look after」修飾「no one」。

6. 不定詞作副詞

不定式作副詞，修飾動詞，在句中表示目的、結果、原因。

例句	中譯	說明
We hurried to the classroom only to find no one there.	我們急忙趕到教室，卻發現那裡沒人。	only to do表示出人意料的結果
He got up very early in order to arrive there on time.	為了準時抵達那裡他很早就起床了。	in order (not) to, so as (not) to 用來引導目的副詞
I'm not such a fool as to believe that.	我沒笨到會相信那件事。	enough, too, so... as to do, such+名詞... as to do作結果副詞。

I'm really puzzled about what to do or say.	我真的不知道該做些什麼或說些什麼。	同一結構並列由and或or連接。
To be or not to be, that is the question.	生存或毀滅，這是個問題。	特殊用法
It is better to laugh than to cry.	笑比哭好。	表示對比

1. Some of the high school graduates go abroad _____.
   A. study　　　B. to study　　　C. to be studying　　　D. to have studied

2. I heard him _____ Spanish fluently.
   A. spoke　　B. to speak　　　C. to be spoken　　　D. speaking

3. I have three final report_____ before I can enjoy the summer vacation.
   A. finish　　B. finished　　　C. to finish　　　　D. to be finished

4. His plan _____ the old lady into buying the fake jewelry failed.
   A. tricking　B. to trick　　　C. tricked　　　　D. tricks

5. This stage show is _____ tribute to the legendary star Audrey Hepburn.
   A. to pay　　B. pay　　　　C. paid　　　　D. pays

6. The politician failed _____ the public's trust for he was once involved in a bribery scandal.
   A. to win　　B. won　　　　C. winning　　　　D. to have won

7. The story has not ended yet. It is _____.
   A. continuing　　　　　　B. to continue
   C. to have continued　　　D. to be continued

8. What remains _____ is to clean up the mess in the house after the party.
   A. to do　　B. doing　　　C. to be done　　　D. to be doing

9. _____ regular hour is said _____ good for your health.
   A. Keeping; being　　　　B. To keep; to be
   C. Keeping; x　　　　　　D. To keep; as

10. Some local residents claimed _____ unidentified flying objects before.
    A. witness　　　　　　　B. witnessing
    C. to have witnessed　　　D. to witness

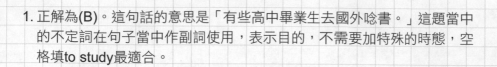

1. 正解為(B)。這句話的意思是「有些高中畢業生去國外唸書。」這題當中的不定詞在句子當中作副詞使用，表示目的，不需要加特殊的時態，空格填to study最適合。

2. 正解為(D)。本題意思是「我聽到他很流利地説西班牙文。」這題考的是hear後面接的受詞補語形式，應用動詞原型或者種詞ing的形式。若改為被動，則是「He was heard to speak Spanish fluently.」

3. 正解為(C)。這題意思是「我還有三個期末報告要完成才能享受暑假。」其中「to finish」修飾「final reports」，是作為受詞補語。

4. 正解為(B)。這句話的意思是「他想要騙老太太買假珠寶的計畫失敗了。」這裡用不定詞「to trick」修飾plan。

5. 正解為(A)。本題的句子是「這個舞台劇是要向傳奇明星奧黛麗·赫本致敬。」這裡的「to pay tribute」作為主詞補語修飾「the stage play」。

6. 正解為(A)。句子的意思是「這名政客因為曾經涉及收賄的醜聞而無法贏得大眾的信任。」這句話當中的不定詞to win是作為「fail」的受詞。

7. 正解為(D)。這句話的意思是「這個故事還未完結。它仍待續。」這裡的「to be continued」是不定詞加上被動語態的continue表示故事會繼續下去。

8. 正解為(C)。這句話是説「現在有待進行的事情是要把派對過後房子裡的髒亂清理乾淨。」要表示「等待被完成的事情」也可以説「the things which remains to be done」。

9. 正解為(B)。本句意思是「據説作息規律對你的健康是有好處的。」這句話的主詞可以用To keep regular hours或者 Keeping regular hours來當作主詞，而「被説是」會接「to be」再接修飾語。

10. 正解為(C)。本題題目的意思是「有些當地居民宣稱以前有看過不明飛行物體。」這一句當中「to have witnessed」作為claimed 的受詞，強調的是「經驗」所以會使用不定詞加上完成式。

Day

16

動名詞
Gerund

Day 16 動名詞 Gerund

第一節：概述

1. 動名詞的構成

基本為「動詞 + ing」，既有名詞的特徵，又有動詞的特徵。依句子的意思會有如下的變化：

	主動語態	被動語態
一般式	doing	being done
完成式	having done	having been done

或者：

肯定形式	否定形式
doing	not doing

2. 動名詞的性質

動名詞具有動詞性質，它有時態與語態的變化，可以接受詞或副詞，並構成動名詞片語。

例句	中譯	說明
Entertaining audiences is the purpose of movies.	娛樂觀眾是電影的目的。	動名詞Entertaining後面接了受詞audience，構成動名詞片語，在句子當中作主詞用。

例句	中譯	說明
He prided himself on having never been beaten in competition.	他為自己在比賽中從未被擊敗而自豪。	這裡的「having never been beaten」可代換為「not having been beaten」

第二節：動名詞的用法

1. 動名詞作主詞

動名詞作主詞時，動詞用第三人稱單數

例句	中譯	說明
Watching TV too much is bad for your health.	看太多電視對你的健康有害。	be 動詞用第三人稱單數的is
Phubbing on the smartphone takes up much of my leisure time.	滑手機佔據我很多休息的時間。	動詞take加上第三人稱單數的s

2. 動名詞作主詞補語

例句	中譯	說明
Her favorite sport is running.	她最喜愛的運動是跑步。	running 修飾主詞He favorite sport
The only thing she is interested in is dancing.	她唯一感興趣的就是跳舞。	跳舞作為 the only thing she is interested in 的説明。
Your greatest weak point is not knowing yourself.	你最大的弱點是沒有自知之明。	這裡使用了否定用法。

3. 動名詞作受詞

(1) 有些動詞後面固定要接動名詞作受詞：

suggest, finish, avoid, stop, can't help, mind, enjoy, require, practice, miss, escape, pardon, advise, consider, imagine, keep, appreciate, permit。

例句	中譯
I enjoy working with you.	我很開心跟你們一起工作。
Have you all finished doing the test?	你們大家都做完試題了嗎？
Would you mind lending me your English-Chinese dictionary for a while?	請把你的英漢字典借我用一下，好嗎？
I am very sorry I missed seeing you while in Taipei.	很遺憾在台北時我沒見著你。
She couldn't help crying after she listened to the sad story.	聽了那悲傷的故事，她忍不住哭了起來。
I suggested trying it in a different way.	我建議換一種方法試試。

重點深度學： Day 16 進階挑戰

★還有一些動詞片語後面要接動名詞：

leave off, put off, give up, feel like, have trouble/ difficulty (in) doing sth., be fond of, be worth。

例句	中譯	說明
I have trouble in understanding the Scottish accent.	我聽不懂蘇格蘭的口音。	have trouble in 加上動名詞作受詞，片語中的in常常會省略。

(2) 動名詞作介系詞的受詞

動名詞也可用作介系詞片語的受詞，而介系詞後要接動名詞。例如：

what about, how about, without, be fond of, be good at, abstain from, amount to, apologize for, succeed in, believe in, dream of, object to, insist on, take to, think of, worry about, agree on, aim at, forget about, think about, aid sb. in, accuse sb. of, congratulate sb. on, devote...to..., excuse sb. for, pay attention to, prevent sb. from, assist sb. in, look forward to, be opposed to, be (get) used to 等。

例句	中譯	說明
He insisted on finishing the work before going home.	他堅持在回家前一定要先完成工作。	動名詞 finishing 作為 insist on 動詞片語的受詞。

(3) 有些動詞片語當中的 to 是介系詞，要接動名詞作受詞，如：

get used to, devote to, pay attention to, look forward to, object to, due to, stick to, owing to, prefer...to。

例句	中譯	說明
We look forward to seeing you.	我們期盼見到你。	動名詞 seeing 前面的 to 為介系詞

重點深度學： Day 16 進階挑戰

有些動詞後接不定詞和動名作為受詞時，代表不同的意思：

★begin, start, continue, like, love, dislike, hate, prefer, can't stand

例句	解析
It began to rain. It began raining. It was beginning to snow. I love lying (to lie) on my back. I like listening to music, but today I don't like to. I don't prefer to swim in the river now.	意思無差別，但動詞用進行時，後面只跟不定式。表示一種傾向多接動名詞作受詞，如果表示某一特定的或具體的行動，多接不定式。

★remember, forget, regret, try

例句	解析
I remember to meet her at the station.	remember to do sth. 記住要做的事
I remember seeing her once somewhere.	remember doing sth. 回顧過去發生的事
I forgot to tell you about it. Now here it is.	forget to do sth. 忘記要做的事
I forgot giving it to you yesterday.	forget doing sth. 忘記做過的事
I regret to hear of your sister's death.	regret to do sth. 對將要做的事感到抱歉
I regret not having worked hard.	regret doing sth. 對發生過的事後悔
We must try to get everything ready.	try to do sth. 設法～，試圖
Try knocking at the back door.	try doing sth. 試試看，試一試
I had meant to go on Monday.	mean to do sth. 打算做～，想要
That will mean flooding some land.	mean doing sth. 意味著，就是

★want, require, need

例句	解析
These desks need repairing. These desks need to be repaired. The patient required examining. The patient required to be examined.	此處主、被動意思差別不大

(4) 動名詞接在about, against, at, before, after, by, besides, for, from, in, on, upon, without等介系詞之後，作為句子的副詞

例句	中譯	說明
Upon returning from New York, he went to visit his friend.	一從紐約回來，他馬上就去拜訪朋友。	「Upon returning from New York」句子的副詞

(5)「名詞 + 介系詞 + 動名詞」結構

常見的有：advice on, delay in, difficulty in, experience in, fancy for, interest in, habit of, idea of, method of, object of, plan for, possibility of, surprise at, skill in, apology for, hope of, success in, way of, chance of, opportunity of, means of, right of, excuse for, objection to等。

例句	中譯	說明
Have you any objection to going there on foot?	你們反對走路去那裡嗎？	動名詞going作為objection to 的受詞

(6)「形容詞 + 介系詞 + 動名詞」結構

常見的有：aware of, busy in, capable of, confident of, angry about (of), equal to, equivalent to, fond of, guilty of, hopeful of, awkward at, fearful of, keen on, intent on, tired of, sick of, responsible for, suitable for, right in, wrong in, proud of 等。

例句	中譯	說明
To keep the money you have found is equal to stealing.	撿到錢而佔為己有等於偷竊。	stealing 作為equal to 的受詞。

第三節：動名詞的特殊用法

1. 動名詞的複合結構

用代名詞所有格+動名詞，在句子當中作主詞、受詞、主詞補語等。

例句	中譯	說明
Do you mind my smoking here?	你介意我在這裡抽菸嗎？	代名詞所有格 + 動名詞 作為 mind的受詞
His coming late made them unhappy.	他來晚了，這讓他們很不高興。	代名詞所有格 + 動名詞作為句子的主詞

2. 動名詞的完成式

如果要表示動名詞的動作發生在句子主要動詞所表示動作之前，通常用動名詞的完成式。例如：

例句	中譯	說明
I still remember having ever worked together with him.	我還記得曾經與他一起共事過。	強調work這個動作在 remember 之前。

3. 動名詞的被動式

例句	中譯	說明
She came without being invited.	她不請自來。	被動式的動名詞，用being + Vp.p，作為without 的受詞
I really couldn't stand being criticized without any reason.	我真的無法忍受毫無理由的指責。	被動式的動名詞，用being + Vp.p，作為stand的受詞
I don't remember having ever been given such a chance.	我不記得誰曾給過我這樣的機會。	動名詞的現在完成被動式，用being + Vp.p，作為 remember 的受詞

重點提示：必學文法小要點

　　★在 need, deserve, require等動詞及worth等介系詞後所接的動名詞，雖然是主動的形式，卻表示被動的含義：

例句	中譯	說明
The problem deserves explaining.	這個問題值得解釋。	用explaining 而不是 being explained。
This phenomenon requires studying carefully.	這種現象需要仔細研究。	用studying 而不是 being studied。
The book is worth reading.	這本書值得一看。	用reading 而不是 being read。

4. 名詞化的動名詞

　　有些V-ing的單字已經完全成為名詞，例如：

例句	中譯	說明
The movie has a sad ending.	電影結局令人傷心。	前面加了冠詞a
The leaders from the both parties spoke at the gathering.	雙方的領導人都在會上講了話。	前面加了冠詞the

1. The critique pointed out three reasons why the latest Disney movie is worth _____.

   A. watch   B. to watch   C. being watched   D. watching

2. It is said that your immune system would start to deteriorate if you stop _____ water.

   A. to drink   B. drinking   C. being drunk   D. having drinking

3. He served in jail for ten months after _____ of _____ bribes.

   A. being convicted; taking   B. convicting; being taken

   C. convicting; taking   D. being convicted; being taken

4. His _____ annoyed the representatives of our client. He should have arrived on time.

   A. coming   B. being late   C. lecturing   D. meeting

5. I regret _____ worked harder to prepare for the interview.

   A. having   B. being   C. not having   D. not being

6. If you can't find the word in the dictionary, try _____ on the Internet.

   A. looking it up   B. to look it up

   C. being looked up   D. having looked up

7. Several men in black came to Mr. White's campaign rally without _____.

   A. inviting   B. being invited

   C. invited   D. having invited

8. Her dream of _____ as the leading actress for the new movie didn't come true.

   A. being chosen   B. choosing

   C. having chosen   D. having been chosen

9. I remember _____ philosophical questions with Professor Hawking when I was studying in the university.

   A. to discuss   B. being discussed

   C. having been discussed   D. having discussed

10. He was glad at _____ the opportunity to express his opinion.

   A. giving   B. having given

   C. gave   D. having been given

1. 正解為(D)。這句話的意思是「評論家指出三個最新迪士尼電影值得去看的原因。」這題當中的worth後面雖然有被動的意思,但是習慣接主動的動名詞。

2. 正解為(B)。本題意思是「如果你停止喝水,你的免疫系統會開始惡化。」這題考的是stop後面接動名詞表示「停止做某事」。

3. 正解為(A)。這題意思是「在被定罪收賄之後,他入監服刑十個月。」其中「被定罪」要用被動式的動名詞,而「收賄」是用主動式的動名詞。

4. 正解為(B)。這句話的意思是「他的遲到讓客戶代表很不開心。他應該要準時到達。」透過後半句的提示可知,空格要填入的單字是「遲到」。

5. 正解為(C)。本題的句子是「我後悔沒有更加努力準備面試。」這裡的 regret + V-ing 是表示「為了已經發生的事感到後悔」,而使用完成式在於強調「work harder」是在強調動作是很早發生的。

6. 正解為(A)。句子的意思是「如果你在字典裡面找不這個單字,試試看上網查。」這句話用動名詞「looking it up」作為try的受詞,表示嘗試一個方法。如果用「try to look it up」有嘗試做某件事情但是最後沒有成功的意思在。

7. 正解為(B)。這句話的意思是「有幾名黑衣男子不請自來到懷特先生的造勢活動上。」這裡的「without being invited」是介系詞加上被動的動名詞,表示「沒有被邀請」。

8. 正解為(A)。這句話是說「她獲選為新電影女主角的夢想沒有實現。」要表示「被選為」需使用被動的動名詞「being chosen」。

9. 正解為(D)。本句意思是「我記得唸大學的時候有和霍金教授討論過哲學的問題。」這句話強調「discuss」這個動作是很早發生的,使用完成式的動名詞「having discussed」。

10. 正解為(D)。本題題目的意思是「他很高興被給予機會表達他的意見。」這一句當中「被給予機會」強調時態很早發生,所以用完成式,而被給予機會,用被動語態,空格應填入「having been given」。

Day

17

分詞
Participle

Day **17** 分詞
Participle

第一節：概述

　　現在分詞是由動詞原形加字尾 ing 構成，過去分詞一般是由動詞原形加字尾 ed 構成。可以用在句子中扮演形容詞和副詞角色。分詞和動名詞、不定式相似，也可以有自己的受詞或副詞，有時也有它單獨的邏輯上的主詞。例如：

例句	中譯	說明
Do you know that man carrying a stick?	你認識那位拿著拐杖的人嗎？	現在分詞carrying有自己的受詞 a stick
Given enough time, we are sure to do it well.	如果給予我們足夠的時間，我們一定能做好。	過去分詞given有自己的受詞 enough time

第二節：現在分詞

1. 現在分詞的構成

動詞＋ing

2. 現在分詞的用法

(1) 現在分詞作副詞

　　現在分詞作副詞時可置於句首，亦可置於句尾，但表示結果時，常置於句尾；表示條件時，則可置於動詞之前或之後。

　　①表示時間

例句	中譯	說明
Hearing the good news, he jumped with great joy.	聽到這個消息，他高興得跳起來。	Hearing 前面省略了 When，由 when he heard 簡化而來。

②表示原因

例句	中譯	說明
Not having received any answer, he decided to write her another letter.	由於沒收到回信，他決定再寫封信給她。	分詞not receive的動作在主要動作write之前發生，就須用完成式。

③表示條件

例句	中譯	說明
Knowing all that, they needn't ask him question.	假如瞭解這一切，他們就沒有必要再問他任何問題了。	分詞Knowing 由 If they know 簡化而來。

④表示結果

例句	中譯	說明
A plane crashed near the South Pacific, killing 24 passengers on board.	一架飛機在南太平洋附近墜毀，造成機上24名乘客遇難。	分詞killing 由 and the accident killed 簡化而來。

⑤表示讓步

例句	中譯	說明
Knowing all this, they asked him to write down what happened.	儘管瞭解這一切，他們還是叫他把發生的事寫下來。	分詞 knowing 由 Although they know 簡化而來

(2) 現在分詞作形容詞

　　現在分詞構成的形容詞通常描述事物，可有比較形式， 也可被very等副詞修飾，表示「很」或「非常」的概念，例如：amusing, charming, disappointing, exciting, interesting, astonishing, encouraging, convincing, pressing, surprising, confusing。

例句	中譯	說明
That the philanthropist made a donation to the orphanage was an inspiring news.	慈善家捐款給孤兒院是一個激勵人心的消息。	也可以用「The news inspired people.」或「People are inspired by the news.」

(3) 現在分詞作主詞補語

例句	中譯	說明
The movie *Fly Away Home* is very touching.	電影《返家十萬里》相當感人。	touching 為形容詞，在句當中作主詞補語。

(4) 現在分詞作受詞補語

例句	中譯	說明
I saw him sneaking into your house in the middle of the night.	我看到他半夜偷偷跑進去你家。	看見某人做某事這個句型中的受詞補語用Ving表示動作正在進行。

(5) 獨立分詞結構

作副詞用的分詞，和主要子句並不共用主詞。

例句	中譯	說明
Weather permitting, we'll go to do some shopping tomorrow.	假如天氣允許的話，明天我們想去買些東西。	表示條件的分詞，主詞示weather，而主要子句的主詞是we。

有些作為副詞用的現在分詞，可以當成是慣用的片語：

例句	中譯	說明
Generally speaking, to learn a foreign language well is not an easy job.	一般來說，要學好一種外語不是一件容易的事。	「Generally speaking」為一個慣用語。
Judging from her accent, this lady is from New Zealand.	從她的口音判斷，這位女士是紐西蘭人。	「Judging from~」為一個慣用語。

第三節：過去分詞

1. 過去分詞的構成

動詞原形加詞尾-ed

2. 過去分詞的用法

(1) 過去分詞作副詞

①表示時間

例句	中譯	說明
Seen from the hill, the city looks like a garden. =When the city is seen from the hill, it looks like a garden.	從山上看，這個城市像座花園。	由「When the city is seen from the hill」簡化而來。

②表示原因

例句	中譯	說明
Tired by the trip, he soon fell asleep.	由於旅途勞累，他很快就睡著了。	由「Because he was tired by the trip」簡化而來。

③表示伴隨狀態

例句	中譯	說明
The teacher came in, followed by some students.	老師進來了，後面跟著一些學生。	由「and was followed by」簡化而來。

④表示條件

例句	中譯	說明
Once discovered, the mistakes must be corrected.	一旦發現錯誤就必須改正。	由「Once the mistakes are discovered」簡化而來。

⑤表示讓步

例句	中譯	說明
Born in a rich family, he lived a simple life.	雖然出生在一個富裕的家庭，但他還是過著簡樸的生活。	由「Although he was born in a rich family」簡化而來。

(2) 過去分詞作主詞補語

例句	中譯	說明
She looked very disappointed.	她看起來很失望。	disappointed 是disappoint的過去分詞，是修飾主詞she 的補語

(3) 過去分詞作受詞補語

例句	中譯	說明
I would keep you informed of what's going on here.	我會讓你知道這裡所發生的事情。	informed修飾keep的受詞you。

(4) 過去分詞作形容詞

過去分詞做形容詞用，通常描述人的感受，例如：

excited, amused, disappointed, interested, astonished, encouraged, convinced, confused, surprised, amazed, exhausted, worried, satisfied

例句	中譯	說明
We have a copy of signed agreement.	我們有一份簽過字的協議書。	signed表示「被簽署過的」。
We need more qualified educators badly.	我們急需更多合格的教育工作者。	qualified表示「合格的」。

(5) 獨立分詞結構

例句	中譯	說明
The door unlocked, the monkeys all escaped from the cage.	門沒鎖好，猴子就都跑出籠子了。	表示原因的過去分詞unlocked前面的主詞是door，而主要子句的主詞是monkeys。
The manager sat quietly in the office, with his eyes closed.	經理閉著雙眼靜靜地坐在辦公室裡。	with + 受詞 + 受詞補語的結構，closed是描述eyes的狀態

1. We were much _____ because of the manager's short talk at the meeting this morning.
   A. to encourage
   B. encouraging
   C. encouraged
   D. encouragement

2. _____ the news that his flight was cancelled, the passenger lost his temper at the ground attendant.
   A. Once heard
   B. Upon hearing
   C. While he sees
   D. With him seen

3. The _____ sea level may cause Tuvalu to disappear within few decades.
   A. rise
   B. rose
   C. risen
   D. rising

4. She looked at the _____ vase and gave a long sigh. Then, she picked up the _____ fragments.
   A. breaking; scattering
   B. broken; scattered
   C. broken; scattering
   D. breaking; scattered

5. With more and more people _____ in English around the world, it has become more and more important to have a good command of the language.
   A. communicating
   B. communicated
   C. to communicate
   D. being communicated

6. _____ from home for so long, he was very glad to see a friend from his hometown.
   A. Going
   B. Gone
   C. Without going
   D. To go

7. _____ with your composition, Johnny's work leaves a lot to be desired.
   A. Compare
   B. To compare
   C. Compared
   D. Though comparing

8. _____ with many difficulties, he persisted in carrying out his plan.
   A. Faced
   B. Facing
   C. To face
   D. Face

9. A: May I speak to Mr. Smith? B: This is Mr. Smith _____.
   A. speak
   B. to speak
   C. speaking
   D. speaks

10. _____ his final report, Chris felt relieved when he packed his luggage for the summer trip.
    A. To submit
    B. Submitted
    C. Having submitted
    D. While submitting

文法實戰解析

1. 正解為(C)。這句話的意思是「我們因為經理今天早上在會議上的簡短談話受到鼓勵。」這題中用encourage的過去分詞來形容we，表示「感到被鼓勵」。

2. 正解為(B)。本題意思是「一聽到他的航班被取消，這名旅客就對地勤人員發脾氣。」這題考的是利用現在分詞表示「一～就～」，用現在分詞的片語作為在句子中的時間副詞。

3. 正解為(D)。這題意思是「正上升中的海平面將會使吐瓦魯在幾十年內消失。」其中現在分詞「rising」作為形容詞描述sea level。

4. 正解為(B)。這句話的意思是「她看著被破掉的花瓶深深嘆一口氣。接著，她把摔破的碎片撿起來。」形容vase和fragments都是用過去分詞，表示動作已經發生了的狀態，所以第一個空格用broken，而第二個空格用scattered填入。

5. 正解為(A)。本題的句子是「由於世界各地有越來越多人使用英文溝通，將這個語言學好變得越來越重要。」用With+受詞+受詞補語，communicating修飾people，是主動的，所以用現在分詞。

6. 正解為(B)。句子的意思是「由於久離家鄉，他因碰到一位來自家鄉的朋友而感到很高興。」這句話用過去分詞的片語「Gone from home」，由「Because he was gone from home for so long」簡化而來。

7. 正解為(C)。這句話的意思是「和你的作文比起來，強尼的作品還有很大的改進空間。」這裡用過去分詞「compared」表示作文是被拿來做比較，所以用過去分詞來修飾。

8. 正解為(A)。這句話是說「儘管面對許多困難，他還是堅持執行計畫。」這句話用過去分詞片語修飾he，是由「Although he was faced with many difficulties」簡化而來。

9. 正解為(C)。本句是講電話時A說「請找史密斯先生。」而B說「我就是」用現在分詞「speaking」來修飾Mr. Smith。

10. 正解為(C)。本題題目的意思是「因為已經繳交期末報告，克里斯為暑假的旅行打包準備時覺得心情輕鬆。」表示原因現在分詞片語是由「Since he has submitted the final report」簡化而來。

Day

18

句子的組成
Sentence Structure

Day 18 句子的組成 Sentence Structure

第一節：概述

句子是包含主詞和動詞。句子開頭第一個字母要大寫，句子末尾要有句號、問號或感嘆號。

1. 按照使用目的分類

句子類型	例句	說明
陳述句 (Declarative Sentence)	He is a good student.	由主詞+動詞構成。
疑問句 (Interrogative Sentence)	Is he a good student?	Be動詞或助動詞置於句首。
祈使句 (Imperative Sentence)	Be a good student.	用動詞原形開頭。
感嘆句 (Exclamatory Sentence)	What a good student he is!	What a + Adj. + N. 表示驚嘆的句型。

2. 按照結構分類

句子類型	例句	說明
簡單句 (Simple Sentence)	I am sure he can pass the exam.	只有一組主詞+動詞
並列句 (Compound Sentence)	He has worked very hard, and I am sure he can pass the exam.	有兩組主詞+動詞，中間用對等連接詞and連接。
複合句 (Complex Sentence)	He who studies hard can surely pass the exam.	含有一個從屬子句(who studied hard)

第二節：陳述句、疑問句、祈使句、感嘆句

1. 陳述句

用來說明一個事實或陳述說話人的看法。例如：

句子類型	例句	說明
The building has been completed.	那棟建築已經完工。	事實
I am sure he will keep his words.	我肯定他能信守承諾。	看法

2. 疑問句

疑問句有四種：一般疑問句、特殊疑問句、選擇疑問句和附加疑問句。

(1) 一般疑問句

用yes或no回答的疑問句，叫做一般疑問句。這種疑問句通常把be動詞或助動詞放在主詞之前。

例句	中譯	說明
--Do you have a car? --Yes, I do. (No, I don't.)	--你有汽車嗎？ --是的，我有。 （不，我沒有。）	助動詞置於句首。
--Is this your watch? --Yes, it is. (No, it isn't.)	--這是你的手錶嗎？ --是的，它是。 （不，它不是。）	Be 動詞置於句首。

(2) 特殊疑問句

用what, who, which等疑問代名詞或when, where, why, how等疑問副詞引起的疑問句，叫做特殊疑問句。

例句	中譯	說明
—What are those? —They are photos.	--那些是什麼？ --是照片。	what + be 動詞

—When did you get up this morning? —I got up at six this morning.	--你今天早晨什麼時候起床的？ --我今天早晨六點起床的。	When + 助動詞

(3) 選擇疑問句

提出兩種或更多的情況，要求對方選擇一種，這種疑問句叫做選擇疑問句。

例句	中譯	說明
—What is your uncle, a doctor or a teacher? —He's a doctor.	--你叔叔是做什麼工作的，是醫生還是教師？ --他是個醫生。	問句之後會加上 "A or B?" 這樣的結構。

(4) 附加疑問句

在陳述句之後附上一個簡短問句，對陳述句所敘述的事實提出相反的疑問，如前一部分為肯定，後一部分則用否定。反之，如前一部分為否定，後一部分就用肯定。

例句	中譯	說明
He works for the League, doesn't he?	他為聯盟工作，不是嗎？	用助動詞+否定形式形成附加問句
The Sound of Music is a wonderful musical, isn't it?	《真善美》是一部精彩的音樂劇，不是嗎？	用be動詞+否定形式形成附加問句

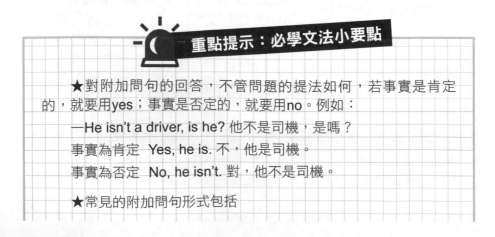

重點提示：必學文法小要點

★對附加問句的回答，不管問題的提法如何，若事實是肯定的，就要用yes；事實是否定的，就要用no。例如：

—He isn't a driver, is he? 他不是司機，是嗎？

事實為肯定　Yes, he is. 不，他是司機。

事實為否定　No, he isn't. 對，他不是司機。

★常見的附加問句形式包括

例句	中譯	說明
Let's have a rest, shall we / shan't we / OK?	休息一下，好嗎？	Let's...後面附加問句，常用shall we / shan't we
Let us go home now, will you / won't you?	讓我們現在回家，好嗎？	以let us / me / him開頭的祈使句，其後用will you, won't you
Nothing is impossible in the world, is it?	世上無不可能的事，是嗎？	主詞為everything, nothing, something, anything時，其附加部分的主語應用單數代名詞it
Everybody enjoys the movie, don't they?	大家都喜歡這部電影，不是嗎？	主詞是no one, nobody, everybody, someone, somebody, anyone, anybody, none, neither時，附加問句用複數代名詞they（與複數動詞連用）
Those are their books, aren't they?	那些是他們的書，不是嗎？	主詞為this / that，附加問句用it 主詞these / those，附加問句用they
They've never seen such beautiful scenery, have they?	他們從沒有見過這麼美的風景，是嗎？	帶有否定詞few, little, seldom, hardly, never, not, no, nobody, nothing, none, neither時，附加問句用肯定。
I don't suppose you are serious, are you?	我並不認為你是當真的，是嗎？	陳述部分的主句是I think (suppose, expect, believe, imagine...)加that子句時，附加部分的主詞與動詞要和子句中一致。
He is a teacher, but his wife is a nurse, isn't she?	他是位老師，而他的妻子是位護士，不是嗎？	陳述部分若是並列句，附加部分與最近的子句一致。
You must have been to Yangmingshan, haven't you?	你們一定去過陽明山，對嗎？	當must表示「推測」意義時，附加問句與推測的部分內容一致。

3. 祈使句

用來表示請求、命令、叮嚀、號召等。祈使句用動詞原形開頭，它的否定形式多以do not（常用don't）或never開頭。例如：

例句	中譯	說明
Be sure to get there in time.	一定要及時到那裡！	用be動詞開頭
Don't forget to buy me some ketchup on your way back.	別忘了在你回來的路上幫我買一些番茄醬。	否定祈使句用Don't開頭
Never judge people by their appearance.	千萬不要以貌取人。	否定祈使句用Never開頭

4. 感嘆句

(1) 構成

> What a / an+名詞 （+主詞+動詞）！
> How + 形容詞（副詞）（+主詞+動詞）！

(2) 用法

例句	中譯	說明
What fine weather it is today!	今天天氣多好啊！	也可以說What pleasant weather!
How interesting the film is!	那電影多麼有趣呀！	也可以說What an interesting film it is!

第三節：簡單句、並列句和複合句

1. 簡單句

最小的句子單位就是簡單句，它一定會包含一個主詞和一個動詞，包含五大類型：

基本句型	例句	中譯
S+V（主詞+不及物動詞）	He smiled.	他笑了。
S+V+O （主詞+及物動詞+受詞）	The hotel offers a host of leisure activities.	這家旅館提供很多休閒活動。
S+V+P （主詞+連綴動詞+主詞補語）	She's ready for a new challenge.	她準備迎接新挑戰。
S+V+IO+DO （主詞+及物動詞+間接受詞+直接受詞）	Michael supplied us a list of the guests.	麥可提供了一份客人的名單給我們。
S+V+O+OC （主詞+及物動詞+受詞+受詞補語）	We call the dog Lucky.	我們叫那隻狗「Lucky」。

2. 並列句

由並列連接詞把兩個或者兩個以上的簡單句連在一起而構成的句子叫並列句。常見的並列連接詞有and, and then, but, for, nor, or, so, yet, either...or, neither...nor..., only...but...(also /as well / too)。這些並列連接詞可用以表示另加(and)，對比(but，yet)，選擇(or)，理由(for)，連續 (and then)以及結局或結果(so)等。

例句	中譯	說明
We were talking and laughing.	我們又說又笑。	表示另加（= in addition to 又）
He fell heavily and broke his arm.	他摔得很重，手臂都摔斷了。	表示結果（= so 因此）
Weed the garden and I'll pay you £5.	除去花園的雜草，我就付給你5英鎊。	表示條件（= If...then 如果……那麼）
He finished lunch and went shopping.	他吃完午飯之後去買東西。	表示連續（=then 然後）

例句	中譯	說明
Tom's 15 and still sucks his thumb.	湯姆15歲了，還在吮大拇指。	表示對比（=despite this 儘管如此）
She sold her house, but / yet (she) can't help regretting it.	她賣掉了她的房子，但（她）不禁感到惋惜。	表示對比
He either speaks French, or understands it.	他可能是會講法語，或是懂法語。	表示選擇（I'm not sure which 我不清楚是哪一種情況）
We rarely stay in hotels, for we can't afford it.	我們很少住旅館，因為我們住不起。	表示原因（for為所陳述的事說出原因。它與 because不同，不能用於句首。）
He couldn't find his pen, so he wrote in pencil.	他找不到鋼筆，所以他用鉛筆寫。	表示結果（在so之後通常要重複主詞）

3. 複合句

由一個主句和一個或者一個以上的子句構成的句子叫複合句。子句有主詞子句、受詞子句、副詞子句、形容詞子句、主詞補語子句等。

例句	中譯	說明
What I want to emphasize is this.	我想強調的是這一點。	子句作為主詞
There is something in what you said.	你說的話有些道理。	子句作為介系詞的受詞
The days when big powers dictated the destiny of the world are gone forever.	大國主宰世界命運的日子已經一去不復返了。	子句作為修飾語
He expressed confidence that the enemies' schemes would never succeed.	他表示相信敵人的陰謀是絕對不會得逞的。	子句作為同位語

其中，子句又可歸為三種：名詞子句（主語子句、受詞子句、表語子句、同位語子句）、關係／形容詞子句（關係子句）和副詞子句（各類狀語子句）

例句	中譯	說明
He told me that the match had been cancelled.	他告訴我比賽已經取消了。	名詞子句作為told的受詞
Holiday resorts which are very crowded are not very pleasant.	那些擁擠的渡假場所令人感到很不愉快。	形容詞子句作為修飾語
However hard I try, I can't remember people's names.	不管我怎麼用心，還是記不住人們的名字。	「However + Adv. + 主詞 + 動詞」作為副詞子句

文法實戰演練

1. We must double our efforts, _____ we will never be able to catch up with others.
   A. and　　　　　B. so　　　　　C. but　　　　　D. or

2. New Zealand has a mild sea climate, _____ the north is subtropical.
   A. while　　　　B. for　　　　　C. then　　　　D. or

3. A majority of the committee members objected to continue this project, _____ it came to a halt.
   A. for　　　　　B. but　　　　　C. so　　　　　D. or

4. She must be very tired, _____?
   A. mustn't she　　B. didn't she　　C. wasn't she　　D. isn't she

5. He could hardly offer any evidence for his innocence, _____?
   A. was he　　　B. could he　　C. wasn't he　　D. couldn't he

6. _____ you are not good at figures, it is pointless to pursue a career as an accountant.
   A. What　　　　B. Unless　　　C. However　　　D. If

7. _____ hard they tried to convince the supervisor, the proposal got rejected.
   A. Whatever　　B. However　　C. Whichever　　D. Whenever

8. I miss the old days _____ online scams were not so common.
   A. what　　　　B. which　　　　C. that　　　　D. when

9. He expected _____ every employee could submit a quarterly report of their sales record.
   A. that　　　　B. which　　　　C. what　　　　D. when

10. Distant education will help people study _____ they go.
    A. whichever　　B. wherever　　C. whatever　　D. whenever

1. 正解為(D)。這句話的意思是「我們一定要更加倍努力，否則我們會永遠趕不上別人。」這題考連接詞的用法，前後句子表示對比，故選擇or連接最為適當。

2. 正解為(A)。本題意思是「紐西蘭是溫和的海洋氣候，而北部則是亞熱帶氣候。」這題考的是連接詞的用法，前後子句內容有對比的意味，可以使用but, yet, while等連接詞在空格當中。

3. 正解為(C)。這題意思是「委員位成員大多數反對繼續進行這個計畫，所以它被擱置了。」這句當中，前後子句有因果關係，所以用so在空格中。

4. 正解為(D)。這句話的意思是「她一定很累吧，不是嗎？」這句話裡的must be 為推測，附加問句依照推測的內容 She is very tired 來變化，應為「isn't she?」

5. 正解為(B)。本題的句子是「他幾乎提不出證明自己清白的證據，不是嗎？」這裡主要敘述的部分有hardly這個表示否定的詞，所以附加問句應用肯定的「could he？」來表示。

6. 正解為(D)。句子的意思是「如果你對數字不在行，追求成為會計師的夢就沒有意義了。」這句話前面的子句是後面子句內容成立的條件，用If 這個連接詞在空格中最為符合語意。

7. 正解為(B)。這句話的意思是「無論他們怎麼努力去說服主管，這個提案還是被駁回了。」這題的空格後接上副詞hard（努力），前半句是however hard 開頭的副詞子句。

8. 正解為(D)。這句話是說「我懷念以前網路詐騙還沒有那麼普遍的時候。」其中用when開頭帶出表示時間的修飾語子句「when the online scams were not so common」。

9. 正解為(A)。本句意思是「他期望每位員工都可以每季繳交一次銷售紀錄的報告。」用that帶出作為expect受詞的名詞子句。

10.正解為(B)。本題題目的意思是「遠距教育可以讓人們無論去到哪裡都能學習。」用wherever 帶出表示地點的副詞子句。

Day

19

主語
Subject

主語
Day 19 Subject

第一節：概述

　　主詞是句子要說明的人或者物，是句子的主體。一般放在句首。名詞、代名詞等常常在句子中當作主詞。此外V-ing形式、動詞不定式（to V）、名詞子句等也可以當作主詞。

主詞的類型	例句	中譯
名詞	Thrill rides use technology and special effects to give you a thrill.	動感電影利用高科技和特技效果帶給人刺激感。
代名詞	He told a joke but it fell flat.	他說了一個笑話，但沒有引人發笑。
數詞	Three's enough.	三個就夠了。
名詞化的形容詞	The idle are forced to work.	懶漢被迫勞動。
副詞	Now is the time.	現在是時候了。
名詞化的介系詞	The ups and downs of life must be taken as they come.	我們必須承受人生之浮沉起落。
不定式to V	To find your way can be a problem.	你能否找到路可能是一個問題。
動名詞	Watching a film is a pleasure, making one is hard work.	看電影是樂事，製作影片則是苦事。
名詞化的過去分詞	The disabled are to receive more money.	身障者將得到更多的救濟金。

介系詞片語	From Taipei to Kaohsiung was a two-hour ride on high speed rail train.	從台北到高雄要搭高鐵兩個小時。
子句	How the Pyramids were built is still a mystery.	金字塔是怎麼建造的仍然是個謎。
句子	"How do you do?" is a greeting.	「你好！」是一句問候語。

第二節：虛主詞

1. 虛主詞it

在由 it引導的表示天氣、溫度、時間、日期、距離等的句子中，it的語法功能是明確的（作主語），而意義卻是含糊的，可以說是沒有辭彙意義的，所以叫做「虛義it」。

it 的意義	例句	中譯
表示天氣	—What's the weather like? —It's sunny (cloudy).	--天氣怎麼樣？ --天晴（多雲）。
表示溫度	—How hot (cold) is it outside? —It's 38°Celsius (5°C below zero).	--外面有多熱（冷）？ --攝氏38度(攝氏零下5度)。
表示時間、年月	—What day is it today? —It's Wednesday.	--今天星期幾？ --星期三。
表示距離	—How far is it from Nanjing to Shanghai? —It is 300 kilometers.	--南京離上海多遠？ --300公里。

2. 由「先行it」作主詞

另一種it句型是在句中用it 作「先行主詞」而將真正的主詞後移。這種後移的「真主詞」可以是不定式結構。

it 代表的真主詞	例句	中譯
不定式結構	It is everyone's duty to abide by the law.	遵守法律是每個人的責任。
-ing結構	It's no good complaining.	抱怨是不會有好處的。
名詞子句	It is a pity that you didn't meet him.	你沒有見到他，真可惜。

3. 由it引導的強調句型

分裂句的結構模式是：It + be + 中心成分 + that / who 分句。 強調的中心成分可能是主詞、時間、地點等。

例句	中譯	說明
It is a book that he bought yesterday.	他昨天買的是一本書。	原句為He bought a book yesterday. 強調受詞 a book。

第三節：存在主詞

1. 構成：

存在句又叫there存在句。是由「There + be+ 名詞片語（＋狀語）」構成的，表示「存在」概念的句子結構。

2. 用法

例句	中譯	說明
The weatherman says there'll be a strong wind in the afternoon.	天氣預報說下午起大風。	真正的主詞是在大風。
There oughtn't to be too great a discrepancy in our views.	我們在看法上不應當有太大的分歧。	否定加在後面的動詞上。

| Is there any water left in your thermos (bottle)？ | 你的熱水瓶裡還有水嗎？ | 疑問句時，there作為主詞和be動詞互換位置。 |

第四節：名詞子句作主詞

1. 由what等代名詞引起的主語子句

例句	中譯	說明
What little she said has left us much to think about.	她說的短短幾句話很發人深思。	what表示「……所……的（東西）」，是一個關係子句。
Whatever was said here must be kept secret.	這裡說的話都應當保密。	whatever表示「所……的一切」
Whoever fails to see this will make a big blunder.	誰要是看不到這一點就是犯下極大的錯誤。	whoever引起，表示「一切……的人」

2. 由連接詞that引起的主詞子句

例句	中譯	說明
It's not your fault that this has happened.	發生了這樣的事不是你的錯。	= That this has happened is not your fault.
It is quite obvious that we need more equipment.	我們需要更多設備，這是很明顯的。	= That we need more equipment is obvious.

3. 由連接代名詞或連接副詞（或whether）引起的主詞子句

例句	中譯	說明
Whether he will join us won't make too much difference.	他是否加入我們不會造成多大的差別。	= It won't make too much difference whether he will join us.

1. Everybody makes mistakes. _____ nothing to be ashamed of.
   A. Here is   B. There is   C. There isn't   D. It isn't

2. _____ occurred to him that he forgot to being the portable hard drive with him.
   A. What   B. Who   C. It   D. That

3. _____ they cared about was to make profit.
   A. That   B. What   C. Which   D. It

4. _____ the solution to the math problem took us thirty minutes.
   A. To find   B. Found   C. Finds   D. To finding

5. _____ the alien crafts have visited the Earth remains a mystery.
   A. What   B. Whether   C. Who   D. Which

6. _____ the next meeting will be convened is not announced yet.
   A. That   B. What   C. When   D. If

7. _____ solve the puzzle before midnight can win a big prize.
   A. Whatever   B. However   C. Whichever   D. Whoever

8. _____ is against the law to drive after drinking.
   A. It   B. What   C. That   D. There

9. _____ in this café that we signed a contract with the client.
   A. It is   B. There is   C. What was   D. That is

10. They will definitely visit our school, but _____ they will do so hasn't been made clear yet.
   A. whether   B. where   C. who   D. when

文法實戰解析

1. 正解為(B)。這句話的意思是「每個人都會犯錯。不需要感到羞恥。」這題用虛主詞there開頭。

2. 正解為(C)。本題意思是「他忽然想到他忘記帶隨身硬碟了。」這題考的是用虛主詞It代替後面的that子句。

3. 正解為(B)。這題意思是「他們所在乎的就是要獲取利益。」這句話用What開頭的名詞子句作為主詞。

4. 正解為(A)。這句話的意思是「我們花了三十分鐘想出這題數學的解法。」這題用不定詞作為句子的主詞，空格當中也可以填Finding。

5. 正解為(B)。本題的句子是「外星人的飛行船是否來過地球仍是個謎。」這裡用Whether帶出的名詞子句作為句子的主詞。

6. 正解為(C)。句子的意思是「下次會議何時召開還未宣布。」這個空格中如果填that，則語義不完整。其他可填入空格中的詞包括whether（是否）、Where（何處）等。

7. 正解為(D)。這句話的意思是「無論是誰在午夜前解開這個謎題，就可以獲得大獎。」這題要用whoever作為名詞子句的主詞。

8. 正解為(A)。這句話是說「酒後開車是違法的。」原句可以說是「To drive after drinking is against the law.」用虛主詞It代替真正的主詞。

9. 正解為(A)。本句意思是「我們就是在這家咖啡廳跟客戶簽約的。」這句話為強調句型，中心的部分是地點，放在 It is 和 that 的中間。

10. 正解為(D)。本題題目的意思是「他們一定會來我們學校參觀，但是什麼時候來還不清楚。」用when代替二個對等子句中的主詞。

Day

20

謂語
Predicative

Day 20 謝語 Predicative

第一節：概述

　　謂語就是說明主詞的動作或狀態的部分，在這裡是一個句子的成分，是比Day 11 當中所提到一個單字本身性質為動詞更大的概念。實義動詞可以直接擔任句子的動詞；be動詞必須和主詞補語一起構成複合動詞；助動詞必須和其他動詞一起構成複合動詞。

例句	中譯	說明
The new school year begins on the 1st of September.	新學年在9月1日開學。	謂語部分由實義動詞begin組成。
His wife is a worker.	他妻子是位工人。	謂語部分由be動詞和主詞補語a worker 組成
Mr. Xie looked tired.	謝先生看起來很累。	謂語部分由動詞look和主詞補語tired組成。
You may go home now.	你現在可以回家了。	謂語部分由助動詞may和go 組成。

第二節：謂語＝情態動詞+動詞原形

例句	中譯	說明
You needn't come over yourself. You could have sent us an email.	你其實可以不必親自來的，你寄封電子郵件給我們就行了。	謂語部分=否定的情態動詞needn't + 動詞原形 come

| We'd better have a doctor in. | 我們最好請個醫生來。 | 謂語部分=情態動詞 had better + 動詞原型 have |

重點提示：必學文法小要點

★不定式還可和個別情態動詞、另一些動詞或其他詞構成複合謂語：

例句	中譯	說明
We ought to have done better.	我們應該要做得更好的。	謂語部分=情態動詞ought to + 助動詞 have + 動詞過去分詞 done
They aren't going to make any concession.	他們不打算做什麼讓步。	謂語部分=否定的情態動詞 aren't going to + 實義動詞 make
Do you happen to know his address?	你（碰巧）知道他的地址嗎？	謂語部分=助動詞 + 情態動詞 happen to + 實義動詞 know

★有些句子變為被動結構後，包含了一個複合謂語：

例句	中譯	說明
We were made to pay very heavy rents.	我們被迫繳很重的租金。	原本是Somebody made us pay very heavy rents.
He was often heard to sing the song.	人們常常聽到他唱這首歌。	原本是People often hear him sing the song.
They should be kept informed of what we are doing here.	應當經常讓他們知道我們這裡在做什麼。	原本是Somebody should inform them of what we are doing here.

上述這種複合謂語緊密結合在一起，說明主語的情況，分析句子時最好不要把它們分開來。

第三節：謂語=連綴動詞+主詞補語

謂語可由一個連綴動詞加表語構成，主要說明主語的特徵、類屬、狀態、身份等。

(1) 第一類單純表示一個特徵或狀態，用：be, feel, look, sound, taste, smell, seem, appear

例句	中譯	說明
He looked very agitated.	他看起來很焦急不安。	謂語部分= looked agitated

(2) 第二類表示由一種狀態變為另一種狀態，用：become, grow, get, turn, fall, go, come, run

例句	中譯	說明
The leaves have turned yellow.	樹葉已經變黃了。	謂語部分 = have turned yellow

(3) 第三類表示保持某種狀態等，用：remain, continue, stay, keep, rest, prove, turn out

例句	中譯	說明
This method proved quite efficient.	這方法最後證明非常有效。	謂語部分= proved efficient

(4) 有些動詞如wear, flush, blush, break, flash, lie, ring 有固定接某些形容詞的特殊表達法

例句	中譯	說明
He flushed crimson with anger.	他氣得滿臉通紅。	謂語部分 = flushed crimson
The whole area has lain waste for many years.	整個地區荒蕪了多年。	謂語部分 = has lain waste

重點提示：必學文法小要點

★常見出現在主詞補語中的介系詞片語

of the same age 同樣年齡	of great help 很有幫助	of little value 價值不大
in high spirits 情緒很高亢	of great importance 很重要	of different sizes 不同尺寸
of no use 沒有用	in difficulty 碰到困難	in line with 符合
in good order 有條有理	out of order （機器）壞了	out of cigarettes 煙抽完了
In trouble 處境困難	In danger 有危險	out of control 失去控制
out of danger 脫離危險	out of work 失業	under the weather 身體不適
out of patience 不耐煩了	under investigation 正在調查	under the impression 有……印象，覺得……
under discussion 正在討論	under the weather 身體不舒服	under medical treatment 正在治療

第四節：主詞與謂語的一致

1. 主詞的單複數

　　有的主語，形式上是複數，但實際上是單數的；又有的主語，形式是單數，但實際上是複數的，或是又可當作複數的。這就必須根據實際情況

判斷用何種形式的謂語動詞。

例句	中譯	說明
Every means has been tried.	每一種方法都試過了。	means表示方法，是單數的名詞
The audience were carried away by the attractive performance.	觀眾們為這場富有吸引力的演出感動得出了神。	audience 是集合名詞，描述觀眾成員的狀態用複數的謂語。

2. 連帶提出者不影響單複數

　　主語是單數，後面有其他干擾的部分，如with, together with, along with, as well as, no less than, like, but, except等片語時，仍和單數形式的謂語動詞連用。

例句	中譯	說明
The emperor, along with his ministers, was in the palace.	皇帝和他的大臣們一起在宮殿裡。	謂語的單複數以emperor為主。

3. 謂語之單複數視鄰近詞而定

　　謂語動詞的形式常常根據和它最靠近的名詞或代名詞的個數及人稱來決定，而不是取決於真正主語的個數及人稱。

例句	中譯	說明
Neither you nor I am right.	你和我都不對。	謂語的單複數以I為主。
Either he or his children are going to accept the prize.	他或是他的孩子們將接受獎品。	謂語的單複數以his children為主。

4. 抽象名詞的謂語用單數

　　一段時間、一筆錢或一段距離作主語時，謂語用單數。

例句	中譯	說明
Twenty years is needed to realize the scheme.	要實現這項計畫需要二十年時間。	twenty years 被當成是一段時間整體看待。

5. What 和 all 為主詞的謂語

　　what和 all是單數或複數的謂語往往取決於後面的成分。

例句	中譯	說明
All he needs is knowledge.	他所需要的就是知識。	knowledge 為單數，謂語動詞為單數
What I have are the books on the table.	我所有的東西就是桌上的書本。	the books 為複數，謂語動詞為複數。

文法實戰演練

1. He _____ know much about laws. We should consult someone else.
   A. seems to
   B. appears to
   C. doesn't seem to
   D. doesn't appear

2. Soon, the child _____ sound asleep.
   A. went
   B. fell
   C. felt
   D. looked

3. You can _____ assured that the goods will be delivered on time.
   A. stay
   B. keep
   C. rest
   D. remain

4. The officer of Central Weather Bureau reminded people to _____ for a typhoon is approaching the island.
   A. prove wrong
   B. stay alert
   C. flush crimson
   D. sit silent

5. Please leave the computer _____ for the simulation software is still working.
   A. up
   B. on
   C. off
   D. out

6. The daily necessities are _____ abundant supply.
   A. in
   B. about
   C. around
   D. above

7. We know what they are _____. They did this to avoid taxes imposed on their products.
   A. before
   B. after
   C. under
   D. against

8. Struggle is _____ the significance of life lies.
   A. what
   B. when
   C. how
   D. where

9. What he brought us _____ a bottle of wine.
   A. was
   B. were
   C. are.
   D. has

10. Neither you nor your brother _____ the right to inherit the castle.
    A. have
    B. has
    C. are
    D. is

1. 正解為(C)。這句話的意思是「他似乎不太懂法律。我們應該去問別人。」由上下文可知，空格應填入否定的連綴動詞，連綴動詞後加to再接動詞。

2. 正解為(B)。本題意思是「這個孩子很快就睡得很熟了。」這題考的是「fall asleep」這個片語。

3. 正解為(C)。這題考的是「rest assured（放心）」這個片語。這句話的意思是「你們可以放心，訂的貨品會準時送達的」。

4. 正解為(B)。這句話的意思是「氣象局的官員提醒民眾要保持警戒，因為颱風正接近本島。」這題考的是謂語的意思，選項(A)是證明錯誤，選項(C)是滿臉通紅（形容生氣），選項(D)是安靜地坐著。

5. 正解為(B)。本題的句子是「請保持電腦開機，因為模擬程式還在運作中。」這裡用副詞on表示電腦開機的狀態。

6. 正解為(A)。句子的意思是「日用品的供應充足。」這裡考的是介系詞，供應充足固定會使用「in abundant supply」。

7. 正解為(B)。這句話的意思是「我們知道他們在追求什麼。他們在試圖避免加諸在商品上的稅。」這題考的是「what they are after」這個片語。

8. 正解為(D)。這句話是一個諺語，意思是說「奮鬥就是生命的意義所在。」空格考的是用副詞子句當作謂語的成分，用表示地點的where填在空格中才符合語意。

9. 正解為(A)。本句意思是「他帶給我們的是一瓶酒。」這句話主詞是What 開頭的名詞子句，動詞視後面名詞單複數變化，故須用單數的was。

10. 正解為(B)。本題題目的意思是「你跟你的哥哥都沒有權力繼承這間城堡。」謂語中的動詞單複數視鄰近的詞決定，所以用單數的has。

Day

21

受詞
Object

Day 21 受詞 Object

第一節：概述

受詞表示動作的物件，是動作的承受者。英語中的及物動詞必須有受詞，稱為動詞受詞；介系詞後面的名詞或者代名詞稱為介系詞受詞。名詞、代名詞、數詞在句子中常常用作受詞。此外動詞不定式、動名詞和子句等也可用作受詞。

受詞的類型	例句	英譯
名詞	Paper catches fire easily.	紙是易燃的。
代名詞	Where did you buy that?	你在哪裡買那個東西的呢？
數詞	If you add 5 to 5, you get 10.	5加5得10。
名詞化的形容詞	I shall do my possible.	我將盡力而為。
副詞	You must tell me the when, the where, the how.	你必須告訴我事情是何時、何地和怎樣發生的。
不定詞	Remember to buy some stamps, won't you?	記得買一些郵票好嗎？
動名詞	He quit smoking last week.	他上星期戒煙了。
名詞化的分詞	More and more people like wearing ready-mades now.	現在愈來愈多的人愛穿現成的服裝。
子句	Studies show that only 7% of the communication in daily life is verbal.	研究表示，言語只佔日常生活交際的百分之七。
句子	He said, "You're quite wrong."	他說道:「你全錯了。」

第二節：直接受詞與間接受詞

　　有些動詞需要接直接受詞和間接受詞，直接受詞一般指動作的承受者，間接受詞指動作所向的或所為的人或物（多指人）。

　　可跟雙受詞的及物動詞以give為代表，大都具有「給予」之意，後面常跟間接受詞，所以這類動詞也叫做授與動詞，常見的有：answer, bring, buy, deny, do, fetch, find, get, give, hand, keep, leave, lend, make, offer, owe, pass, pay, play, promise, read, refuse, save, sell, send, show, sing, take, teach, tell, throw, wish, write等。

　　通常的結構為：主詞 + 動詞 + 間接受詞 + 直接受詞，如：

主詞	動詞	間接受詞	直接受詞	中譯
He	never made	me	such promise.	他從來沒承諾過我這件事。
I	have found	him	a position.	我幫他找到一個職位。

　　有時可改為：主詞 + 動詞 + 直接受詞 + 介系詞 + 間接受詞

主詞	動詞	直接受詞	介系詞	間接受詞	中譯
I	gave	my address	to	him.	我把我的地址給了他。
He	passed	the ball	to	me.	他把球傳給我。

第三節：受詞補語

　　如受詞帶有補語，即構成複合受詞，可以擔任複合受詞的有名詞、數詞、形容詞、介系詞、非限定動詞等。

受詞補語的類型	例句	英譯
名詞	Mr. Alvis entitled the book "A Handbook of English Patterns".	艾維斯先生把這本書名定為《英語句型手冊》。
形容詞	No one ever saw him angry.	從未有人見他惱怒過。

介系詞片語	They found treasure in the chest.	他們在那只箱子裡找到了珠寶。
不定式to V	The comrades asked Dr. Bethune to take cover.	同伴們請白求恩醫生迴避一下。
現在分詞	Aren't you ashamed to have everybody laughing at you?	大家都嘲笑你,難道你不覺得羞恥嗎?
過去分詞	The kings had the pyramids built for them.	這些國王為他們自己建造了金字塔。

第四節:受詞子句

受詞子句在句中作受詞,常用的連接詞有:that, whether, if, who, what, which, when, where, how, why等。

1. 第一個受詞子句的that 可省略

例句	中譯	說明
I think (that) he'll be back in a moment.	我認為他等一下就會回來。	that可以省略
I believed (that) the law was made of for man and that the government should be the servant rather than the master of the people.	我相信法律是為人制定的,而政府應該是人民的公僕,而不是他們的主人。	第一個that可以省略。第二個that 不能省略。

2. 受詞子句的疑問詞之後用「主詞 + 動詞」的語序

問句:

Where　　does　　he　　live?
疑問詞 + 助動詞 + 主詞 + 動詞?

受詞子句:

Can you tell me where　he　lives?
　　　　疑問詞 + 主詞+ 動詞

重點提示：必學文法小要點

★在下列情況下只能用whether而不能用if:

說明	例句	中譯
受詞是不定式 to V	We really don't know whether to go or to stay.	我們真的不知道是否該去。
後面有接or not	Can you tell me whether or not he will come to our party?	你能告訴我他是否會來參加我們的晚會嗎？
受詞是介系詞引導的子句	Success depends on whether we make enough effort.	成功取決於我們是否做出了足夠的努力。
受詞子句放在句首時	Whether the story is true or not, I don't know yet.	故事是否屬實，我還不知道。

第五節：直接引用句及間接引用句

1. 用法

當我們引用別人的話時，我們可以直接用別人的原話，也可以用自己的話把意思轉述出來。被引用的部分就是直接引用，轉述的部分則稱為間接引用。由直接引用變間接引用時，要注意以下三方面的變化：

(1) 人稱的變化

直接引用	間接引用
She said, "I am busy."	She said that she was busy.
她說她很忙。	

(2) 時態的變化

259

直接引用（原句）	間接引用
現在簡單式	過去簡單式
現在進行式	過去進行式
現在完成式	過去完成式
過去簡單式	過去完成式
過去完成式	過去完成式
未來簡單式	would/should + 動詞
未來進行式	would / should + be V-ing
未來完成式	would/ should have + Vp.p

例如：

直接引用（原句）	間接引用
"Where have you been?" he said to me. →他問我去哪裡了。（現在完成式 ）	He asked me where I had been.（過去完成式）

(3) 指示代名詞、時間副詞、地點副詞和某些動詞的相應變化

直接引用（原句）	間接引用
He said to her, "Where did you meet Mr. Smith three days ago?" 他問她三天前在哪裡遇見史密斯先生。	He asked her where she had met Mr. Smith three days before.

2. 各種不同句型的轉變方法：

(1) 直接引用是陳述句，一般間接引用中要用that引導，當然 that也可省略

直接引用（原句）	間接引用
Tom said, "I was in the library this morning." 湯姆說那天早晨他在圖書館。	Tom said (that) he was in the library that morning.（用that帶出的名詞子句作said的受詞）

(2) 直接引用是一般疑問句時，間接引用用 **whether** 或if引導，動詞用過去完成式

直接引用（原句）	間接引用
Billy said to me, "Have you seen the film?" 比利問我有沒有看過那部電影。	Billy asked me if / whether I had seen the film. （疑問句改為if/ whether + 主詞 + 動詞）

(3) 直接引用是特殊疑問句時，間接引用以原本的疑問詞作連接詞，並改成陳述句的語序，陳述句就是主詞+動詞的語序。

直接引用（原句）	間接引用
"Where is the station?" said Tim. 提姆問火車站在哪裡。	Tim asked where the station was. （疑問句改為where + 主詞 + 動詞）

(4) 直接引語是祈使句時，用**ask / tell / order sb. (not) to do sth.** 句型

直接引用（原句）	間接引用
"Don't run so quickly," Mr. Black said to him. 布萊克先生叫他別跑這麼快。	Mr. Black told him not to run so quickly. （用tell + 受詞 + 受詞補語替代）

1. Can you tell me _____?
   A. what is the article about
   B. how can I open the jar
   C. where the nearest supermarket is
   D. when will he come back

2. NASA will give a big prize to _____ can come up with a good name for the newly found asteroid.
   A. whoever   B. whenever   C. whatever   D. wherever

3. I am really thankful for her because she _____ in a multinational company.
   A. give me a job
   B. gave a job me
   C. found me a position
   D. found a position me

4. I have never heard him _____ about his family.
   A. to talk   B. talks   C. talked   D. talking

5. She is considering _____ to join the sorority of the university.
   A. if   B. whether   C. that   D. what

6. Can you explain _____ the electric car sales drop so much in June?
   A. what   B. when   C. where   D. why

7. The laborers requested _____ they can get paid for working overtime and _____ all full-time workers of the company can have health insurance.
   A. x ; that   B. x ; x   C. that ; x   D. that ; where

8. The patients' family requested the doctor _____ the patient's condition.
   A. explain   B. explains   C. explained   D. to explain

9. I was reminded _____ the utility bills before the deadline.
   A. of paying   B. to pay   C. pay   D. paid

10. He told me that he _____ the catalogue of our products to the clients.
   A. sends   B. sent   C. had sent   D. has sent

文法實戰解析

1. 正解為(C)。這句話考的是用疑問詞帶出受詞子句時，其中的語序，應為主詞+動詞的順序。選項(A)應改為 what the article is about，選項(B)應改為how I can open the jar，選項(D)應改為when he will come back。

2. 正解為(A)。本題意思是「NASA會獻出一份大禮，給任何可以為這個新發現小行星取個響亮名號的人。」這題考的是用whoever帶出受詞子句的用法。

3. 正解為(C)。這題考的是直接受詞和間接受詞的語序，可以用動詞＋間接受詞＋直接受詞，或者動詞＋直接受詞＋介系詞＋間接受詞。這句話的意思是「我很感謝她，因為她幫我找到一份在跨國公司的工作」。

4. 正解為(D)。這句話的意思是「我從來沒聽過他談論他的家庭。」這題考的是hear受詞補語的形式，可以用動詞原形或動詞-ing。

5. 正解為(B)。本題的句子是「她在考慮是否要加入大學的姐妹會。」這裡用whether 表示「是否」，空格後面用to接動詞，不可用if。

6. 正解為(D)。句子的意思是「你可以解釋為何電動車銷售量六月的時候下滑這麼多嗎？」這裡考的適用疑問詞帶出的受詞子句，根據子句的語意可判斷，應填入詢問原因的why。

7. 正解為(A)。這句話的意思是「勞工要求他們可以有加班費，以及所有正職員工都可以有健康保險。」這題考的是第二個子句的that不可以省略的概念。

8. 正解為(D)。這題的意思是説「病人家屬要求醫生解釋病情。」空格考的是request+受詞+to V 作為受詞補語的用法。

9. 正解為(B)。本句意思是「我被提醒要在期限內繳水電費帳單。」這句話如果是主動，可以説「Somebody reminded me to pay the utility bill.」。改用被動式，受詞後面的補語是用to V形式。

10. 正解為(C)。本題題目的意思是「他告訴我他已經將商品型錄寄給顧客了。」這裡考的是間接引用句中的動詞時態，空格中的動詞，強調比過去時間點更早就發生的事，使用過去完成式。

Day

22

修飾語
Modifier

Day 22 修飾語 Modifier

第一節：概述

修飾語用來修飾名詞或代名詞，說明人或物的狀態、品質、數量等；形容詞是最常見的修飾語，而其他詞性的字也可以當作修飾語，如：

修飾語的類型	例句	中文
形容詞	Privacy is a very important part of western cultures.	隱私是西方文化的一個重要的組成部分。
名詞	We read the works of Shakespeare in literature class.	我們在文學課閱讀莎士比亞的作品。
代名詞	He is a friend of mine.	他是我的一個朋友。
數詞	Do it now, you may not get a second chance!	現在就做吧，你可能再也沒有機會了！
副詞	Innovation is the only way out.	創新是唯一的出路。
不定式 to V	She has a wish to travel round the world.	她有環遊世界的願望。
動名詞	This washing machine makes little noise.	這個洗衣機不會發出很多噪音。
分詞	Don't wake the sleeping baby.	不要吵醒睡眠中的寶寶。
介詞片語	The tender look in her eyes displays her affection for her child.	她的溫柔目光展現出她對小寶寶的愛。
子句（限定）	The car that's parked outside is mine.	停在外面的汽車是我的。
子句（非限定）	Your car, which I noticed outside, has been hit by another one.	我在外面看見你的汽車，它被另一輛車撞了。

表示單位的修飾語有：

a basket of eggs 一籃雞蛋　a bunch of flowers 一束花

a mass of buildings 一群建築物　a number of people 若干人

第二節：關係子句

關係子句就是修飾名詞的子句，被修飾的名詞稱為先行詞。關係子句由關係代名詞和關係副詞引導，前者在子句中作主語、受詞或表語，後者在子句中作狀語。

1. 關係代名詞

先行詞	關係代名詞
事物	which / that
人	who / that

需注意的是，在某些情況下只能用that，如：

例句	中譯	說明
He has got all the tools that we need.	他有我們需要的所有工具。	先行詞前面有不定代名詞時要用that
This is the funniest film that has come from the studio.	這是那個製片廠製作最滑稽的電影。	先行詞前面有形容詞最高級時要用that
The first statement that was issued gave very few details.	最先發佈的聲明沒有公佈什麼細節。	先行詞前面有序數詞時要用that
The government has promised to do everything that lies in its power to alleviate the hardships of the people.	政府承諾盡其一切力量減輕人民的苦難。	先行詞前面有不定代名詞時要用that

★關係代名詞在子句中作主詞補語時，只能用that或which，不能用who或whom，但可以省略，如：

John is not the man that he was years ago.
約翰已不再是多年前的他了。

★先行詞為集合名詞時，如果該詞指一個整體，則關係代名詞用which；如果指組成整體的所有成員，則關係代名詞用who，如：

Our team, who are all in good form, will do well in the coming matches.
我們隊員狀態都很好，在未來賽事中一定會表現出色。

Our team, which placed second last year, played even better this year.
去年排名第二的我們隊今年打得更為出色。

2. 介系詞+關係代名詞

有時關係代名詞之前要用介系詞。「介系詞 + 關係代名詞」在子句中作副詞。

例句	中譯	說明
Behavior is a mirror in which everyone shows his image.—Geothe	行為是一面鏡子，每個人都把自己的形象顯現於其中。—（德國）歌德	in which 可以換成 where
The world is a stage, on which every role will find a player.—Middleton	世界是個舞臺，各種角色都由人扮演。—（英）米德爾頓	on which 可以換成 where
He was born on the day on which his father died.	他在父親去世的那一天出生。	on which 可以換成 when
This is the reason for which he was late.	這就是他遲到的原因。	for which 可以換成 why

重點深度學： **進階挑戰**

對於關係子句，基於意義上的需要，可以在 some, any, few, several, many, most, all, both, none, neither, either, each, enough, half, one, two 等詞之後接of whom或of which。

例句	中譯	說明
The North Island is famous for an area of hot springs, some of which throw hot water high into the air.	北島是著名的溫泉勝地，有些溫泉的熱水能高高地噴向半空。	先行詞為事物，用some of which
I met the table tennis players, two of whom were studying in university.	我見到了那些乒乓球選手，其中有兩人正在大學就讀。	先行詞為人物，用some of whom

3. 限定關係子句 v.s. 非限定關係子句

限定關係子句 = 幫助讀者了解先行詞所指的特定對象，沒有這段描述，就可能不知道指涉的對象為何者，通常不會用逗號隔開。

非限定關係子句 = 補充説明先行詞的指涉對象的特徵，沒有沒有這段描述，還是可以知道指涉的對象為何者，通常會使用逗號隔開。

類型	例句	中譯
限定關係子句	My uncle is a man who believes in discipline.	我叔叔是個十分守紀律的人。
非限定關係子句	My uncle, who believes in discipline, is very strict with his children.	我那十分守紀律的叔叔對他的孩子們很嚴格。

1. He has all the features _____ we expect to see in a good teacher.
   A. who   B. which   C. that   D. what

2. The poet described the _____ leaves as the flying butterflies in autumn.
   A. falling   B. fell   C. fall   D. fallen

3. The veteran worker showed us the way _____ the machines in the factory.
   A. operate   B. to operate   C. operating   D. operated

4. The _____ girl gave up halfway through the marathon.
   A. injure   B. injures   C. to injure   D. injured

5. A report _____ any specification of the data source is not trustworthy.
   A. without   B. within   C. through   D. about

6. The last chapter of the book _____ is the most difficult part, took me three days to finish reading.
   A. that   B. which   C. , that   D. , which

7. There are two paths _____ to the basement. One is near the gate, and the other is behind the reception desk.
   A. up   B. down   C. past   D. above

8. The company is recruiting new employees _____ are competent in developing AI software.
   A. which   B. when   C. who   D. whom

9. I couldn't find the box _____ I keep the bracelet and necklaces.
   A. which   B. in which   C. for which   D. with which

10. The eggs, _____ have gone bad, were thrown away.
    A. half of them   B. several of whom
    C. most of which   D. some of that

文法實戰解析

1. 正解為(C)。這句話考的先行詞前面有不定代名詞修飾時,關係代名詞要用that。這句話的意思是説「他有所有我們期望在好老師身上看到的特質。」。

2. 正解為(A)。本題意思是「詩人把飄落的葉子形容成秋天飛舞的蝴蝶。」修飾語如果是falling表示「正在飄落的」,如果是fallen是「掉落地面上的」。

3. 正解為(B)。這句話的意思是「資深員工告訴我們操作工廠裡機器的方法」。這裡用to V 作為名詞 way 的修飾語。

4. 正解為(D)。這句話的意思是「那個受傷的女孩在馬拉松跑到一半的時候放棄了。」這girl的修飾語是過去分詞injured。

5. 正解為(A)。本題的句子是「沒有註明資料來源的報導不值得相信。」選項(B)是「在～期間內」,選項(C)是「穿過」,選項(D)是「關於」。

6. 正解為(D)。句子的意思是「這本書的最後一章,也是最困難的部分,花了我三天時間才讀完。」這裡考的是要選用非限定關係子句的用法,也就是「, which」。

7. 正解為(B)。這句話的意思是「有兩條路可以向下通往地下室。一個在大門附近,另一個在接待櫃檯的後面」用副詞down修飾名詞path。

8. 正解為(C)。這題的意思是説「公司正在招募會開發人工智慧軟體的人。」這裡的先行詞new employees是指人,關係代名詞用who。

9. 正解為(B)。本句意思是「我找不到我存放手環和項鍊的那個盒子。」句子當中用介系詞+關係代名詞表示先行詞是一個地點副詞,in which 可以換成 where。

10. 正解為(C)。本題題目的意思是「那些雞蛋被丟掉了,其中大部分都壞掉了。」這裡考的是several of + 關係代名詞的用法。

Day

23

同位語
Appositive

Day 23 同位語 Appositive

第一節：概述

同位語可被用來說明或解釋另一個句子成分，通常皆放在其所說明的名詞或代名詞之後。

1. 同位語可能會由不同詞性的字表示：

同位語的類型	例句	中譯
名詞	We have two children, a boy and a girl.	我們有兩個孩子，一男一女。
代名詞	They all wanted to see him.	他們都想見他。
數詞	Are you two ready?	你們兩位準備好了嗎？
不定式 to V	Their latest proposal, to concentrate on primary education, has met with some opposition.	他們最近提出的集中全力於初等教育的提議遭到了某些人的反對。
動名詞	The first plan, giving coupons, was turned down.	第一個提案是送折價券，被回絕了。
of 片語	He wishes to master the art of writing.	他希望可以精通寫作的藝術。
子句	The news that we are having a holiday tomorrow is not true.	明天放假的消息不是真的。
動詞	Asked about the likelihood of a recession, he responded, "We're going to continue to expand, to continue to have an increase in productivity."	當被問到衰退的可能性時，他答道：「我們將繼續擴展，繼續增強生產力。」

| 形容詞 | She is more than pretty, that is, beautiful. | 她不只好看而已，而是漂亮。 |
| 副詞 | He is working as hard as before, that is to say, not very hard. | 他工作的幹勁和過去一樣，也就是說，不是很努力。 |

2. 同位語的位置

　　同位語一般皆緊跟在其所說明的名詞之後，但有時二者亦可被其他詞語隔開。例如：

例句	中譯	說明
They spread the lie everywhere that Tom was guilty of theft.	他們到處散佈謠言說湯姆犯有盜竊罪。	同位語前面隔了一個 everywhere

　　同位語與其所說明的名詞之間常見的插入詞語包括：namely（即）、that is（亦即）、that is to say（那就是說）、to wit（即）、in other words（換言之）、or（或）、or rather（更正確地說）、for short（簡略言之）、for example（例如）、for instance（例如）、say（比如、假定說）、let us say（假定說）、such as（比如）、especially（尤其是）、particularly（特別是）、in particular（特別是）、mostly（多半）、chiefly（主要）、mainly（基本上）、including（包括）等等。

例句	中譯	說明
I am pleased with only one boy, namely, George.	我只對一個男孩滿意，那就是喬治。	同位語George前面插入namely
He works all day, that is to say, from 9 to 5.	他工作全天，也就是說，從上午九時至下午五時。	同位語from 9 to 5 前面插入that is to say

第二節：同位語子句

1. 通常的結構為：

> 先行詞 ＋ that ＋ 同位語子句

2. 同位語子句的先行詞多為fact, news, idea, thought, reply, report, remark等抽象名詞

例如：

例句	中譯	說明
The fact that the money has gone does not mean it was stolen.	那筆錢不見了這一事實並不意味著是被偷了。	先行詞是 fact
Where did you get the idea that I could not come?	你為什麼會認為我不能來？	先行詞是idea

3. 引導同位語子句的關聯詞 that 在非正式文體中可以省去，如：

例句	中譯	說明
He grabbed his suitcase and gave the impression he was boarding the Tokyo plane.	他拿起了手提箱，給人的印象是他要登上飛往東京的飛機了。	同位語子句 he was boarding...省去了 that

4. 疑問詞亦可引導同位語子句

例句	中譯	說明
She asked the reason why there was a delay.	她問之所以發生延誤的原因。	疑問詞 why引導同位語子句，why子句亦可看作是一關係子句

第三節：同位語子句的注意事項

1. 同位語子句的作用是對皆在其前面，包含抽象名詞的先行詞進行解釋或說明。同位語子句的that 通常不能省略。

例句	中譯	說明
The fact that she was a foreigner made it difficult for her to get a job.	她是個外國人，這一點使得她難以找到工作。	fact 後面的that 不可省略

Your proposal that the money should be used to build a nursery school is admirable.	你主張把錢用於建造一座幼稚園的建議是極好的。	proposal 後面的that 不可省略
The idea that you can do the thing without thinking is quite wrong.	你不加以考慮就可以做這件事，這個想法是相當錯誤的。	idea後面的that 不可省略

2. 有些同位語子句使用should + 動詞原型的

這類同位語子句在 suggestion, request, motion, proposal, order, recommendation, plan, idea 等詞之後。

例句	中譯	說明
He made the suggestion that we should invite Shankira, known as Latin Queen, to come here to perform.	他建議我們邀請拉丁舞后夏奇拉來這裡表演。	同位語子句中的 should 可以省略。

第四節：同位語子句與關係子句的區別

分析角度	同位語子句	關係子句
從文法角度上看	that 是連接詞，不是屬於句子的成分	that是關係代名詞
從語義角度上看	同位語描述前面名詞的內容	關係子句修飾先行詞的特徵
that 的性質	連接詞that一般不能省略	關係代名詞that，當其在子句中作受詞時，常常可以省略

這種差別從下列的例子看出：

例句	中譯	說明
The news (that) he told me just now is true.	他剛才告訴我的消息是真的。	關係子句
The news that I have taken the first place in English is true.	我英語考第一名的消息是真的。	同位語子句

1. The fact _____ he failed the test does not mean he is good for nothing.
   A. which　　　　　B. that　　　　C. why　　　　　D. who

2. The idea _____ daily necessities to the children in Africa was rejected.
   A. that donation　B. of donating　C. to donating　　D. by donating

3. His determination _____ his goal impressed his mentor.
   A. to achieve　　　　　　　B. for achievement
   C. have achieved　　　　　D. achieves

4. We visited several large European cities, _____, Istanbul and Rome.
   A. mostly　　　　B. or rather　　C. especially　　D. for instance

5. The company has produced several blockbusters, _____ action movies.
   A. mostly　　　　B. let us say　C. that is　　　　D. in other words

6. The report _____ made by the radical journalist was not considered just.
   A. that　　　　B. which　　　C. x　　　　　D. , which

7. The news _____ Senator Warren called to impeach the president surprised all of us.
   A. who　　　　B. which　　　C. that　　　D. x

8. The thought _____ he might go bankruptcy because of the inappropriate investment made him very upset.
   A. which　　　　B. when　　　C. who　　　　D. that

9. The suggestion that all plastic straws _____ was supported by many people.
   A. should ban　　　　　　B. should be banned
   C. to be banned　　　　　D. to ban

10. The hope that he _____ is faint.
   A. recover　　　B. recovered　　C. may recover　　D. to recover

文法實戰解析

1. 正解為(B)。這句話考的是同位語子句用that帶出並且不能省略的概念，題目的意思是「他考試失敗並不代表他一無是處。」。

2. 正解為(B)。本題意思是「捐贈日常物資給非洲兒童的想法被拒絕了。」這題考的是用of + Ving作為同位語的用法。

3. 正解為(A)。這句話的意思是「他要達成目標的決心令他的導師印象深刻」這裡用to achieve 做為determination 的同位語。

4. 正解為(D)。這句話的意思是「我們去了幾個歐洲的城市，例如伊斯坦堡和羅馬。」這題考的是同位語子句插入語的意思。選項(A)是「大部分」，選項(B)是「更正確地說」，選項(C)是「特別是」。

5. 正解為(A)。本題的句子是「該公司製作好幾部賣座電影，大多是動作片。」選項(B)是「假定」，選項(C)是「也就是說」，選項(D)是「換句話說」。

6. 正解為(C)。句子的意思是「由偏激記者所作的報導被認為是不公正的。」這句話用的是形容詞子句，需注意與同位語子句的區別，這裡的關係代名詞that在關係子句中作為受詞，可以省略。

7. 正解為(C)。這句話的意思是「參議院華倫呼籲要彈劾總統的新聞令我們很驚訝」這題句子用的是同位語子句，that不可省略。

8. 正解為(D)。這題的意思是說「不當投資可能會令他破產的想法讓他很難過。」這題的that子句是thought的同位語。

9. 正解為(B)。本句意思是「應該禁止所有塑膠吸管的提案受到很多人的支持。」作為suggestion的同位語子句中，會使用should + 動詞原形。

10. 正解為(C)。本題題目的意思是「他復原的希望是渺茫的。」這裡考的是hope 的同位語子句中，用助動詞+動詞原形。

Day

24

狀語
Adverbial

狀語 Adverbial

Day 24

第一節：概述

　　狀語修飾動詞、形容詞、副詞以及全句，說明動作或狀態的特徵，或對某一特徵作補充說明，狀語其實就是句子中作為副詞角色的成分。

第二節：狀語的表示法

1. 副詞作狀語的位置

　　副詞最常用作狀語，位置比較靈活，可置於句末、句首、句中。

例句	中譯	說明
He speaks the language badly but reads it well.	這種語言，他講得不好，但閱讀能力很強。	置於句末
Naturally we expect hotel guests to lock their doors.	當然我們期望旅館的旅客把房門鎖上。	置於句首
He has always lived in that house.	他一直住在那棟房子裡。	置於句中，位於助動詞與主要動詞之間
I couldn't very well refuse to go.	我不大好拒絕去。	位於句中

　　副詞通常置於形容詞或副詞的前面作為修飾。

例句	中譯	說明
The kitchen is reasonably clean.	廚房還算乾淨。	副詞當作狀語修飾形容詞
He did the work fairly well.	那工作他做得還算好。	副詞當作狀語修飾另一副詞

　　副詞enough當作狀語時須後置。

例句	中譯	說明
Is the room big enough for a party?	這個房間容得下一個晚會嗎？	副詞enough後置，修飾形容詞
He didn't run quickly enough to catch the bus.	他跑得不夠快，沒有趕上那台公車。	後置，修飾副詞

2. 不同詞性的詞作為狀語使用，會有不同的用法

例句	中譯	說明
The soldiers were taught to serve country heart and soul.	軍人被教導要全心服從國家。	名詞作狀語，多置於句末
We have walked this far without stopping.	我們不停地走了這麼遠。	指示代名詞、不定代名詞作狀語多置於其所修飾詞語之前
Can you move along a little?	你可以往前面挪一挪嗎？	形容數量的詞如 any, some, a little 作為狀語時後置
Many people use checks or credit cards to avoid carrying cash with them in the west.	在西方，許多人為避免攜帶現金而使用支票或信用卡。	不定式作狀語多置於句末
To kill bugs, spray the area regularly.	為了殺死蟲子，這地方要經常噴灑殺蟲劑。	強調時可置於句首
Arriving at the station, we learned that the train had already gone.	到了車站，我們得知火車已開走了。	分詞作狀語，多置於句首與句末，有時也置於句中
At the moment he's out of work.	他目前沒有工作。	介系詞片語作狀語多置於句末和句首
Where on earth is it?	它到底在哪裡呀？	有時亦可置於句中
We chatted as we walked along.	我們邊走邊聊。	子句作狀語多置於句末或句首

第三節：狀語的種類

狀語按其句法功能可分為三大類，如下：

1. 按其辭彙意義可分時間、地點、方式、程度、目的、原因、結果、條件、讓步等狀語。

例句	中譯	說明
Our country has experienced great changes in the last sixty years.	我們國家在過去的60年中經歷了巨大的變化。	時間狀語
Poets and artists often draw their inspiration from nature.	詩人和藝術家往往從大自然中吸取靈感。	地點狀語
She carefully picked up all the bits of broken glass.	她仔細地撿起了所有的碎玻璃片。	方式狀語
It was too hot to work.	天氣太熱，無法工作。	程度狀語
To improve the railway service, we are electrifying the main lines.	為加強鐵路服務，我們正在主幹線上實施電氣化。	目的狀語
I lent him the money because he needed it.	因為他需要，我借了錢給他。	原因狀語
He mistook me for a teacher, causing me some embarrassment.	他錯把我當成了老師，使我有些尷尬。	結果狀語
In case of rain bring your raincoat with you.	你最好帶著雨衣以防下雨。	條件狀語
Though no good swimmer, Mary splashed about happily in the sea.	儘管瑪麗游泳游得不好，她還是在海裡潑弄得很開心。	讓步狀語

2. 通常位於句首，常用逗號與句子隔開，表示說話人講話的方式，例如：seriously, frankly, literally, specifically, generally, broadly, honestly, confidentially, truly, truthfully, briefly, parenthetically, relatively, personally, candidly, flatly, crudely, bluntly, simply, metaphorically, strictly, paradoxically等等。

例句	中譯	說明
Generally, the two writers were against any censorship.	一般來說，這兩位作家是反對審查制度的。	Generally 作為評註性狀語置於句首。

| Briefly, there are too many people and too little food. | 簡而言之，有太多人太少食物了。 | 也可以說是Briefly speaking。 |

(1) 表示話語可靠程度的有：

probably, apparently, evidently, obviously, plainly, conceivably, possibly, presumably, arguably等等。

例句	中譯	說明
Obviously, he will lose the tennis game.	他顯然要輸掉這場網球比賽。	Obviously表示很明顯地

(2) 表示「確定」的有：

certainly, surely, admittedly, allegedly, undoubtedly, definitely, incontestably, unarguably, clearly等。

例句	中譯	說明
Undoubtedly, he is more intelligent than his brother.	他肯定比他的哥哥聰明。	Undoubtedly表示可確定程度很高

(3) 表示驚訝、迷惘、失望、安慰、諒解、遺憾等感情的有：

amazingly, astonishingly, astoundingly, bewilderingly, surprisingly, disappointingly, annoyingly, comfortingly, amusingly, understandably, regrettably, strangely, curiously等。

例句	中譯	說明
Curiously, all this stone walling seems totally out of place.	奇怪的是，所有這些石牆看來完全不合適。	置於句首的狀詞表示情感的狀態。

(4) 表示悲傷、高興、希望、感謝、幸運等感情的有：

sadly, happily, thankfully, hopefully, unhappily, fortunately, luckily, unfortunately, unluckily等。

例句	中譯	說明
Thankfully, everyone returned to the camp safe and sound.	謝天謝地，每個人都安全回到了營地。	表示感謝的狀語置於句首。

(5) 表示正確、錯誤、聰明、愚蠢等意義的有：

rightly, correctly, cleverly, wisely, incorrectly, wrongly, foolishly, unwisely, absurdly, preposterously, unreasonably, unjustly 等。

例句	中譯	說明
Rightly, the judge received praise for his decision.	那位法官因為他的裁決理所當然地獲得了讚譽。	表示正確的狀語置於句首。

(6) 表示尋常、罕見等意義的有：

conventionally, rarely, traditionally, (not) unusually等。

例句	中譯	說明
Traditionally, second-hand car prices drop in the autumn and rise in the spring.	按慣例，二手車的價格秋季下跌春季上揚。	表示慣例的狀語可說是Traditionally或 Conventionally

　　3. 具連接性，只是在意義上將句子聯繫起來。連接性狀語多為副詞和介系詞片語，常用的有：

　　(1) 表示列舉：first(ly), second(ly), third(ly)...; one, two, three...; for one thing...(and) for another (thing); to begin / start with; next, then; finally, lastly 等等

　　(2) 表示增補：besides, moreover, in addition, what is more等等

　　(3) 表示意義等同：likewise, similarly, in the same way等等

　　(4) 表示話題改變：by the way, incidentally等等

　　(5) 表示概括：in all, in conclusion, in a word等等

　　(6) 表示同位關係：namely, in other words, for example, that is, that is to say等等

　　(7) 表示結果：so, therefore, consequently, as a result等等

　　(8) 表示推論：then, in that case, otherwise等等

　　(9) 表示意義轉折：instead, on the contrary, in contrast, by comparison, (on the one hand...) on the other hand等等

　　(10) 表示讓步：anyhow, however, nevertheless, still, though, yet, in spite of that, after all 等等

第四節：狀語子句

　　就是在句子中扮演副詞功能的子句，可以表示時間、地點、原因、結果、目的、方式、條件、讓步等意義。下面分別敘述各種狀語子句。

1. 時間狀語子句

(1) when表示一個時間點或一段時間，**while**只能表示一段時間，**when**常可代替 **while**。**as**強調一個動作發生，另一個動作緊接著發生

例句	中譯	說明
He was swimming in the lake when he heard a cry for help.	他正在湖裡游泳時，忽然聽見呼救聲。	swimming 和 heard 兩個動作是在同個時間發生

(2) after 和 **before** 為表示動作或事件先後關係的連接詞

例句	中譯	說明
The train had left before I reached the station.	我到車站前火車已經開走了。	left 這個動作在 reached 這個動作之前發生

(3) since 表示從起點到現在的一段時間，所以主句必須用完成式或完成進行式

例句	中譯	說明
I have been wearing glasses since I was three.	我三歲以後就一直戴眼鏡。	動作從三歲持續至今。

2. 地點狀語子句

　　地點狀語子句由where引導。

例句	中譯	說明
Where there is a river, there is a city.	凡是有河流的地方，必有城市。	where 為副詞子句，至於句首

3. 原因狀語子句

(1) because引導的子句常常在主句之後，而as和since引導的子句多位於主句之前。

例句	中譯	說明
Ice cream is junk food because it has a lot of fat and sugar.	霜淇淋屬於垃圾食品，因為它含有大量的脂肪與糖分。	Because的子句置於主句之後
Since you desire it, I will look into the matter.	既然你希望，我會研究此事。	Since 的子句置於主具之前

(2) seeing that和now that表示的意義與 as一樣

例句	中譯	說明
Seeing that I was in the same class as George, I used to be with him all day long.	因為我與喬治以前同班，所以我和他成天在一起。	Seeing that 表示原因，可以代換為As 或Since

(3) that 引導的子句主要用在表示感情意義的形容詞或不及物動詞之後

例句	中譯	說明
We were alarmed that Bob swam in deep water.	鮑伯在深水中游泳，我們很吃驚。	alarmed可換成astonished 表示非常驚訝

4. 結果狀語子句

結果狀語子句由so...that, such...that, so that引導。

例句	中譯	說明
The room is so quiet that one can hear even a pin drop.	這房間安靜得能聽見一根針落地的聲音。	so + Adj. + that 子句，表示子句當中的狀況是前面句子的狀況造成的

5. 目的狀語子句

目的狀語子句由 in order that, so that, lest, for fear that, in case 等引導。

例句	中譯	說明
He listened attentively so that he might not miss a single word.	他注意地傾聽以便不錯過任何一個字。	so that 之後的子句表示目的

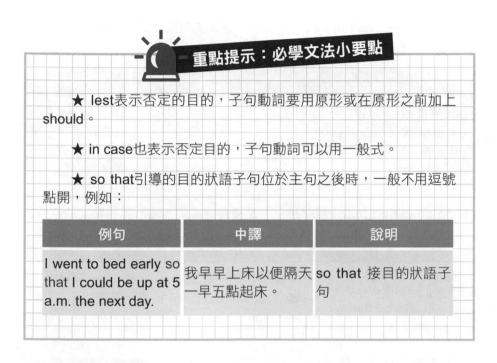

重點提示：必學文法小要點

★ lest表示否定的目的，子句動詞要用原形或在原形之前加上should。

★ in case也表示否定目的，子句動詞可以用一般式。

★ so that引導的目的狀語子句位於主句之後時，一般不用逗號點開，例如：

例句	中譯	說明
I went to bed early so that I could be up at 5 a.m. the next day.	我早早上床以便隔天一早五點起床。	so that 接目的狀語子句

6. 條件狀語子句

引導條件狀語子句的連接詞有：if, suppose, supposing, unless, providing, provided, on condition that, if。

(1) if 為最常見的連接詞，句子中可以根據需要使用各種動詞形式

例句	中譯	說明
I will return the book to you on Monday if I have read it by then.	如果我星期一讀完了，那我會把書還給你的。	If 後面是是表示前半段句子狀況的條件。

(2) once「一旦」，強調的是條件

例句	中譯	說明
Once you show any sign of fear, he will attack you.	你一旦露出任何恐懼的跡象，他就會攻擊你。	Once 表示條件

(3) so long as / as long as「只要」，強調主句所述的情況和子句所述的情況同時並存。

例句	中譯	說明
Rice will grow well so long as it is given enough sunlight and a good supply of water and fertilizer.	只要能得到充足的陽光、水和肥料，水稻就能長得很好。	So long as 後面接的是前半段句子狀況要實現的條件。

(4) on condition that「條件是」，是複合連接詞，暗示某種特定的條件

例句	中譯	說明
She will join us on condition that you also be there.	她會和我們一起去，條件是你也必須在場。	on condition that 後面接的是要讓前面子句成立到條件。

(5) in case「如果，萬一」

例句	中譯	說明
Send me a message, in case you have any difficulty.	萬一有什麼困難，請傳個訊息給我。	in case 用條件句型

(6) unless 經常等於if...not

例句	中譯	說明
Unless you polish your resume before you send it, you would not get a chance for an interview.	除非你寄出履歷之前先修改一下，否則你是不會有面試機會的。	Unless 接的子句發生（先修改履歷），後半部子句的狀況（沒有面試機會）才不會發生。

(7) provided，providing

多用於正式文體

例句	中譯	說明
Provided that the statistical data has been verified, the result was considered robust.	因為數據資料被證實過，實驗結果被認為是合理的。	Provided that 接的是讓後半子句狀況成立的條件句。

7. 讓步狀語子句

讓步狀語子句由though, although, even if, even though以及「when等詞 + ever」或「no matter + when」等詞引導。

例句	中譯	說明
Even if you lose the match, you shouldn't lose heart.	即使你輸了比賽，你也不該喪失鬥志。	Even if 表示讓步
Wherever he went, doors were shut upon him.	不管他走到哪，所有的大門都關上了。	Wherever 可以換成 no matter where
While there are many different interpretations of our body language, some gestures seem to be universal.	儘管我們對肢體語言有許多不同的理解，但有一些手勢似乎應是通用的。	While可以表示儘管的意思

1. _____ the Dengue fever from spreading, we should clean the garden regularly.
   A. Preventing   B. Prevented   C. To prevent   D. Prevention

2. _____ the restaurant without making a reservation in advance, we realized that we have to wait for an hour to have a table.
   A. Arriving   B. Arrived   C. To arrive   D. Arrival

3. He tend to be late for the first class in the morning, _____ on Monday.
   A. briefly   B. personally   C. honestly   D. especially

4. _____, the amateur athlete broke the world record.
   A. Amazingly   B. Presumably   C. Arguably   D. Relatively

5. The protestors did not yell irrational words; _____, they held their slogans and sat quietly outside the municipal building.
   A. consequently   B. instead   C. similarly   D. in addition

6. The hopeful people see opportunities _____ others see challenges.
   A. where   B. when   C. which   D. what

7. Ketogenic diet may help people lose weight _____ it enhances metabolism.
   A. while   B. so that   C. because   D. however

8. You should pay attention to the dress code _____ you go to a job interview.
   A. which   B. when   C. how   D. where

9. _____, all of the kid who got trapped in the cave were rescued.
   A. Conventionally   B. Regrettably   C. Seriously   D. Fortunately

10. You will never achieve you goal _____ you reflect on yourself and amend your mistakes.
    A. since   B. for   C. provided that   D. unless

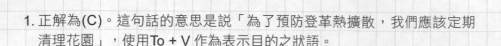

1. 正解為(C)。這句話的意思是說「為了預防登革熱擴散，我們應該定期清理花園」，使用To + V 作為表示目的之狀語。

2. 正解為(A)。本題意思是「我們沒有訂位就到達餐廳，才發現要等一個小時才有位置。」這句用現在分詞作為描述時間的狀語。

3. 正解為(D)。這句話的意思是「他常常在早上的第一堂課遲到，特別是星期一」。這題測驗的是評註性狀語的意思，選項(A)是簡短地，選項(B)是個人地，選項(C)是誠實地。

4. 正解為(A)。這句話的意思是「令人驚訝地，那位業餘的運動員打破了世界紀錄。」這裡考副詞的意思，選項(B)是想必，選項(C)是按理說，選項(D)是相對來講。

5. 正解為(B)。本題的句子是「抗議者沒有大喊不理性的話語，反而是拿著標語靜坐在市政大樓前面。」選項選項(A)是結果，選項(C)是相似地，選項(D)是此外。

6. 正解為(A)。句子的意思是「懷有希望的人在別人看見挑戰的地方看見機會。」空格中應填入一個表示地點的副詞。

7. 正解為(C)。這句話的意思是「生銅飲食可以幫助人減重因為它促進新陳代謝作用。」這裡用表示原因的狀詞子句。

8. 正解為(B)。這題的意思是說「去參加面試的時候，你應該要注意服裝儀容。」這裡用的是when所引出，表示時間的狀語子句。

9. 正解為(D)。本句意思是「幸運的是，所有受困於洞穴中的孩童都順利獲救了。」這裡考的是副詞的意思，選項(A)是傳統上來說，選項(B)是令人遺憾地，選項(C)是認真地說。

10. 正解為(D)。本題題目的意思是「你永遠無法達到目標，除非你能自我反省並且改正錯誤。」選項(A)是自從，選項(B)是因為，選項(C)是如果、只要的意思。

Day

25

獨立成分
Independent
Elements

Day 25 獨立成分 Independent Elements

🚩 第一節：概述

當一個單字、短句或子句用在句子裡，而與句子的其他成分沒有語法上的關係時，就被稱為「獨立成分」。獨立成分包括：感嘆語及插入語。

🚩 第二節：獨立成分的類型

獨立成分可分為下面幾種常見的類型。

1. 感嘆語

例句	中譯	說明
Ah, there you are, the very man I've been looking for.	啊，你在那兒。我要找的就是你。	放在句首的感嘆詞，還有hey、here、Oh等。

2. 插入語

對一句話作一些附加的解釋說明，常見的結構有：I hope, I guess, I think, I'm afraid, I believe, I suppose, I wonder, you know, I tell you, it is said, it is suggested, it seems, it seems to me等等。

例句	中譯	說明
The performance, I think, was very interesting.	我認為那場表演很有趣。	在句中插入I think 、I am afraid 等詞語表示個人看法

3. 稱謂

例句	中譯	說明
Shylock, how can you hope for mercy yourself when you show none?	夏洛克，如果你不寬恕別人，你自己怎能希望得到別人的寬恕呢？	此用法通常用來強調要求對方的注意，或者是加強後面説話內容的語氣。
Dad, when you sent me to Paris to see if I could really earn a living as a painter, I stayed at my friend's flat for three months.	爸爸，你把我送去巴黎，想看看我是否真正能以繪畫謀生，那時候我就住在我朋友的那套房間裡，住了三個月。	

4. 獨立單字

例句	中譯	說明
Fire! Hurry up, John!	失火了！ 約翰，快走！	此用法做強調之功能。

第三節：插入語的功能

1. 插入語的功能

　　英語句中有時插入一個與全句句義無直接關係的附加部分，這個部分就叫「插入語」。插入語表示説話人的態度，解釋或説明整個句子而不是某個詞。它和句子的聯繫並不緊密，一般位於句首，用逗號和句子分開。

　　插入語一般對一句話作一些附加的解釋説明，常見的結構有：I hope, I guess, I think, I'm afraid, I believe, I suppose, I wonder, you know, I tell you, it is said, it is suggested, it seems, it seems to me等等。例如：

例句	中譯
That book, it seems, is very well written.	那本書看來寫得很好。
That will be a good beginning, I hope.	希望這是一個良好的開端。

You will have to try harder, you know, if you want to succeed.	你知道，如果你想要獲得成功，就必須更加努力才行。
This diet, I think, will do good to your health.	我想這種飲食對你的健康有好處。

2. 插入語對全句解釋的表達形式

(1) 副詞

屬於這一類的副詞有：actually, certainly, definitely, fortunately, frankly, maybe, obviously, perhaps, personally, possibly, probably等等。

例句	中譯	說明
Honestly, that is all the money I have.	老實説，我所有的錢就是這些。	用副詞

其他常見的還有：

例句	中譯	說明
Lots of trees were blown down. Worse still, some people were killed or injured.	許多樹木被風刮倒了。更糟糕的是，還死傷了一些人。	形容詞片語
To tell you the truth, I don't quite agree with you.	説實在的，我不太同意你的意見。	用不定詞片語
By the way, do you happen to know the young man's name?	順便問一下，你知道那個年輕人的名字嗎？	用介系詞片語，另外還有 in his opinion、to my surprise等。
Generally speaking, the species that are able to adapt to the change of environment will survive, while the others will die out.	一般來説，能夠適應環境變化的物種會繼續生存下去；而那些適應性差的物種就會滅絕。	用現在分詞片語，另外還有 frankly speaking、judging from~等説法。

What is more, this "information line" operates 24 hours a day.	此外，這條「諮詢路線」是一天24小時運作的。	也可以寫作What's more y作為寫作文中的轉承語

3. 還有一種獨立成分，是有連接詞作用的插入語

例句	中譯	說明
There was no news; nevertheless, she went on hoping.	沒有消息，然而她繼續抱著希望。	用副詞nevertheless表示連接上下文。
A spouse is, in a sense, a partner in the voyage of life.	從某種意義上來說，配偶是人生旅程中的伴侶。	用介系詞片語in a sense表示連接上下文
After all, this ball is very important.	這次舞會畢竟是非常重要的。	用片語after all 連接上下文
The story happened about a century ago, that is to say, a hundred years ago.	這故事發生在大約一個世紀以前，也就是說，100年前。	用子句that is to say 連句上下文

4. 某些插入成分標點符號的用法

有些詞或片語可插到句子中間，不用逗號隔開。例如：

例句	中譯
What on earth do you mean?	你究竟是什麼意思？
When the devil did you lose it?	你到底什麼時候丟的？
Who in the world is that fellow?	那個人究竟是誰？
What the hell do you want?	你到底要什麼？

1. The classic movie, *Titanic* , _____ , has been remade.
   A. personally   B. frankly   C. surely   D. actually

2. The supervisor gave us some suggestions. _____, we should revise our marketing project.
   A. In his opinion   B. By the way
   C. To be honest   D. Generally speaking

3. You should arrange your time well. _____, you will find yourself striving to catch up with the schedule.
   A. Besides   B. Otherwise
   C. On the contrary   D. Nevertheless

4. A typhoon stuck the island. _____, dozens of flights were canceled.
   A. After all   B. On the other hand
   C. What's more   D. As a result

5. He keeps regular hours. _____, he exercises every day to stay healthy.
   A. What's more   B. To be precise   C. Probably   D. In a sense

6. She has rehearsed dozens of times for her first stage play. _____, her debut will be successful.
   A. Generally   B. Unluckily   C. Personally   D. Hopefully

7. _____ his experience, he shall be the best candidate for this position.
   A. Judging from   B. To think of
   C. With a view to   D. Without a doubt

8. A: I'd like to thank you for you timely assistance.
   B: Oh, _____.
   A. it's my pleasure   B. it doesn't matter
   C. it's a disaster   D. it's pure boredom

9. _____ you the truth, I don't think cutting down the budget on health care is a good idea.
   A. Telling   B. To tell   C. Told   D. Tell

10. _____, Lady Gaga will have a concert in our city. I will definitely go!
   A. To our dismay   B. To his embarrassment
   C. To my great joy   D. To her annoyance

文法實戰解析

1. 正解為(D)。這句話的意思是說「經典電影鐵達尼號其實已經被翻拍過了」。這裡考的是副詞作為獨立成分的意思，選項(A)是「個人地」，選項(B)是「誠實地」，選項(C)是「確定地」。

2. 正解為(A)。本題意思是「主管給我們一些建議。依他之見，我們應該重新修改行銷計畫。」選項(B)是「順帶一提」，選項(C)是「老實說」，選項(D)是「一般來說」。

3. 正解為(B)。這句話的意思是「你應該要好好安排自己的時間，否則你會發現自己總是在為了趕上時程而掙扎。」這題考的是具連接作用的副詞意義。選項(A)是「此外」，選項(C)是「相反地」，選項(D)是「然而」。

4. 正解為(D)。這句話的意思是「有個颱風侵襲本島。因此，數十個航班被取消了。」這裡要選的是表示因果的副詞。選項(A)是「畢竟」，選項(B)是「另一方面」，選項(C)是「此外」。

5. 正解為(A)。本題的句子是「他作息規律。此外，他每天運動來保持健康。」前後兩個句子之間有並列關係，所以用What's more來連接。

6. 正解為(D)。句子的意思是「她為了第一齣舞台劇排練了數十次。但願她初次登台能成功。」這裡要填入適當意義的副詞。選項(A)是「一般來說」，選項(B)是「不幸地」，選項(C)是「個人地」。

7. 正解為(A)。這句話的意思是「從他的經驗看來，他應該是這個職缺的最好人選」。表示「從～看來」的片語用Judging from ~。

8. 正解為(A)。這題的A角色說「我想要謝謝您即時的協助。」B角色說「噢，那是我的榮幸。」的插入語Oh之後要說的話，應該是要能回應的對方，帶有「不客氣」意味的詞。

9. 正解為(B)。本句意思是「老實說，我不覺得減少健康保險的預算是個好主意。」這裡應該用不定式to V的片語作為插入語的開頭。

10. 正解為(C)。這題考的是to + 所有格 + 名詞，需選用正確的意思「令我們愉快的是」以符合其後的句意。

Day

26

強調用法
Emphasis

Day 26 強調用法 Emphasis

第一節：概述

在英文裡，可以用詞彙、句型、或修辭方式來強調句子當中的某個成分。例如強調主詞、時間、地點等，我們可以藉由以下的說明來理解英文中強調的用法。

第二節：用詞彙表示強調

1. only

例句	中譯	說明
Only Tom saw the rabbit (=no one else saw it).	只有湯姆看見了野兔。	強調其他人都沒看見
Tom only saw the rabbit (=he didn't shoot it).	湯姆只看見野兔。	他並沒有打中
Tom saw only the rabbit (=not the tiger).	湯姆只看見了野兔。	他沒看見老虎
Tom saw the rabbit only in the forest (=not in other places).	湯姆只有在森林中看見過野兔。	不是在其他地方
Tom saw the rabbit in the forest only in spring (=not in other seasons).	湯姆只有在春天於森林中看見過野兔。	而不是在其他季節

2. even

例句	中譯	說明
Even a child can understand the book.	即使小孩也能看懂這本書。	一般放在所強調的成分之前。
You are even more beautiful than before.	你比以前更漂亮了。	even還可用來強調比較級。

3. ever

例句	中譯	說明
Why did you ever want to do that?	你究竟為何會想要那樣做？	主要用來強調疑問詞可表示「究竟、到底」的意思。
How could you ever do that to me?	你究竟為何能那樣對我？	

4. just

例句	中譯	說明
The performance was just wonderful.	演出的節目就是好。	放在所強調的成分之前
This is just how things are.	事情本來就是如此。	

5. 其它用法

　　much, still, a lot, a little, far, by far, a good / great deal等常用來強調比較級，much和by far還可用來強調最高級

例句	中譯	說明
I feel a lot better today.	我今天感覺好多了。	a lot 修飾比較級
The Pacific is by far the largest ocean in the world.	太平洋是世界上最大的海洋。	by far修飾最高級

第三節：用句型表示強調

1. 用反身代名詞表示強調

例句	中譯	說明
We ourselves often made that mistake.	我們自己常常犯那個錯誤。	反身代名詞放在所強調的詞的後面

2. 用助動詞do或does強調

例句	中譯	說明
I do hope you'll stay for lunch.	我真希望你留下來吃午飯。	放在所強調的謂語動詞之前

3. 「It is / was...that...」強調句子中主語、受詞、副詞等

例句	中譯	說明
Barack met Michelle in Austin in 1989.	布拉克1989年在奧斯丁遇到米雪兒。	原句
It was Barack who / that met Michelle in Austin in 1989.	正是布拉克於1989年在奧斯丁遇到了米雪兒。	強調主詞布拉克，不是別人。
It was Michelle who / that Barack met in Austin in 1989.	1989年布拉克在奧斯丁遇到的正是米雪兒。	強調受詞米雪兒，不是別人。
It was in Austin that Barack met Michelle in 1989.	1989年布拉克正是在奧斯丁遇到米雪兒的。	強調地點在奧斯丁，不是在別的地方。
It was in 1989 that Barack met Michelle in Austin.	正是在1989年，布拉克在奧斯丁遇見了米雪兒。	強調是在1989年，不是在別的年份。

第四節：用修辭方式強調

1. 提前

把要強調的部分（如：主詞、受詞、時間、地點等）提前到句首

例句	中譯	說明
Even the most complicated problems, a computer can solve in a short time.	即使是最複雜的問題，電腦也能在短時間內解決。	將受詞提前
Of all the books I have, this is the best.	在我所有的書中這本是最好的。	用作修飾語的of介系詞片語提前
Very grateful they were for your help.	他們非常感謝你的幫助。	形容詞提前
To youth, I have but three words of counsel—work, work, and work.	對年輕人，我的忠告只有三個詞－ 工作、工作、工作。	副詞提前

2. 重複

用重複關鍵字、透過同義詞或相似詞來表示強調。

例句	中譯	說明
She looks much, much older now.	她現在看來老得多了。	用重複much強調程度上的差別。

3. 疑問

用附加疑問句表示強調。

例句	中譯	說明
The picture is true to nature, isn't it?	這幅畫畫得逼真，不是嗎？	主要句子用肯定，附加問句用否定。
The picture isn't true to nature, is it?	這幅畫畫得不夠逼真，是嗎？	主要句子用否定，附加問句用肯定。

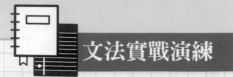

文法實戰演練

1. In the modern society, _____ a toddler knows how to use the tablet computer.
   A. only   B. even   C. such   D. that

2. It was in the fifteenth century _____ the concept of cars was first proposed by Leonardo Da Vinci.
   A. which   B. who   C. that   D. where

3. _____ by applying suitable strategy can you complete the task with great efficiency.
   A. Even   B. Only   C. By far   D. much

4. The temperature today is _____ suitable for us to have a hot spring bath.
   A. only   B. even   C. a lot   D. just

5. The administrator of the bulletin board would remove the offensive remarks from the system _____.
   A. whenever   B. himself   C. by far   D. ever since

6. _____ the priority would be accomplishing the education and obtaining the diploma of higher education.
   A. For him   B. Very important C. It is   D. A lot

7. It was _____ that received award for Best Singer of the Year.
   A. in 2018   B. in Taiwan   C. Jolyn   D. lucky

8. Instagram is _____ more popular than Facebook among teenagers.
   A. very   B. only   C. somehow   D. by far

9. It was _____ that Da Vinci's paintings were exhibited last month.
   A. in Louvre   B. in 2019   C. the art work D. a collection

10. Even _____ can be removed by the detergent.
    A. tough stains   B. a child
    C. a cloth   D. by washing machine

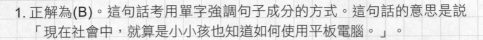
1. 正解為(B)。這句話考用單字強調句子成分的方式。這句話的意思是說「現在社會中，就算是小小孩也知道如何使用平板電腦。」。

2. 正解為(C)。本題意思是「正是在十五世紀時，汽車的概念首度由李奧納多·達文西所提出」。這句強調時間副詞，把表示時間的副詞，放在It is 和 that 的中間。

3. 正解為(B)。這句話將作為手段的副詞提前到句首，句子意思是「只有運用適當的策略，你才能有效率地完成任務」。選項(A)的even是甚至的意思，選項(C) 和 (D)都是修飾形容詞的強調語。

4. 正解為(D)。這句話的意思是「今天的溫度正好適合我們去泡溫泉」。這裡用just放在形容詞之前，表示「剛巧、正好、適當」的意思。

5. 正解為(B)。本題的句子是「系統的管理員會親自把佈告欄上冒犯的留言刪去」。這裡用反身代名詞放在句尾強調句子的主詞是「親自」完成動作。

6. 正解為(A)。句子的意思是「對他來說優先要做的事情是完成學業並且拿到高等教育的學位。」這題考的是將強調的成分往前提到句首，強調的部份是「對他來說」。

7. 正解為(C)。這句話的意思是「獲頒本年度最佳歌手獎的是巧琳」，這句話在that子句後面沒有主詞，可見主詞被提前到it is 和 that的中間作為強調的成分，所以選人名。

8. 正解為(D)。這題的意思是說「Instagram在年輕人之間比臉書受歡迎多了。」這裡考的是修飾形容詞比較級的強調語by far。

9. 正解為(A)。本句意思是「達文西的畫作上個月正是在羅浮宮展示。」在that子句中少了地點的元素，可見地點提前到It was 和 that 的中間表示強調。

10. 正解為(A)。本題題目的意思是「就算是頑強的髒污，也可以用這個清潔劑洗掉。」這裡用Even在句首的強調方式，且在that子句中少了受詞，可知需選擇tough stains填入空格中。

Day

27

倒裝
Inversion

Day 27 倒裝 Inversion

🚩 第一節：概述

　　句子的正常語序是主詞在前，動詞及其他的部分在後。有時為了強調，會採用全部或部分「倒裝」，把要強調的部分移到主詞的前面。

🚩 第二節：全部倒裝和部分倒裝

1. 全部倒裝

例句	中譯	說明
Here are some letters for you.	這裡有你的幾封信。	原本的語序是： Some of your letters（主詞）are（be動詞）here（主詞補語）.
Down fell the rain.	雨傾盆而下。	原本的語序是： The rain fell down.
Here we are.	我們到了。	主詞如果是人稱代名詞時，主詞和動詞則不倒裝。

2. 部分倒裝

例句	中譯	說明
Never have I heard such a thing.	我從未聽說過這樣的事。	原本的語序是： I（主詞）have（be動詞）never（副詞）heard（動詞）such a thing（受詞）.

| Only today did I learn the dreadful news. | 我今天才聽到這可怕的消息。 | 原本的語序是：I（主詞）learned（動詞）the dreadful news（受詞）only today（副詞）.
倒裝後加上助動詞did |

第三節：倒裝的用法

1. 疑問句

例句	中譯	說明
Have you finished writing the report?	你的報告寫好了嗎？	疑問句都會將助動詞往前移，作為倒裝。
What can you do to promote world peace?	你能為促進世界和平做些什麼？	Wh疑問詞置於句首。

重點提示：必學文法小要點

但疑問詞作主語或修飾主語時，句子則不必倒裝。例如：

What is on at the Capital Theatre tomorrow?
明天首都劇院上演什麼？

How many students are making the trip?
有多少學生參加這次旅行？

2. 表示祝願的句型

例句	中譯	說明
May you live a happy life!	祝你生活愉快！	原本的語序是 You may live a happy life.

3. 以副詞引導的句型

如here, there或out, in, up, down, away, now, then等

例句	中譯	說明
Here comes the bus.	公車來了。	原本的語序是 The bus comes here.

4. neither / nor / so + be / have

例句	中譯	說明
Rock music is OK, and so is skiing.	搖滾樂不錯，滑雪也不錯。	動詞is 放在主詞 skiing 的前面

5. 條件子句中的if省略時

例句	中譯	說明
Should you change your mind, let us know.	你如果改變主意，就告訴我們。	原本語序為If you change your mind, ……
Had I realized what you intended, I should not have wasted my time trying to explain matters to you.	如果我本來瞭解你的意圖，我就不會浪費時間向你解釋了。	原本語序為If I had realized what you intended, ……

6. 句首是否定詞或帶有否定意義的詞語時

這類詞語有：at no time, by no means, under no circumstances, few, hardly, scarcely, hardly...when, scarcely...when, in no way, little, much/even/still less, never, no longer, no sooner...than, nowhere, not frequently, not often, not only...but also, not until, on no account, rarely, seldom 等等。

例句	中譯	說明
Nowhere else in the world can there be such a quiet, beautiful place.	世界上沒有別的地方能這樣美，這樣幽靜。	否定意味的字nowhere else in the world 提前至句首。
Not until he was arrested did he begin to think of his future.	他直到被捕後才開始思考自己的前途。	原本的語序是He did not think of his future until he was arrested.

| Hardly had the sailors sighted land when they shouted happily. | 水手們一看到陸地就高興得跳了起來。 | 用 hardly + 助V + 人 + V1 + when + 人+ V2 的句型表示「一～就～」 |

7. 句首由only所修飾

例句	中譯	說明
Only then did I understand what she meant.	只有到了那時候我才明白她的意思。	Only提前，加上助動詞再接主詞
Only by changing the way we live can we save the earth.	只有我們改變自己的生活方式，才能拯救地球。	原本的語序是 We can only save the earth by changing the way we live.
Only wisdom and friendship can light up our advance in darkness.	只有智慧和友誼才能在黑暗中照亮我們的前路。	only修飾主詞，不倒裝。

8. 使上下文緊密銜接

例句	中譯	說明
Also present will be a person who thinks of an idea for an advertisement.	出席會議的還有廣告的策劃者。	原本的語序是 A person who thinks of an idea for an advertisement will also be present.
Attending the meeting were government officials, businessmen and bankers from different parts of the country.	參加會議的有全國各地的政府官員、商人和銀行家。	原本的語序是 Government officials, businessmen and bankers from different parts of the country were attending the meeting.

9. 直接引語對話放在句首時

例句	中譯	說明
"Who's paying?" shouted the fat man at the corner.	「由誰付錢？」角落裡的胖子叫喊道。	句子往前移動至句首，後面先接動詞再接主詞。

1. By no means _____ betray your best friends.
   A. should you   B. you should   C. are you   D. you are

2. _____ you have any question regarding this project, call the assistant of the department and she will help you.
   A. Do   B. Are   C. Should   D. Had

3. Never _____ about giving up. She just persisted in pursuing her goal.
   A. she will think   B. she did think
   C. had she thought   D. she was thinking

4. It was not until midnight _____ back to the dormitory.
   A. did he come   B. had he come   C. that he came   D. was he to come

5. _____ he known your purpose, he would not have answered your question.
   A. Should   B. Have   C. Has   D. Had

6. _____ the press conference were three officials from the Ministry of Foreign Affairs.
   A. Attending   B. Attended
   C. Having attended   D. Who attended

7. _____ whose video of performing tricks went viral on the Internet.
   A. He comes here   B. Here comes he
   C. Here comes the magician   D. Here the magician comes

8. The service of the restaurant is nice, and _____ its food.
   A. neither is   B. so is   C. neither does   D. so does

9. She never tried to cheat in the exams, and _____ I.
   A. neither was   B. so was   C. neither did   D. neither do

10. Little _____ expect that he would break his promise.
    A. had I   B. has she   C. was she   D. did I

1. 正解為(A)。這句話考的是副詞提到句首的倒裝，語序改為「副詞+助動詞+主詞+動詞」= By no means should you betray your best friends. （你無論如何不應該被判你最好的朋友）。

2. 正解為(C)。本題意思是「如果你對這個計畫有任何問題，請打電話給這個部門的助理，她會幫忙你。」這裡原本的語序是「If you have any question regarding this project,...」。

3. 正解為(C)。這句話的意思是「她從來沒有想過要放棄。她只是一直持續地追求目標。」這裡的語序是否定副詞never + 助動詞 + 主詞 + 動詞，應為Never had she thought~。

4. 正解為(C)。這句話的意思是「他直到半夜才回到宿舍。」這裡用「It was not until + 時間 + that + 主詞 + 動詞」的句型。

5. 正解為(D)。本題的句子是「如果他知道你的目的，他就不會回答你的問題了。」原本的語序「If he had known your purpose」是與過去事實相反的假設語氣。

6. 正解為(A)。句子的意思是「出席記者會的有三位外交部的官員。」原本的語序是「Three officials from the Ministry of Foreign Affairs were attending the press conference.」。

7. 正解為(C)。這句話的意思是「那位魔術表演影片在網路上瘋傳的魔術師來到這裡」空格後面有修飾先行詞的形容詞子句，主詞是一個名詞片語，倒裝的語序為「Here + 動詞 + 主詞」。

8. 正解為(B)。這題的意思是說「這家餐廳的服務很好，食物也很好」在這句當中用so + be 動詞 + 主詞的倒裝語序。

9. 正解為(C)。本句意思是「她從來沒有嘗試在考試中作弊，我也沒有。」句子前半部用一半動詞過去式，後半部用倒裝，語序為「neither + 助動詞 + 主詞」。

10. 正解為(D)。本題題目的意思是「我沒料想到他會不守信用。」這題當中用的是「否定副詞+助動詞+主詞+動詞」的語序。選項(A)為過去完成式的助動詞，後面會接動詞的過去分詞(expected)。

Day

28

省略句
Ellipsis

省略句 Ellipsis

第一節：概述

　　英文中為放避免不必要的重複，將一些上文重複、而雙方都不會誤解的部分省略；有時是習慣用法。

第二節：被省略的成分

1. 句子當中的主詞、受詞、不定式to V

例句	中文	說明
Beg your pardon.	請再說一遍。	省略主詞I
Any question?	有什麼問題嗎？	省略前面的 "Are there"
—Who do you think must be responsible? —Hard to say.	—你認為誰應該負有責任？ —這很難說。	答句中省略了受詞it。
We had invited him to take part in the party, but he didn't come.	雖然我們邀請過他來參加晚會，但他沒來。	省略了後半句的不定式to V片語 "to take part in it"
Trouble is we don't know it ourselves.	問題是我們自己也不知道。	省略了trouble前面的定冠詞the。
Glad to see you.	見到你真高興。	省略了主詞和動詞I'm
—Did you like the book? —Oh, very much.	—這本書你喜歡嗎？ —啊，很喜歡。	省略了答句中的主詞+動詞+受詞 I liked it
Looking for me?	在找我嗎？	省略了be動詞和主詞Are you

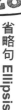
2. 有些慣用的句子只有動詞和副詞

Thanks a lot! 多謝！
No smoking! 禁止抽菸！
Hands up! 舉起手來！

第三節：簡單句中的省略

簡單句中常有一些成分被省略掉。

1. 對話中的回答

例句	中文	說明
—Are you hungry? —Not yet.	一你餓了嗎？ 一還沒有。	完整的答句應為 I am not hungry yet.
—May I smoke here? —No, you'd better not.	一我可以在這裡抽菸嗎？ 一不，你最好不要在這裡抽菸。	完整的答句應為 No, you'd better not smoke here.
—The book is very interesting. —Yes, and very instructive, too.	一這本書很有趣。 一是的，而且很有教育意義。	完整的打句應為 Yes, and it is very instructive, too.

2. 陳述自己的意見、問題或要求

例句	中文	說明
Why not come?	為什麼不來呢？	Why don't you come?
What to do next?	下一步該怎麼辦？	What are we supposed to do next?
No move!	不許動！	Do not move!

3. 在傳統電報中也常用省略句

例句	中文	說明
Arrive Shanghai August the Tenth.	8月10日到達上海。	～arrive at Shanghai on August the Tenth

4. 在報紙標題和文章標題中

例句	中文	說明
Kosovo crisis over, but peace hard to come.	科索沃危機已經結束，但和平難以實現。	The Kosovo crisis is over, but it is hard for the peace to come.

第四節：複合句中的省略

複合句中某些成分省略的情形也很多。主要有：

1. 在回答問題時

例句	中文	說明
—May I smoke here? —I'm afraid not.	一我可以在這裡抽菸嗎？ 一恐怕不行。	完整答句應為I am afraid that you cannot smoke here.

2. 在副詞子句中

如包含有助動詞be，主語又和句子的主語一致，或主語是it 時，就可以把子句中的主詞和動詞的一部分，尤其是助動詞be 省略掉。

例句	中文	說明
Any mistake, once found, must be corrected.	一旦發現任何錯誤，就必須加以改正。	完整句子為If there is any mistake, once it is found, it must be corrected.

3. 在以than或as引起的子句

例句	中文	說明
He is more of a writer than a historian.	他是歷史學家，但更可以說是位作家。	省略 he is 在than 後面的子句中。
He worked as hard as others.	他工作像別人一樣起勁。	others後面用do

4. 在複合句中

　　在複合句中被省略的還可以是主句的一部分，或是子句的一部分，或主、子句中都有省略。

例句	中文	說明
Any question you want to ask me?	你們還有什麼問題要問我的嗎？	句首省略Is there
If not today, I'm sure you will get my answer tomorrow.	如果你今天收不到我的回信，明天你一定能收到。	If 開頭的子句原為 If you don't receive my answer today.

　　或是俗語及諺語，如：

The sooner, the better. 越快越好。

Like father, like son. 有其父必有其子。

第五節：並列句中的省略

1. 在並列句中相同的部分常被省略

例句	中文	說明
Someone has told me that, but I don't remember who.	有人已經告訴我了，但我記不得是誰了。	Who 後面省略 told me
His mother is a teacher and his father a writer.	他母親是個老師，父親是個作家。	his father 後面省略了 is
He majors in English and I in French.	他主修英語，我主修法語。	I 後面省略 major

2. 後面的副詞成分修飾前面的動詞

例句	中文	說明
We tried to persuade her but in vain.	我們想勸服她，但沒成功。	在 but 之後省略了 "we tried"
He started to learn music and quite well in a year.	他開始學音樂了，並且一年後就學得相當不錯。	原句為He started to learn music and (he learned it) quite well in a year.

文法實戰演練

1. Mary is not sure about what career path to take in the future, and _____.
   A. so is her brother
   B. either is her brother
   C. neither is her brother
   D. so does her brother

2. A: My computer is disconnected from the network. B: _____.
   A. Mine, too.　　B. Me, either.　　C. Me, too.　　D. Neither does mine.

3. A: Have you submit the revised version of your thesis to Professor Schmidt?
   B: _____.
   A. No wonder.　　B. Not yet.　　C. No more.　　　D. Not now.

4. He does the job more smoothly _____ before.
   A. as　　　　　　B. by　　　　　　C. than　　　　　　D. for

5. A: Can I exchange the product if I lost the receipt? B: I'm afraid _____.
   A. we don't　　　B. we can't　　C. you don't　　　D. you can't

6. She said she will do what _____ to help us.
   A. she does　　　B. she can　　C. can do　　　　D. is done

7. You will receive the invitation card by this Friday. _____, please contact us.
   A. If not　　　　　B. If don't　　C. If can't　　　　D. If isn't

8. He promised that he will sponsor us _____ always.
   A. than　　　　　　B. as　　　　　C. for　　　　　　D. such

9. The project will end up a failure _____.
   A. if managed not well
   B. if management not well
   C. if not well managed
   D. if not good management

10. Her mother is a lawyer, _____.
    A. and her father a nurse
    B. her father nurse
    C. father is a nurse
    D. while her father is nurse

文法實戰解析

1. 正解為(C)。這句話的意思是說「瑪麗不確定她未來的職業生涯方向，而她弟弟也還沒有。」後半部的句子可以說是 "and her brother isn't sure about his career path in the future, either" 省略掉動詞重複的部分。

2. 正解為(A)。本題中A說「我的電腦從網路中斷線了」，B說「我的也是」，這裡答句可以省略描述的詞disconnected from the network，留下be動詞和主詞，而主詞My computer 也可以直接換成所有代名詞Mine。

3. 正解為(B)。A說「你已經繳交更改過的論文給施密特教授了嗎？」B說還沒，這裡用省略的回答「Not yet.」。

4. 正解為(C)。這句話的意思是「他做這份工作比以前更順手了。」這句話省略了than之後的 "he did this job"。

5. 正解為(D)。本題A說「如果我弄丟了收據的話可以換貨嗎？」B回答說「恐怕不行」，這裡省略了afraid後面的子句動詞部分「you can't exchange the good if you lost the receipt」。

6. 正解為(B)。句子的意思是「她說她會盡力幫助我們。」這裡省略的是can後面的動詞do。

7. 正解為(A)。這句話的意思是「你這個星期五之前會收到邀請函。如果沒有，請聯絡我們。」這裡If後面會省略掉主詞和動詞，not 會保留。

8. 正解為(B)。這題的意思是說「他承諾會像以前一樣贊助我們。」這裡的 as always 也可以說是 as usual，就是一如既往的意思。

9. 正解為(C)。本句意思是「如果管理不善，這個計畫就會失敗。」句子當中if 之後省略了主詞和動詞，還原是「If the project is not well managed」。

10. 正解為(A)。這句話的意思是「她的母親是一位律師，而父親是一位護理師。」後面並列的地方省略了be動詞is。

Day

29

常用交際英語
Communication English

常用交際英語
Communication English

第一節：概述

這篇介紹對話中常用的短句或片語，包括表達情緒、感受、勸告等等的句子，對日常生活溝通或者在考試會話題型作答很有幫助。

第二節：表達感情、觀點等的用語

表達內容	慣用短句或片語
Intention 意願	I'm going to... I'll... I'd like to... I want/hope to...
Like 喜好	I like... love...(very much) I'm fond of... I enjoy doing... My favorite... I like love to...
Dislike 厭惡	I don't like (to) I hate (to do/doing)... I dislike doing...
Agreement 同意	Certainly. Sure. Yes, I think so. OK. That's a good idea. Of course. Yes, please. That's true. All right.

Disagreement 不同意	No, I don't think so. I'm afraid not. I really can't agree with you.
Certainty 肯定	I'm sure. I'm sure that...
Uncertainty 不肯定	I'm not sure whether if... Maybe Perhaps Possibly Probably...
Emotions 情緒	喜悅： I'm glad pleased happy to... That's wonderful great. 焦慮： What's wrong? What's the trouble? I'm worried. 驚奇： Oh, what shall I do? Really? Oh, dear? Is that so? 遺憾： I'm sorry to hear...
提供幫助	Can I help you? What can I do for you? Is there anything I can do for you? Would you like...? What's the matter? Here, take this... Let me...for you.

提供幫助的回答	Thanks. That would be nice. Thank you for your help. No, thanks. Thank you. That's very kind of you, but...

第三節：表達請求的用語

表達內容	慣用短句或片語
Request and response 請求及應答	尋求幫助及回答： Please give/ pass/ hand me... Please wait (here/ a moment). Please wait (for) your turn. Please stand in line. / Line up, please. Please hurry. Excuse me. Will you come to...? Yes, I'd love to... I'd love to, but... Could you...for me? Yes./Certainly. 提供幫助及回答： Would you like to...? Yes, it's very kind nice of you. May/ Could Can I... Yes, please do. Of course (you may). That's OK. All right. I'm sorry, but... 問路及回答： Can you tell me the way to... Go down this street. Turn right/ left at the first second turning. Take the second turning on the right.

Advice, suggestions, prohibition and warnings 勸告、建議、禁止和警告	You'd better... Shall we... You can't mustn't... If you... No noise, please. No smoking fishing/ talking swimming, please. Take care! Be careful! Look out!
Difficulties in language 語言困難	Pardon. Please say that again more slowly. What do you mean by... In what sense do you... I'm sorry I can't follow you. I'm sorry I know only a little nothing about...
Making appointment 約定會面	Are you free this evening? Shall we meet at 4:30 at...? Yes, that's all right. No, I won't be free then. Yes, I'll be free then. How about tomorrow? Let's make it a little earlier/ at 6. But I'll be free at... See you then. You should... Let's... You need (to)... What/How about...

第四節：日常寒暄用語

表達內容	慣用短句或片語
問候	Hello/ Hi/ Fine, thank you. Very well, thank you. How are you?

Greetings, wishes, congratulations and responses 問候、祝賀及回答	祝願： Good luck! Have a nice day/ good time. Congratulations! Merry Christmas! Happy New Year! 回答： Thank you! The same to you!
Thanks, apologies and responses 感謝、道歉及應答	感謝及應答： Thanks for... Not at all. (It's) my pleasure. I'm sorry. Sorry. 道歉及應答： Sorry. That's all right.
Introductions 介紹	This is Mr. Mrs. Miss X. My name is ... How do you do? Nice Glad to meet/ see you.
Farewells 告別	I think it's time for us to leave now. Goodbye! Bye-bye! See you later/ tomorrow. Good night.
Asking the time or date, talking about the weather 問時間、日期，談論天氣等	What day is (it) today? What time is it? What's the weather like today? What's the date today? What's the time? How's the weather in...?

332

第五節：打電話用語

表達內容	慣用短句或片語
電話打不通	The line is busy. I can't get through.
打電話找人	Hello! May I speak to... Is that...(speaking)? Please put me through to...
接電話回應	Hold on, please. This is...(speaking). Please call later. He isn't here right now. Can I take a message for you?

第六節：常見標誌用語

公共場所指標	PUSH 推 PULL 拉 ON 開 ENTRANCE 入口 EXIT 出口 STOP 停 PAUSE 暫停
公告	BUSINESS HOURS 營業時間 OFFICE HOURS 辦公時間
禁止的公告	DANGER! 危險！ NO PHOTOS! 禁止拍照！ NO SMOKING! 禁止吸菸！ NO PARKING! 禁止停車！
包裝與產品上的標語	FRAGILE 易碎 THIS SIDE UP 這面朝上 INSTRUCTIONS 說明 PLAY 播放 OFF 關

1. A: Hello. May I speak to Mr. Chang, please? B: _____.
   A. Can I leave a message?　　　B. There is a long line.
   C. Speaking.　　　　　　　　　D. Can I help you?

2. A: Excuse me. How can I get to the Palace museum?
   B: _____.
   A. I'm afraid not.　　B. Go down for two blocks and make a left.
   C. It's nice to see it.　D. You can get a lot from the trip.

3. A: Is there anything I can do for you? B:____.
   A. Here, take this brochure.　　B. I can give him a hand.
   C. Thanks. It's fine.　　　　　D. I appreciate what you've done.

4. A: Do you mind my turning off the air conditioner? B: _____.
   A. Many thanks.　　B. Not at all.　C. Never mind.　　D. That's right.

5. A: I'm sorry about causing you so much trouble. B: _____.
   A. It's not a big deal.　　　　B. I'm under the weather.
   C. You are welcome.　　　　　D. See you tomorrow.

6. A: _____. B: It's a quarter to five.
   A. Can I take a message?　　　B. Do you have the time?
   C. How is the weather?　　　　D. What's the date today?

7. A: Don't cut the queue. It's rude. B:_____.
   A. Sorry.　　　B. Take care.　　C. Look up.　　　D. Of course.

8. A: Could you pass the ketchup to me? B: _____.
   A. Go down this street.　　　　B. This way, please.
   C. Hold down, please.　　　　D. Sure, here you are.

9. A: Can I speak to Mr. Marvin, please? B:_____.
   A. What can I do for you?　　　B. Line up, please.
   C. Hold on. I'll put you through.　D. I'd like to leave the message.

10. A: Shall we meet at 5:00 at the entrance? B: _____.
   A. I'm afraid you can't.　　B. I'll be free at three o'clock this afternoon.
   C. Ok. See you then.　　　D. There is no need to rush.

文法實戰解析

1. 正解為(C)。這句話是電話的用語，電話中回答說「我就是」可以說This is Mr. Chang speaking.。

2. 正解為(B)。A說的話是在問路，選項(C)是「往前走兩個街區，然後左轉。」

3. 正解為(C)。A詢問「有我可以幫忙你的事情嗎？」而B回答說「謝謝您，不用了。」

4. 正解為(B)。A詢問「你介意我把冷氣關掉嗎？」B回答「不會。」選項(A)是「非常感謝」、選項(C)是「算了」、選項(D)是「沒錯」的意思。

5. 正解為(A)。A說道「抱歉給你造成了那麼多困擾。」B回答「不要緊。」選項(B)是「我身體不舒服」，選項(C)是「不客氣」，選項(D)是「明天見」。

6. 正解為(B)。問句的意思是「你知道現在幾點嗎？」如果說「Do you have time?」就是在問對方有沒有空。回答的意思是「現在四點四十五分。」

7. 正解為(A)。A說「請不要插隊。很沒禮貌。」B回答「抱歉。」選項(B)是「小心」，選項(C)是「注意」，選項(D)是「當然」。

8. 正解為(D)。這裡的A說「可以請把番茄醬遞給我嗎？」B回答說「好的，給你」。

9. 正解為(C)。這是在電話上面的對話。A說到「請找馬文先生。」B說到「稍等，我為您轉接」。選項(A)是「我能為您做什麼？」，選項(B)是「請排隊」，選項(D)是「我想要留言」。

10. 正解為(C)。A說「我們約五點在入口處碰面好嗎？」B回答說「好的。到時候見」。選項(A)是「您恐怕不行」，選項(B)是「我今天下午三點有空」，選項(D)是「不需要趕時間」。

Day

30

常見句型
Common Sentence Structure

Day 30 常見句型
Common Sentence Structure

在這個單元，我們來複習常考的句型：

1. 感嘆句

What	名詞片語	主詞	動詞	中譯
What	an interesting book	it	is!	多麼有趣的書啊！

How	形容詞	主詞	動詞	中譯
How	beautiful	these flowers	are!	這些花多美啊！

How	副詞	主詞	動詞	中譯
How	fast	he	is running!	他跑得多快啊！

How		感嘆的句子	中譯
How		time flies!	時光飛逝！

2. 結果句

句型	例句	中文
so + 形容詞／副詞 +that...	He is so good a teacher that all of us like him.	他是一個好老師，我們都喜歡他。
such + 名詞性片語+ that... 如此……以至……	He is such a good teacher that all of us like him.	

重點提示：必學文法小要點

so + many/ few + 名詞複數 + that...

so + much/ little + 不可數名詞 + that...

There are so many people in the room that I cannot get in.
房間裡人太多，我進不去。

The man has so much money that he can buy a car.
那人有很多錢，能買一輛汽車。

3. 就近原則

有些句型中動詞要以接近的名詞來決定單複數：

句型	例句	中譯
There be... 有……	There is a desk, two chairs and two beds in the room.	房間裡有一張桌子、兩張椅子和兩張床。
not only...but also... 不但……而且……	Not only Brian but also his sisters have been to Turkey.	布萊恩和他的姐妹們都去過土耳其。
either...or... 不是……就是……	Either you or I am right.	不是你對，就是我對。
neither...nor... 既不……也不……	Neither Kevin nor Lawrence is satisfied with the plan.	凱文和羅倫斯都對這個計畫不滿意。

4. 表示「因為……所以……」的詞

連接詞	例句	中譯
because... 因為	—Why didn't you come to school yesterday? —Because I was ill.	—為什麼你昨天沒來上學？ —因為我生病了。
since... 既然	Since you feel tired, you should rest.	既然你累了，就應該休息。
as... 由於	As it was late, we came back soon.	由於天色已晚，我們不久就會回來了。

	The oil must be out, for the light went out.	油一定用完了，因為燈不亮。
for... 由於		

5. 表示「雖然……但是……」的詞

連接詞	例句	中譯
though... 儘管	Though she has some shortcomings, she is a nice girl.	儘管她有些缺點，但她還是一個好女孩。
but... 但是	She has some shortcomings, but she is a good girl.	儘管她有些缺點，但她還是一個好女孩。

注意，以上兩個連接詞不能在一個句子中同時使用。

6. 表示「因為……所以……」的詞

連接詞	例句	中譯
because... 因為	He had to stay at home because he was ill.	他不得不待在家，因為他生病了。
so... 因此	He was ill, so he had to stay at home.	他生病了，因此不得不待在家。

注意，以上兩個連接詞不能在一個句子中同時使用。

7. 足以

句型	例句	中文
enough＋名詞＋ to do...	There were not enough people to pick the apples.	沒有足夠的人手摘這些蘋果。
形容詞／副詞＋ enough to do...	The boy is strong enough to carry the heavy stone.	這男孩力氣夠大，能搬動這塊石頭。

8. 太……而不……

句型	例句	中譯
too + 形容詞／副詞 + to V... 太……以至於不能……	He is too tired to walk on.	他太累了以至於不能再走下去了。

重點深度學：進階挑戰

★「太……而不……」中的兩句也 可以改寫成「so...that...」句型。例如：

She was so excited that she could not say a word.
她如此激動以至於說不出一句話。

9. 以便……／因此……

例句	中譯	說明
They started early so that they could catch the early bus.	他們很早出發，以便能趕上早班車。	引導目的副詞子句。
They started early so that they caught the early bus.	他們很早出發，因此趕上了早班車。	引導的是結果副詞子句

10. 祈使句＋結果句

句型	例句	中文
祈使句, or/and + 陳述句	Hurry up, or we'll be late for school.	趕快，否則我們上學就要遲到了。（轉折關係）
	Work hard, and then you can live happily.	努力工作，你就能生活得愉快。（遞進關係）

11. It's time 開頭的句型

句型	例句	中譯
It's time for sth. 是來做～的時間了	It's time for class.	該上課了。
It's time (for sb.) to do sth. （某人）該做某事了	It's time for you to get up.	你該起床了。

	It's high time that you went to bed. (=It's high time that you should go to bed.)	你該上床休息了。
It's time that sb. did sth. 某人該來做～了		

12. 花費

句型	例句	中譯
It takes sb. some time to do sth. 花費某人一些時間來做～	It takes me ten minutes to come to school on foot.	走路來學校要花費我十分鐘時間。
sb. spend some time on sth./ (in) doing sth. 某人花時間在某事上／花時間來做～	He spends half an hour (in) reading English every morning.	他每天早上花半小時讀英語。
sb. spend some money on sth./ (in) doing sth. 某人花錢在某物上／花錢來做～	I spent ten dollars on this book.	我買這本書花了十元。
sth. cost sb. some money 某事花費某人一些錢	This book cost me ten dollars.	這本書花了我十元。
pay some money for sth. 為某事（物）付錢	I paid ten dollars for this book.	我花了十元買這本書。

重點提示：必學文法小要點

cost 主詞一般為物；spend, pay主詞一般為人。

it用作虛主詞，動詞不定式為真正主詞。

13. 忙於做某事

句型	例句	中譯
keep sb. busy doing sth. 使某人忙於做～	Mary keeps herself busy doing volunteering work.	瑪麗忙著做志工。

| be busy with sth. 忙於某事 | The farmers are busy with the apple harvest. | 農民們正在忙著收成蘋果。 |
| be busy (in) doing sth. 忙於做某事 | Ann's family are busy getting ready for her birthday party. | 安的家人正在忙著為她的生日聚會作準備。 |

14. 停止

句型	例句	中譯
stop + Ving 停止正在做的事	Stop phubbing. Let's do some outdoor activities.	不要再滑手機了。我們來做些戶外活動吧。
stop to + V 停下來去做另一件事	He stopped to have a look.	他停下來看了看。
stop + N + from Ving	The Great Green Wall will stop the sand (from) moving towards the rich farmland in the south.	綠色長城將阻止沙漠侵襲南方肥沃的農田。

15. 繼續

句型	例句	中譯
go on +Ving	He picked up the stick quickly and went on running.	他很快撿起接力棒繼續跑。

重點提示：必學文法小要點

stop doing sth. 停止做～

stop to do sth. 停下來去做另一件事

stop sb. (from) doing sth. 阻止某人來做～

go on doing sth. 繼續做同一件事

go on to do sth. 繼續做另一件事

16. 發現

句型	例句	中文
find sth./ find out...	Have you found your pen?	你找到鋼筆沒有？
find + it + 形容詞 + 不定式	He found it important to learn English well.	他發現學好英語很重要。
find + 受詞 + 受詞補語	Jenny found a wallet lying on the ground.	珍妮發現地上有個錢包。

17. 感官動詞＋受詞＋受詞補語

hear	somebody	doing	強調動作正在進行
		do	強調動作為一事實
see	something	done	強調受詞的情形

I heard them singing. 我聽到他們在唱歌。

I saw him do it. 我看見這事是他做的。

I often hear the song sung. 我常聽見這首歌（被唱）。

18. 倍數表達

句型	例句	中譯
A is ~ 數字 as adj. as B	This house is three times as big as that one.	這間房子是那間房子三倍大。
A is ~ 數字 + 形容詞比較級 + than B	This house is twice bigger than that one.	這間房子比那間房子大兩倍。

19. forget和 remember

句型	例句	中譯
forget/ remember + to V = 表示未完成的動作	Don't forget to post the letter.	別忘了寄信。
forget/ remember + V-ing 表示已做過的動作	I remember seeing her at the product launch event.	我記得在產品發表活動上看過她。

20. 借出、借入與還存

句型	例句	中譯
borrow...from... 從……借……	Miss Yang likes the students to borrow books from the library.	楊小姐喜歡學生從圖書館借書。
lend...to... 把……借給……	Can you lend your bike to me?	你能借我一下你的腳踏車嗎？
return...to... 把……歸還……	You must return the book to the library on time.	你必須準時將這本書歸還圖書館。
keep 借存	How long may I keep the book?	這本書我能借多久？

21. not...until... 直到……才……

句型	例句	中譯
not + V + until + S + V	He did not show up at the party until we were ready to leave.	他直到我們準備離開時才在派對上出現。
Not until + S1 + V1 + 助V + S2 + V2	Not until he got home did he realize that his bike was stolen.	他回到家才發現他的腳踏車被偷了。

It is not until S1 + V1 that S2 + V2	It was not until the police officer called him that he realized that he fell victim to a scam.	直到警察打電話給他，他才知道他被詐騙了。

22. have+過去分詞+for.../since...

句型	例句	中譯
have+過去分詞+for...	I have worked here for ten years.	我在這裡工作十年了。
have+過去分詞+ since...	She has lived there since she was born.	她一出生就住在那裡。

23. 倒裝句

句型	例句	中文
so + be動詞／助動詞／助動詞＋主詞	He can swim. So can she.	他會游泳，她也會。
	He speaks English very well. So do I.	他英語説得好，我也是。
Neither/Nor + be動詞／助動詞／助動詞 + 主詞	Li hasn't read this book. Neither has Lin.	李沒看過這本書，林也沒看過。
	He didn't work out this maths problem. Nor did I.	他沒解答出這道數學題，我也沒解答出來。

24. 詢問句

句型	例句	中文
How do you like...?	How do you like this book?	你覺得這本書怎麼樣？
What do you think of...?	What do you think of this book?	你覺得這本書怎麼樣？

25. There/ Here 句型

句型	例句	中文
There/Here + 動詞 + 主詞	Long, long ago, there lived a king.	很久很久以前,有一位國王。
	Here comes the bus.	公車來了。
Here + 代名詞 + is/ are	Here you are.	給你。
	Here it is.	拿去。

1. I heard someone _____ on the door. Can you check who that is?
   A. knocked　　　B. to knock　　　C. knocks　　　D. knocking

2. The five-year-old boy is four times _____ his baby brother.
   A. as heavier　　　　　　　　　B. as heavy as
   C. heavier as　　　　　　　　　D. more heavy than

3. The driver did not _____the injured man. Instead, he sped up and escaped from the scene of the accident.
   A. stop checking　　　　　　　B. stop to check
   C. go on to check　　　　　　　D. go on checking

4. It _____ him three years to master that foreign language.
   A. spent　　　B. cost　　　C. took　　　D. paid

5. It is high time that we _____ measures to prevent severer climate change.
   A. taking　　　B. to take　　　C. took　　　D. taken

6. So _____ that he couldn't speak clearly.
   A. drunk was he　　　　　　　B. much wine does he drink
   C. drunk he was　　　　　　　D. much wine he drank

7. He is _____ a patient person _____ I have never seen him annoyed by anything.
   A. so; that　　　B. such; that　　　C. too; to　　　D. by far; more

8. She was _____ embarrassed _____ say anything.
   A. so; that　　　B. such; that　　　C. too; to　　　D. so; as

9. What _____!
   A. considerate he is　　　　　B. a considerate boy he is
   C. considerate is the boy　　　D. considerate a boy he is

10. He has been working for the travelling circus _____ he was little.
    A. for　　　B. from　　　C. because　　　D. since

文法實戰解析

1. 正解為(D)。這句話考的see/hear受詞後面接動詞原形或V-ing。這句話的意思是說「我聽到有人在敲門。你可以看一下是誰嗎？」。

2. 正解為(B)。本題意思是「五歲的小男孩是他強褓中弟弟的四倍重。」這邊考的是倍數的說法 A is ~ times as + adj. + as B。

3. 正解為(B)。這句話的意思是「駕駛沒有停下來查看受傷的男子。反而加速逃離車禍現場。」

4. 正解為(C)。這句話的意思是「他花了三年的時間把那個外語學好。」這邊考的是跟花費有關的動詞用法。spend 和 pay 的主詞都是人，而cost後面接的會是金錢而非時間。

5. 正解為(C)。本題的句子是「該是我們採取措施防止更嚴苛氣候變遷的時候了。」It is high time that 後面接過去式的動詞。

6. 正解為(A)。句子的意思是「他醉得如此嚴重以至於說話都不清楚。」這裡考的是倒裝句，需注意前半部子句的語序。

7. 正解為(B)。這句話的意思是「他是如此有耐心的人以致於我從沒看過他因為任何事情而惱怒。」用such + 名詞片語 + that 子句。

8. 正解為(C)。這題的意思是說「她太尷尬了，以至於說不出話來。」這裡用「too ~ to ~」表示「太～以致於無法～」。

9. 正解為(B)。本句意思是「他是多麼體貼的一個男孩啊！」句子的語序應是What + 名詞片語 + 代名詞 + be動詞。

10. 正解為(D)。本題題目的意思是「他從小就在這個巡演馬團工作。」這裡考的是完成式動詞後面接since+子句的用法。

英語學習 系列 010

＿＿用英文文法30天完＿攻略：
逆轉你學了10年都還搞不懂的文法概念

精闢分析英文文法要點，從零開始替你精準打下基礎！

作　　者	許綺 ◎著
顧　　問	曾文旭
總 編 輯	王毓芳
編輯統籌	耿文國、黃璽宇
主　　編	吳靜宜
執行主編	姜怡安
執行編輯	李念茨、陳儀蓁
美術編輯	王桂芳、張嘉容
封面設計	阿作
法律顧問	北辰著作權事務所　蕭雄淋律師、幸秋妙律師

初　　版	2019年08月
出　　版	捷徑文化出版事業有限公司——資料夾文化出版
電　　話	（02）2752-5618
傳　　真	（02）2752-5619
地　　址	106 台北市大安區忠孝東路四段250號11樓-1

定　　價	新台幣399元／港幣 133 元
產品內容	1書

總 經 銷	知遠文化事業有限公司
地　　址	222新北市深坑區北深路3段155巷25號5樓
電　　話	（02）2664-8800
傳　　真	（02）2664-8801

港澳地區總經銷	和平圖書有限公司
地　　址	香港柴灣嘉業街12號百樂門大廈17樓
電　　話	（852）2804-6687
傳　　真	（852）2804-6409

▲本書圖片由 Shutterstock、123RF提供。

捷徑 Book站

現在就上臉書（FACEBOOK）「捷徑BOOK站」並按讚加入粉絲團，
就可享每月不定期新書資訊和粉絲專享小禮物喔！

http://www.facebook.com/royalroadbooks
讀者來函：royalroadbooks@gmail.com

國家圖書館出版品預行編目資料

萬用英文文法30天完全攻略：逆轉你學了10年
都還搞不懂的文法概念／張慈庭英語研發團隊
著. -- 初版. -- 臺北市：捷徑文化, 2019.08
　面；　　公分（英語學習：010）

ISBN 978-957-8904-83-5(平裝)

1. 英語　　2. 語法

805.16　　　　　　　　　　　　　108008491